SPIRIT OF THE VIOLINISTS

Maddie Evans

Spirit of the Violinists, Copyright © 2021, Maddie Evans.

Print ISBN: 978-1-942133-44-5
Library of Congress Control Number: 2020952672

Cover art by Crowe Covers
Editing by Michaela DeToma

DEDICATION

Two years ago, I covered a charity 5K for the local paper. A high school senior organized it to promote awareness of early-onset frontotemporal dementia, the illness that was taking her father from her family at far too young an age. I was impressed by her and by her family, touched by their perseverance and their resourcefulness, and by how in the midst of their struggle, they cared about making the way easier for others. Long after the 5K, their experience stuck with me.

Although the Castleton family is in no way based on the Krauss family, I'd like to dedicate the Castleton String Quartet trilogy to the memory of Mark Krauss and to all those who loved and supported him.

CHAPTER ONE

Jason had been upstaging Lindsey all evening, but when he stole the first violin line, that's when she wanted him gone.

This Christmas party wasn't anything special. Not to Lindsey, that was. Lindsey had played dozens, so any given party was less about the spirit of the season than about the acoustics, the schedule, and the playlist. Guests mingled throughout the hall paying no attention to the quartet that played through the arrangement of seasonal favorites that Lindsey had seamed together into one forty-five-minute medley. The quartet had played it so often since Thanksgiving that they could do it without thinking.

Except for now, when they'd transitioned into "O Holy Night," and her second violinist started playing the first violin line.

It took four measures before Lindsey finally locked eyes with Jason, and by now they were committed. Ashlyn and Hannah didn't hesitate, and they shouldn't. But Lindsey hadn't played the second violin part since before her father got sick, and Jason had never, as far as she knew, played the first one.

Jason looked unnerved, as if he realized he'd gone too far. It wasn't even clear how they should recover from this, or whether he would step back into his real line if she cued him to.

"O Holy Night" was a soloist's piece to begin with, not a thing you could get an entire congregation singing on Christmas Eve. Now that they were well into the song, Jason was playing it differently than Lindsey had arranged it. Long ago he must have memorized a different version, and he'd clicked into it tonight. Hannah kept adjusting to maintain her harmony with him, whereas Ashlyn had already dropped her volume because her line and his were going to clash.

Lindsey cued Ashlyn to improvise, and she acknowledged. That freed up Lindsey to reach back in time for the second violin line from last year. Last year, when her father played first.

And should still be playing first, blast everything. If Dad weren't sick—weren't dying—then Lindsey wouldn't be in first chair, and Jason wouldn't be gunning for her position at every opportunity.

If any of the party-goers were paying attention, it made more sense to seem as if Jason were supposed to take over for this one segment. Hannah had very nearly a solo at one point, and so did Lindsey. In retrospect, she should have cued the other two to stop playing. The arrangement transitioned to "Angels from the Realms of Glory" at the end of this song, after which they could all step back into their normal roles.

Jason kept checking Lindsey for a cue, but it was taking most of her concentration to remember what she would have played last year. The longer she worked at it, though, the more she remembered. Maybe it was her violin. Violins remembered the songs they'd played.

Also, she'd rather freeze Jason out right now. He created

this mess. He needed to solve it.

Solve it, he did. He soared through the higher parts, voiced the lower ones, and executed all the difficult transitions. As far as the violin was concerned, Jason was a technical master.

Despite that technical mastery, though, the performance felt flat. He was hitting all the notes and missing all the soul. Dad would have wrung so much emotion from this melody. The thrill of hope? The weary world rejoicing? Not under Jason's hand. For him, falling on your knees was just another stage direction, executed to perfection. The night Christ was born? That was December 25th, why? Jason's performance was as emotional as a birth certificate.

At the end of the segment, where the second violin line would swell to allow the key to pivot into "Angels from the Realms of Glory," Lindsey cued Jason to play his own line for once. She resumed her line, and now they were all playing what they should.

She remained furious. Playing tense, it was hard to get a decent vibrato, and if she didn't get back her composure, she was going to start making mistakes. Mistakes Jason would lambaste her for afterward, of course. If she couldn't handle one teenie problem, like having to cover for him stealing the first violin line, how could she be expected to lead a whole quartet?

She fought to relax her wrist and shoulder. Ten minutes more and they could have a break. Play through this. Just get through the arrangement.

So much of Lindsey's life was like that right now. Just get through this. Just do that other thing. Don't look at the overall picture or it will destroy you.

She put it all out of her mind and kept her attention on the music, on the moment, on the other three players. Jason was playing more subdued now, and Hannah sounded shaken. Ashlyn had picked right up again as though nothing had gone wrong. Maybe to non-musicians the quartet sounded great, but to Lindsey, tonight's performance sounded like a loosely linked chain of mistakes.

They reached the final measures of the medley, and none of the guests were paying attention. For a moment it was all futility: Lindsey's life's work—and her father's life's work—only no one cared. Chamber music was merely something for the background of a banal party, nothing to move the soul or breathe flame into the spirit. Music was nothing more than the reason you had to speak a little louder while trading small talk with the husband of the partner of your law firm.

The quartet gave a fanfare, and the piece ended.

To his credit, Jason looked unsettled. Gorgeous, but unsettled. Lindsey turned to Hannah. "Can you play solo for about five minutes?" When Hannah nodded, Lindsey faced Jason with a smile like ice, then laid her violin and bow on her chair. "Jason Vanderbilt Woodward, we have to talk."

Jason followed her, but he brought his violin. Maybe he thought she was about to fire him. Maybe she was.

Ashlyn accompanied them, either to prevent a murder or serve as a witness. Both would do.

Hannah began the first of the six Bach cello suites before the other three were out the back and heading to their prep room behind the banquet hall. Lindsey tried to keep her brain from misfiring before she got the door shut behind them.

Jason preempted her. "I shouldn't have done that."

He was always preempting her. "No, you shouldn't have. That was the most unprofessional thing I've ever seen you do."

Jason had his super-expensive violin tucked under his arm. It matched his super-amazing hair and super-sweet eyes, and in his custom-tailored tuxedo, he looked like a million bucks. Right now, Lindsey would have traded him for ten bucks and a second violinist who was willing to work with her.

"What do you want me to do? I can't turn back time."

His eyes narrowed. "I'm exhausted. We're all exhausted. My mind wasn't where it needed to be, and when it came up, I just played what I've played before."

He sounded so reasonable, except— "Except it's convenient how it's always the first violin line you're stomping all over. You wanted to be first violin from the moment you came back from California, and you've done everything in your power to upstage me every time we've played, from rushing transitions to playing louder than the main line to flourishing things that don't need to be flourished."

Jason's expression was perfectly flat, either because he was bored or he didn't agree that his behavior was a problem.

Lindsey said, "If you wanted to be a soloist, you shouldn't have come back to Maine."

Jason said, "I came back to Maine for your father, and ironically, it's only because of your father that you're first violinist. It's not my fault that I should be the first violin. It's just that you can't hear talent."

"I can't hear your talent over the sound of your raging ego." She stepped closer to him, and he pivoted to move his violin away from her—as if she'd ever willingly damage a violin. "I'm not having the first violinist of the Castleton String Quartet not be a Castleton. You want to be first violin? Awesome. Go start your own quartet."

He looked into her eyes. "You're not your father."

"That's obvious—because you respect my father. But showing up here and disrespecting *me* is the same as disrespecting my father by trying to destroy his quartet. If you came back to Maine to play, play."

Jason grimaced. "I thought that's what I was doing."

Ashlyn said in a low voice, "I think they can hear us in the hallway."

Lindsey pitched her tone down. "You didn't come back here to help my father. This benefits you somehow, even if I have no idea why."

Jason huffed. "Then I'll just have to maintain an air of

mystery to keep you dreaming about me. Can we go back now? We have party guests to entertain."

He was infuriating. First the grandstanding. Then the admission of wrongdoing with no apology. For the finale, an attempt at sounding like the reasonable one.

Lindsey said, "Entertain them with our music, not your shenanigans," and she left the room.

CHAPTER TWO

Lindsey toned down her nasty glares for the rest of the party, so that was nice at least. Any guests who were paying attention—and Jason knew there was one—wouldn't know she'd effectively tugged him from the room by the ear to scold him like a toddler caught with his sneakers untied.

Without incident they played through a Haydn string quartet that had nothing to do with the holidays. Jason kept his focus on the music and not on the fact that Lindsey hated him, nor the fact that he hated being here, nor the fact that they'd already played two Christmas events today, nor worst of all, the fact that they hadn't even started playing tonight before someone had called Jason's name like an old friend.

Lindsey had accused him of not having his head in the game, and for a critical moment, he hadn't. Trying to track his former acquaintance in the banquet hall, Jason had registered that the medley was coming up on "O Holy Night" and automatically played it. By the time he'd realized he'd taken the main line, it was too late to swap back, not without every party-goer hearing the jolt. Bob Castleton always stressed that you never stop playing when you make a mistake. You might have to pivot. You might have to improvise. But what you do not do is stop, give a nervous cough, and start over.

In retrospect, Jason had done that with his life last March. At the time, he hadn't seen it for what it was. Maine: the musical nervous cough.

In addition to a Thursday night performance at the Friends of the Library holiday party, and a Friday evening holiday dinner, they'd done three gigs today. It started at nine with a town square Christmas tree thing in the cold, where he'd had to play the graffitied-up violin he'd borrowed from the school. They'd followed that with a luncheon performance where he could use his real violin, and now this dinner that had started late and was ending late.

What on earth was John Mullen doing here?

If anyone had noticed the "O Holy Night" gaffe, it would be Mullen, and Mullen would smirk about it to anyone who'd listen. It was already going to make the rounds that oh, Jason Woodward was playing second violin in a no-name quartet, and what a fall from grace that must be. Mullen belonged in California, for crying out loud, not in Maine. He belonged in sixty-eight degrees and sunny, not in five degrees and six inches of snow predicted overnight.

Quit it. Head in the game. Head in the game.

Lindsey shot Jason a nasty look, and he edged down his volume. Not his fault that she wasn't getting more power out of her violin, but fine.

By now they had only fifteen minutes remaining, and Lindsey started them on another Christmas medley. This stuff was forgettable. The arrangements were nice, but you'd have to set off a rocket in the middle of the piece in order to catch anyone's attention, let alone get them to remember you. Unless they already knew who you were.

The party was breaking up. The medley ended. Lindsey had clocked the performance perfectly, ending at one minute past their contracted number of hours. She sat momentarily, breathing deep, and then stood to start taking down.

When the host approached, Lindsey marshaled herself into the appearance of a reasonable human being. She wore a performance smile, but the host did seem genuinely pleased. While Jason took care of his violin, the client passed Lindsey some cash, and she thanked him.

Jason's skin crawled, and he looked up to find Mullen in front of him. Mullen said, "Great to see you here!"

Jason shook his hand. "I have to say, you surprised me. Why are you in Maine?"

"You looked like you were about to jump out of your skin!" Mullen's voice was a welcome break from the assortment of Maine accents that had surrounded Jason for the past ten months. "One of my cousins booked a ski lodge for a Christmas wedding, so I made it a long vacation."

Lindsey watched the interaction sidelong. Ashlyn was putting away her music, but Hannah left hers on the stand to carry her cello back to the prep room.

Jason said, "Is Maine treating you well?" because the more impersonal the conversation, the better.

Mullen beamed. "Terrific! You're looking good too. The slower speed here is great for you."

Jason caught the look Ashlyn and Lindsey exchanged.

Mullen turned an inquisitive glance over the quartet, "Frank—the host—told me this quartet lineup had changed recently...?"

And there was the information-fishing. Jason tried to sound casual. "I thought I'd told folks before I left. Robert Castleton was my mentor, and I played second violin for him before I joined the Philharmonic. When he got sick, his daughter took over the quartet, and I stepped back in to help out for a year."

Mullen rubbed his chin. "The timing was good for you, considering."

Lindsey appeared not to be paying attention, but her radar was up. Mullen turned to her and shook her hand, and Jason braced himself for whatever obnoxious thing she'd say. Like, "Wasn't my family nice to cushion Jason's crash landing?" Or even better, "Yeah, my father kicked Jason out of the quartet to make room for me, so it was only fair that when my father got sick, we decided we could use him again."

Mullen said, "Well, Ms. Castleton, you've got yourself a good one here."

"Thank you." She was all smile, all performance. "Jason was generous to step in, and we appreciate the sacrifice he's making to be with us."

She made it sound like military service, but it impressed Mullen. It also confused Jason because Lindsey wasn't hanging him out to dry.

Then she caught Jason's eye, and he realized she'd read him.

Musicians in such a small group needed to adjust and bend to one another mid-play (because, back to Bob's guidance, you never stopped until the end of the piece). Over time a good quartet learned to read one another's slightest cues. It was in the motion of the bow or the tightness of the eyes, the speed of the breathing, the tension in the shoulders. Or maybe it was in something else entirely, but after three years, Bob had been able to cue Jason and read Jason's questions.

Bob's wife was able to read people she knew. And now here stood Lindsey, reading Jason with all her mother's intuition and all her father's musicianship. She saw right past the false front to his discomfort, and instead of ripping off Jason's mask, she was saving her ammunition.

Mullen looked appropriately consoling. "I'm sorry to hear about your father's illness. A man who turned out both of you must have been an amazing teacher."

A portrait of gentleness and sorrow, Lindsey said,

"Thank you. He taught all four of us."

Mullen clapped Jason on the shoulder. "Hard to imagine Castleton let you go. Well, let me know when you decide to come back to California. We should have lunch."

Unease left Jason's hair standing on end. "Definitely. It was great seeing you."

Lindsey studied Jason momentarily, then gathered her things and Hannah's music. Jason, more than a little worried that Mullen might have brought a friend, chose the lesser of two evils and stuck close to Lindsey as she exited.

In the prep room, Hannah said, "Oh, thank you!" when Lindsey set her music binder on the table. Hannah had her cello back in the case, and a moment later she was ready to leave.

While Jason got his things together, Lindsey did her typical Princess and the Pea routine. It was too much discomfort to ride home in concert blacks, so off came her blouse and skirt. Beneath those she wore a sport bra and biking shorts, and over those went a flannel shirt, a sweatshirt, and a pair of jeans. As a point of honor, Jason stayed in his tuxedo. He didn't even loosen his bow tie.

Lindsey pulled the tip money from the skirt pocket. "You know..." Of course, the guy had tipped them three twenties.

Ashlyn said, "It's late. Keep it and send it straight to the bank account."

"No, give me a minute. We got tipped twice before already. We should be able to break this."

No, she *should* just do what Ashlyn said: keep the cash and then spend three lousy minutes on the bank account website. Instead they ended up with their wallets out, breaking bills until there were five tens and two fives on the table. Jason got fifteen, Hannah got fifteen, Ashlyn got twenty, and Lindsey took the ten. Ashlyn and Lindsey lived together, so they'd figure out that last five on their own.

Which, interestingly, was what Ashlyn had told her to do from the start. Jason snapped, "Since we're into perfection tonight, shouldn't we turn out our pockets and figure out how to break that last ten?"

Lindsey pulled on her coat. "Speaking of perfection, pretty boy, I thought maybe you and I could chat." She handed her car keys to Ashlyn. "I'll catch up."

Hannah looked worried, but she followed when Ashlyn left.

Lindsey folded her arms. "You can thank me later for getting that guy off your case."

"No thank you. I didn't ask for your defense." Jason stared at her. "What did you want to say that you didn't say before when you raked me over the coals?"

"I want to know what was going on. I'm used to you upstaging me because you do it all the time, but I don't believe for a second that you were exhausted. I've seen you play four weddings in thirty-six hours without losing the plot."

Jason tilted his head. "Congratulations. You've finally caught me making a mistake."

Unimpressed, Lindsey said, "One word from that guy, and your composure went up the chimney."

Heat rose in Jason's throat. "Since you're a psychic, tell me why."

Arms folded, Lindsey kept her eyes riveted to his face. A frisson of anxiety shot through Jason in case she really were reading his mind, but then her eyes crinkled. "See, I can't pin it down, except that gentleman left a few tantalizing clues. I'll leap to all the wrong conclusions, so help a girl out. What's going on?"

With his stomach tight like an E string, Jason managed, "If it matters, I'll tell you."

"It mattered because you mucked up our performance badly enough that all of us had to cover, or we'd have been toast."

Jason said, "You covered fine. No toast."

She shifted her weight, undeterred, subject unchanged. "It all seemed friendly, and yet his friendly hello left you looking for an escape."

Jason huffed. "As if anyone would want to get caught here, doing this."

Lindsey opened her hands and looked around. "A musician...playing music?" Then her eyes widened. "Oh! The great Jason Woodward, caught as a mere *second* violinist?"

Jason got his coat from the hook. "Do you think your father spent that much time on me so I'd wither away as some forgotten small-town musician in a state no one goes to?"

Lindsey's mouth opened, and she was momentarily breathless. Then, "You jerk."

He slipped his arms into the sleeves but left the coat unbuttoned. "Well?"

"And my father? The greatest violinist you have ever met—and I don't care who you met in California, pretty boy. The greatest violinist you have ever met or ever will meet was exactly what you just described. A musician in a small town in a state no one ever goes to."

Blast. He shouldn't have said that.

Bob Castleton had been a wonder to Jason—and wonderful. He'd loaned Jason a fifteen-thousand-dollar violin at a time when Jason couldn't have afforded it. He'd offered advice and guidance and encouragement and then a job—and then connections. Bob had reached out to every orchestra he knew offering Jason as a soloist, and every time Jason had gotten another headline, Bob had redoubled his efforts.

That support only made it worse when Bob forced Jason out of the quartet to make room for Lindsey. Sure, Jason had landed in the Los Angeles Philharmonic, one of the best and most highly-paid in the world, but look at the fallout afterward. That's what happens when you get fired out of a cannon: you'll soar for a while, but eventually you'll slam into something.

If he backtracked, Lindsey would pounce, so instead he glared. "You're the one who told Mullen we were both in the quartet for the same reason. Your father is the only reason you're the first chair. Bob told me himself I was his best student, but you're trading on the family name and calling shotgun on a position you inherited without deserving."

Lindsey's eyes narrowed. "Don't even talk to me about trading on the family name, Jason Vanderbilt. Sure, remind us about your robber-baron relations and whatever institutes they founded."

He nodded. "Yes, I chose my middle name, the same way you chose yours. Please get to the point because as you've observed, it's been a long day, and Ashlyn's burning the gas in your car."

Lindsey's dark eyes bore into him. "You can pretend all you like that I'm prancing around like the bratty heir to the great musical empire. Meanwhile the reality is that you could be headlining at Carnegie Hall and my father would still be more successful than you'll ever be."

Rather than storm out, Jason opted for a distracted sigh. "Do tell."

She arched her eyebrows. "He had heart, and his playing had heart. You're technically perfect, but no one walks out of a concert thinking, 'Wow, that violinist was technically perfect.'"

All the hair stood on Jason's arms.

She pointed at him. "You have no heart. Whatever you play, it's well-executed and soulless, whereas Hannah plays and there's errors but that cello bleeds in her hands. Ashlyn's viola sobs when she wants it to, and it's brilliant when she wants joy. You play quarter notes and semi tones and they're perfect. Let's all admire Woodward's virtuosity." She slung her backpack over her shoulder, followed by the strap of the violin case. "Awesome, congrats. No one cares. Least of all me."

Fire and dizziness warred between Jason's brain and stomach, and he wasn't sure which would win or how it would come out—only that he wanted it to stop.

As if she hadn't just peppered him with venom, Lindsey went to the door. "I only want you to play the correct line in the same song the rest of us are playing. If you're feeling generous, you can even play it at the right volume. Three months from now, you can fly back to your throne on the Left Coast, and I'll have hired a second violinist who doesn't treat every performance like we're going to war."

Jason followed her into the hallway. "Going to war. Not at all hyperbole."

She gave him a thumbs up. "Playing linguistic games rather than addressing a legitimate concern. Not at all infuriating."

"I can't address your so-called concerns when there aren't any to address. You give me smoke and accusations, convinced you've got some grievance against me, when it's actually the opposite."

Lindsey didn't break pace. "Jason the Martyr, maligned by my awesome might. And the fact that I called shotgun."

Lindsey had a patent on verbal warfare. The only surprising thing was that she hadn't kept Ashlyn around for an audience, since that's what she generally did when aiming for the kill. Jason preferred just to direct the bullet to the heart, no audience required. "You're entirely predictable. Everything about you comes straight off the assembly line."

Lindsey raked her hair back from her eyes. "Quite an assessment, considering it comes from a pretty boy fashion plate."

"Even your insults are predictable." Jason shifted his violin case on his shoulder. "Am I worried about what you're going to do? Not in the slightest because even when you're angry, I can read you like a cheap paperback."

Lindsey looked him up and down, and Jason tried not to give in further to the anger. Her judgment. Her glare. The way she shut him off while putting herself on a pedestal. The way she accused him of musical incompetency by saying he was *too* competent.

Bob had said Jason was his best student, and Lindsey was also Bob's student. Jason had nothing to prove. In every way that mattered, it was already proven.

Lindsey pushed the elevator button. "I'm so wounded. Nothing I've done has ever surprised you?"

Jason glanced at the ceiling. "Not even once."

She stepped up to him and kissed him.

He didn't even gasp because she was right up against him, her lips to his, one hand behind his neck and the other at the small of his back. Heat flashed through him from stem to stern. Then, before he had a chance to react, she stepped away, her eyes brilliant and her smile triumphant. "Consider yourself surprised."

Off-balance, Jason snapped, "Not at all. It was a lousy kiss."

Zero points for that surprise attack. None.

She snickered, self-congratulatory in a way that always made him want to make her see herself the same way he saw her.

His gaze bored into her. "You're still predictable. There's nothing you wouldn't do to one-up me, and I *had* pegged you as a lousy kisser."

The elevator door opened, and she stepped inside, still smug. No, she was not going to win like this. Just before the doors closed, he stepped in after her. As she pushed the button for the lobby, though, he had no idea: neither what he wanted to happen next nor what would make that unknown thing happen.

He kind of wanted her to kiss him again. Which, if he admitted it, was a surprise. But that was him surprising himself, not her surprising him.

He glanced at the ceiling. "If you want to be unpredictable—"

She came at him again, crushing him into the elevator wall as it descended. Her mouth met his, and she ran both hands up through his hair. Her lips were warm, her kiss strong, her scent beguiling. He closed his eyes and let her lean against the whole length of him, his violin pushed to one side and hers to the other. This time he let himself respond, hands beneath her coat, fingers through her belt loops, tugging her hips into his. She was here, right here, all of her, and he didn't even want to come up for air.

The elevator lurched to a stop. She withdrew, cheeks flushed.

Breathing hard, he gripped the railing at his back. The elevator doors slid open. She stepped out.

Brain abuzz, he nearly didn't follow. His body screamed at him to do that again. Yes, even with her, even in the face of her mockery, even though she not only didn't care but actively despised him.

He did get out of the elevator. She stood with her hands on her hips.

She looked good. Curvy, limber, bewitching. He wanted to grab her and surprise her right back. Vanilla clicked in his brain. She smelled like vanilla.

She cocked her head. "Rating, please? Was that good enough to surprise you?"

He wanted to say no. He wanted to dare her to do it again. He wanted to win. He wanted—

No, he was done for tonight. He wanted it over with.

"Fine." He let his eyes roam over her. The strong body, the wool coat that flared around her long legs in those riding boots, the mostly-tamed hair with a few wisps escaping, the bright eyes, the angle of her shoulders... He wanted her. "You surprised me."

She folded her arms. "And was that in fact an excellent kiss?"

Now he did step toward her, but she sidled back. He gave a wicked grin. "That was a surprisingly excellent kiss. If you ever want to surprise me again, feel free to do so anytime."

She pointed at him. "Then it won't be a surprise."

He spread his hands. "Once again, entirely predictable."

He did want her to do it again. How unfair was that? But if she could escalate their war with a kiss that bore no feelings, he could at least enjoy the experience for what it was.

It was never about feelings. His ex-girlfriend had said that back in California, and it was no less true in Maine: it was always about the show, about the storyline, about getting and keeping attention.

Lindsey sighed. "I guess that's what they'll have to put on my tombstone. 'Here lies Lindsey Castleton, entirely as predicted.'"

As epitaphs went, it wouldn't be a bad one. "Can you at least give me advance notice of the date, that way I can mark it on my calendar?"

"Stay classy." She turned away as though she hadn't just come onto him in the elevator and left him restless in a way that defied description. "The minute I die, you'll be the first to know. Wait for the burst of joy in your heart, followed by the dawning of a new era."

CHAPTER THREE

Jason was right. Lindsey was nothing special.

Her car sat in the lot with the engine running, which Jason had also been right about. In the past, Jason had mocked her vinyl decals: "4/4" "Make some treble!" and "Musicians take notes." They made Lindsey happy, so of course Jason had to be hateful about them.

As Lindsey got in, Ashlyn clicked off her phone and shoved it in her pocket. "Did you fire him?"

She must have been texting Michael about the blow-up. Lindsey's eyes burned.

"I didn't fire him." Lindsey buckled her belt and slackened into the seat. "Something set him off tonight, but he won't tell me what."

She let the car idle a moment longer, aching and angry and helpless, the taste of Jason enough to send her digging in her purse for the cinnamon-vanilla lip balm. *Dad, I'm sorry. You worked so hard to establish the quartet, and I'm going to be the reason it falls to pieces.*

Lindsey was nothing special. This was true.

She put the car in gear and eased out of the parking lot, hoping Jason wasn't sitting in his own car, smirking at her retreat. Ashlyn was just as tired as Lindsey, and she didn't say anything else.

The headlights swung through a ghost in the road, and Lindsey smiled. These ghosts happened only on clear nights with the temperatures barely above freezing, hovering over the storm drains for the same reason your breath frosts up in the chill. The sewers were warm, and they breathed into the night. When there were no street lights, your headlights revealed the ghosts.

Ghosts in the road also meant the possibility of black ice, so Lindsey would have to be careful.

Being nothing special wasn't a problem, except that Jason had flung it in her face.

Lindsey had accepted this truth ages ago. The universe hadn't singled her out as its musical savior. She wasn't in possession of a locked box brimming with undiluted talent. She was man-and-woman-made, taught from Day One to love music and from about Day Four Hundred to go ahead and make some herself. In no way was it talent or specialness; she was not set apart. No prophets had foretold her coming. She was, as Jason was all too willing to share, ordinary and predictable.

Given who her parents were, it was predictable she'd learn music. Given how often she'd messed around with different instruments, it was ordinary that she'd get good at it. The daughter of an auto mechanic wouldn't brag, "I was destined by the gods to repair transmissions." She'd remember how as a kid she'd stood at Dad's elbow, passing him tools while he restored a 1966 Mustang. She'd remember the day she smuggled a carburetor to school for Show and Tell. As a teen she'd have hung out after the auto shop class, laughing about how a local mechanic had dropped a car off the lift.

Same thing with Lindsey.

For no reason at all, fate had blessed Lindsey with the best life possible. She'd been born into a home where music flowed as easily as tap water. It was a gift she never could have deserved, and there was no reason this gift had gone to her rather than to anyone else. An irreverent muse had seen the universe unfolding and thought, "I want to give someone a really extravagant gift. I want something so outrageous it could never be deserved—so brilliant it couldn't have been earned." Lindsey's pre-made soul was just then clicking past on the assembly line, so the muse kissed it, then rearranged the world so Bob would marry Susan.

Maybe that's why Lindsey was losing her father. She had the perfect life, but she'd never deserved it in the first place. Creation had finally recognized the rebel muse's overindulgent act of generosity, then analyzed how little Lindsey had moved toward deserving it. It was time for a correction.

She reached the highway and got up to speed. Half an hour to home. Gosh, she just wanted to crawl into bed and forget about it all. Forget about her father dying and forget about the crumbling quartet.

Jason? Now, that man had talent. He had a lightning-quick mind and lightning-quick fingers, and unfortunately also a lightning-quick temper. He'd worked hard and played hard and practiced hard since he was five years old. He had the looks. (Gosh, did he have the looks.) He had the poise. If anyone had been touched by the muses to become someone special in the annals of music, it would be him.

Kissing him was impulsive and dumb. The moment she'd done it, she'd known it was a mistake, but Jason made her so angry that she'd lost judgment. In her determination to win, she'd idiotically handed him the victory. He knew now just how much he could get under her skin. He knew he could insult her father to manipulate her like a marionette.

As for Lindsey, it would be nice if she could scour the memory from her brain. During theater productions, she'd given guys luxurious kisses to convince hundreds of viewers she felt something she didn't. This was just one more kiss with a gorgeous guy who felt nothing, a performance to startle an audience of exactly one. Electrifying and tantalizing, but nevertheless a performance. It meant nothing and it should mean nothing other than he'd made her angry enough to act rashly.

That's how you win the hand and lose the game. That's how you signal to a guy that he's right and you just want to derail the conversation.

They reached the highway. Ashlyn had her head back against the seat, eyes closed. Lindsey could turn on the radio, but she didn't want to awaken Ashlyn. It was fine. There wasn't any chance Lindsey would fall asleep, not when she was this upset with herself.

Really, what was a musical Adonis like Jason doing in Maine? Jason had flown to Los Angeles to render his name a household word. Whatever he figured he'd accomplish in the Pine Tree State, it wasn't going to happen. Not in her quartet.

Lindsey's father had become a local legend, and the rest of the world didn't know him at all. Oh, but he'd been good. Dad had the whole package of Jason, plus a rich heart and a deep understanding of human nature. In the ancient world, people would have talked about Bob Castleton as the offspring of a minor god and a wise mortal, arriving from a far-away land in order to bless their communities with divine song. Then in his wake would have come Lindsey, Corwin, and Sierra, not even demi-gods, just delivering gifts of music as was expected.

"Do you think your father spent so much time on me so I'd wither away as some forgotten small-town musician in a state no one goes to?"

That was uncalled for. Her father was a small-town musician. Her father was withering away. Her father was still the best musician alive, and for all Jason's perfect looks and perfect technique, Jason would never come close.

Jason accused her of inheriting her father's station—*shotgun!*—but Lindsey had been halfway out the door. Another year, and one of their substitutes would have been able to step in as second violinist.

This, though. This ending...her father flickering out like the Northern Lights at dawn...this wasn't right.

When Corwin was an obnoxious ten-year-old, as opposed to now when he was an obnoxious twenty-three-year-old, he'd told a story at the dinner table about a guy who'd gotten his chest crushed in a railroad accident and ended up suspended between the train and the platform. The victim was alive as long as no one tried to move him, but as soon as they got the pressure off his pulverized chest, his ribs would collapse and he'd die. The only thing the paramedics could do was hold up a cell phone so the doomed man could say goodbye to his loved ones.

Lindsey felt that same crushing weight whenever she thought of the future: the same pain and the same inevitability, but with no one to hold the phone as a final act of kindness. The universe wasn't giving her kindness, only that load on her chest and everything broken inside that should be holding her up.

Tears came to her eyes. She blinked them down but didn't wipe them off her cheeks. Ashlyn wouldn't see. The car was dark, the highway nearly empty.

When Jason said Lindsey was only where she was because of her father, he was right. Her father had created a legacy, and no other Castleton could steer that legacy into the future. It was easiest to kiss Jason because the only other way to have startled him would have been to say, "You're right."

Only then he'd have followed up with, "So you agree I should play first violin," and she'd have to say no. The Castleton String Quartet was not going to have a non-Castleton on first violin. Her father's legacy wouldn't flame out that quickly. "I'm a great violinist," Jason might have said, to which she'd have replied that great men can play second violin too—and they'd do it with greatness.

What had he been like in the Los Angeles Philharmonic? A brilliant musician surrounded by a hundred seven other brilliant musicians—had he tried to upstage the concertmaster? Had he argued with the conductor? During rehearsal, had the first chair of his section walked over to him and said, "You're too strident. Back off"?

Fifteen minutes to home. Then she could sleep and get up to do it all over again tomorrow.

She saw another ghost in the road, and it was good. Maine was breathing.

An organization like the L.A. Philharmonic was filled with individuals proficient enough to be soloists in their own right. Maybe it was a shock to Jason that he wasn't as exceptional as he thought. Or maybe it was a shock to Jason that he was. According to her father, there had been four hundred applicants for a violinist. There had been fifty-six auditions. There had been one man chosen.

There had been zero applicants for her quartet's first violinist. There had been one daughter chosen. There had been one afternoon when her mother texted with, "You've got a second violinist. He'll be here in a week."

There had been one endless fight ever since.

CHAPTER FOUR

Monday morning. What time did Lindsey start working?

Ages ago, or at least what seemed like ages ago, when Jason was in his junior year at the New England Conservatory of Music, a friend had sent him a photo of a cup of black coffee, a tumbler of whiskey, and a cigarette. Those stood next to a blank page of sheet music, several pencils, an eraser, and a ton of pencil- and eraser-shavings. The caption read, "Musician's breakfast," and Jason had laughed. He didn't smoke, and the drinking never appealed. This morning, the rest of his table looked the same.

On the docket: Jason had to get work done on this composition, and as a sign of how badly he was procrastinating, he kept thinking he should call Lindsey.

The music... Yeah. So.

His agent was on his back about this. "I know it's Christmas, but you didn't *get* the assignment at

Christmas." Edward sounded so...well, diplomatic. That's why agents got paid: because instead of saying, "You're jeopardizing your contract and possibly your career by not doing the thing you got paid to do," they say, "Please manage your time and get this in by deadline."

Every time Jason looked at the screenplay, though, he had the same cold gut-clench he'd felt on seeing Mullen last night, and that led to him spontaneously standing from the tiny table and walking to the tiny window over the stainless steel double sink so he could look out at a back yard full of trees and, it should be added, no inspiration whatsoever.

The blank notebook was already a fallback position to create inspiration. Usually Jason composed directly on the computer. This time, nothing happened. He'd play with melodies in his head, rearrange progressions, mess around with key changes or rhythm changes, and nothing. He'd had the delusion that putting a nice pen to actual paper would help him regain the spontaneity of a kid with his first music notebook, but the notebook had arrived and the pen clicked open...and nothing.

Jason paced the apartment, similarly devoid of inspiration, from the very small sitting room (it fit a love seat, not even a full couch) to the cramped bedroom to the three-quarter bathroom. His mother had pitched it as a "garret apartment," and it had sounded charming. He'd let her send him video, and then he'd signed the lease via overnight mail. Somehow it was actually "loaded with chahm" as promised by the landlord with his thick Maine accent. Jason liked it, but he hadn't realized charm would be so compact.

His ex-girlfriend had worn a "charm" bracelet, loaded with charms, and those were pretty small too. He preferred this kind. Here he had a lease for a whole year and no expectation that the apartment would love him.

Regardless, with no inspiration (nor charm) in any of the corners nor in the crooks of any of the windows, Jason returned to the table and stared at the page. He needed to compose three songs for this movie, and he needed to do it without torching his career for the second time.

Well, torching it or loading it with rocket fuel. It depended on which vitriolic quarter of the internet you asked, and he wasn't about to ask the internet ever again.

Instead he texted Lindsey. "Call me when you get a chance."

The status went from "delivered" to "read" to the three dots to indicate a reply in progress. Then, "Call? Are we back in the Bronze Age?"

Of course, she had to make everything as difficult as possible—and even her attempts to increase the degree of difficulty had to be something she made still more difficult.

He replied, "I'd rather not text. Too many chances to misread tone."

His phone rang. Well, that was faster than anticipated.

"What's so important you need to hear my voice now rather than waiting for tonight?" Speaking of tone, Lindsey sounded both irritated and concerned. "You do remember we've got a Monday night practice, right?"

For crying out loud. "Both of us were out of sorts last night, and you were trying to make sure that didn't happen again. I wanted to clarify where things stand."

"Oh." The concern evaporating, leaving only irritation. "Then clarify. Where do you think things stand?"

It was common knowledge in California that in financial negotiations, the first person to name a number loses. Jason said, "You're the first violinist. You go first."

She huffed. "For crying out loud, Jason, I have ten minutes before I have to teach a class of preschoolers how to march in a circle with egg shakers and a colorful parachute. You asked me to call you to straighten out where we stand, and then you opted for an attack and tossed in a veiled insult for good measure. That's a better assessment of where things stand than anything I could have come up with."

Jason went for a mystified tone. "What fast food chain

offers an extra pump of hypersensitivity syrup in their takeout coffee? Because that was both paranoid and beautiful."

"Isn't it, though? Almost as beautiful as someone texting to work things out and opening with a defensive salvo, then accusing his conversation partner of being oversensitive when she calls out the behavior." Lindsey sounded cheerful, but she knew what notes to strike with her voice, the same way she knew how to get them from her violin. "Speaking of behavioral call-outs, though, I'll save you some trouble and admit I should not have kissed you. That would fall under the definition of sexual harassment, and as your immediate supervisor, I overstepped the boundaries."

Did it? That was wild. Jason said, "I think it only becomes sexual harassment if you're threatening my job."

Or if he hadn't enjoyed the heck out of it. Or if she'd done it again. Any decent lawyer would claim one single event was a proposition, whereas harassment required a pattern of behavior and a threat. One kiss plus a follow-up he'd baited her to give was not a pattern.

Lindsey sounded matter-of-fact. "Power imbalance. No matter how much you enjoyed me coming on to you in the elevator, my legal and ethical obligation was to stand on the opposite side and let you push the 'door open' button when we reached the lobby. I apologize, and it won't happen again."

A momentary disappointment surprised Jason now as much as his assent had surprised him last night. "I wasn't about to phone my lawyer."

"Now you don't have to. However, we need to discuss the next three months because if we're not talking through our respective attorneys, we need to deal with each other directly. Are you still firm on going back to California in March?"

Jason glanced at the music he hadn't yet written. "Yes."

His coffee felt sour in his stomach even as he said it. Of course he was going back. It was just...he had to go back.

He realized he was pacing. Lindsey continued, "In that case, we have about a dozen performances before your time ends. The majority of those will be in December. In January and February, we'll have nothing to do."

Jason would have music to write, plus at least one trip back to Los Angeles to record it. That was something to do.

Lindsey continued, "Until then, I am going to ask you to continue in the second violin slot. However, I'll offer you a compromise. If you want to play first on one or two pieces, let's negotiate that ahead of time so no one's surprised when you go ahead and do it."

Speechless, Jason stopped in his tracks.

Lindsey said, "We can flip around the 'O Holy Night' part of the medley before the next performance. But if you can come up to speed on any of the Haydn or Beethoven quartets, name one and it's yours."

She'd done it. She'd just surprised him.

Jason managed, "You're not offering me Mozart's D Minor quartet?"

"The one written in the key of death? For reasons I can't fathom, that piece is not in hot request for weddings. I'm not sure if my father ever needed to play it, but if a morose bride begs us, sure." She chuckled. "That's all the time you get, pretty boy. I have preschoolers itching to make my eardrums bleed."

He said, "Were you talking while driving? Texting while driving?"

"I texted you from the drive-thru lane at Paranoia Coffee Company, and I have all that hands-free stuff."

"Not safe," he scolded. "A car is not a toy."

"Why do you care? You'll enjoy my death that much sooner, after which you can be first violinist all the time."

He huffed. "Classy."

"See you tonight, pretty boy," she said, and hung up.

She would let him play first violin?

Lindsey, bratty heir to the Castleton musical empire (as she'd so eloquently put it) would yield first chair, even for a little bit? What was she getting from this?

Jason hummed tunelessly on the way to his parents' bed and breakfast, where he'd get lunch in exchange for helping his father spruce up the place for Christmas. It wasn't tuneless, of course. He was experimenting with tunes, getting five or six notes into them before backing out and trying something else. Every so often, he'd record an audio note (no pun intended) on his phone, hoping to keep it as a form of audible tickle file. He had three songs to write and zero songs written.

At a red light, he dictated a text to his agent. "I'd like to talk to Walt Ingram before I get too much further into the process."

That sounded awesome, didn't it? Without lying, Jason had made it sound as if he were knee-deep in musical compositions and merely needed input from the man directing the movie so he could finalize the details.

California had been all about the way it sounded or the way it looked. Looks were primary, and Jason had fine-tuned his look within the first month. From there he became fluent in all aspects of appearance—not just how you looked but where you were when you looked that way, how often you looked it, and what subtle changes you made to the look. Who you looked it with—now that was even better. Crafting the externals was more like a game of blackjack than Jason had anticipated, but at first he'd even found it fun. Then it became addicting when it turned out he was skilled at the game. He learned when to ante up. He learned when to deliberately lose. He learned in the worst way possible that there were too many people whose expertise at the game made him nothing but an amateur.

His ex, for example, had been mystified at how upset he was when she casually dumped him. "I thought we had something here," he'd protested, to which Mimi had replied, "We did, and we had fun. What more did you expect? It's about keeping your fans talking about you, showing up and staying on their minds. You have to do that, or they forget."

He shouldn't call her Mimi anymore. To her fans, she was Mitzy Maxwell, power pop star extraordinaire. To him, she was also back to being Mitzy. Blast it.

After social media had detonated on Jason, *Mitzy* hadn't wanted her name associated with his. She'd penned a sweet and sad breakup tweet that had gotten her a hundred thousand likes and retweets and replies.

As for Jason, he had to accept that he'd lost the hand. He'd played by their rules and bombed.

He'd get back into the game, but not now. In March, he'd fly back for good. Take up where he left off, other than with Mitzy. Return to the game with more experience and better armor around his heart. If you had no expectation that they'd like you, it wouldn't matter when they didn't.

With a three-hour time difference, Jason didn't expect his agent to reply right way, but instead he got, "I'll see what I can do."

Jason added, "Maybe the writer too."

The agent replied, "As if. No one cares about the writer."

Mom and Dad's house (well, Mom's bed and breakfast) had a parking lot for ten cars, but no one was parked in it. Jason left his Audi in the spot nearest the door and headed inside with a backpack that held his music notebook, a few awesome pens, and an unwarranted optimism.

He and Dad had climbed all over the Victorian two weeks ago with ladders and strands of lighting for the outdoor decorations, now all in place. The windows had electric candles on timers. Ropes of pine wound around the railings, and even the mailbox was decorated, but not so decorated that it obscured the sign hanging down: Juniper Hill Bed & Breakfast.

"Hello?" Jason called when he stepped into the pine- and potpourri-smelling foyer.

Mom came from the back. "Oh, just in time! I was wondering if you weren't coming."

He shrugged. "Lunch and manual labor. I'm not punching a time clock."

"Your father wanted to get an earlier start." Mom kissed him on the cheek, and Jason left his jacket on a hook by the door. The dining room had an assortment of smaller tables near a fireplace, but the tables were unset and the fireplace cold. Instead they went into the kitchen where Mom had set out lunch meat and rolls on the wooden table. She texted Dad, then nodded. "He'll be down in a minute." She smiled at Jason. "It's so good having you home this year."

Every so often Mom would drop that into conversation, and Jason cringed. It wasn't that his parents didn't want him to go back to California. In fact, they did. They accepted that California was the only place Jason could accomplish everything he'd ever dreamed, but as long as he was living in Maine for this year, they'd treat him like a very expensive violin on loan to a soloist. There would be admiration and appreciation. Then at the end of the tour, the soloist would go home, and so would the violin.

"Are you fully booked for Christmas?" Jason asked.

"The final deposit came in last night, thank goodness." Mom got a pitcher of filtered water from the fridge. "The last family was at the deadline, and then I'd have had to start calling the wait list. It's better this way. Last year, a family missed the deadline and then acted as though I'd ruined their entire holiday."

Jason said, "Ruined their holiday by posting your terms and conditions on the website? And doubtless sending three reminder emails?"

"Only two, plus a phone call. I was the devil himself,

stealing their holiday joy." Mom huffed. "And before you tell me owning a bed and breakfast was my dream, I'll remind you your father had to deal with outrageous customers at Woodward Restaurant Supply too."

"I get it. I rode along on some of those deliveries." Jason laughed as he took a seat at the table. "*How dare you deliver white table linens! I mean, we ordered white, and we've had white for the past four years, but you should have known starting this week we wanted tan!*"

Dad came downstairs. "Finally here?"

Jason looked at himself. "Apparently so."

Mom snickered. "Eat first, and then you can get started."

Mom and Dad talked about the preparations still to be done, which Jason would get told about again right before doing them. He didn't need to pay attention. Then they asked him about his performances over the weekend, and the memory of Lindsey crashed into him the same way the body of Lindsey had slammed up against him in the elevator.

His throat burned. "One of yesterday's parties was really high-end."

Mom sighed. "I'd love to host an event like that."

Dad said, "Getting guests in the door would be a trick."

"That's why I haven't done it. Even so." She reached for the water filter.

Jason's phone buzzed. Likely his agent getting back to him with threats or sweet encouragement that ought to be interpreted as threats. Or maybe an appointment to talk to the director. How to weasel out of that one? "I'd prefer not to play anything for you just yet, otherwise you might get attached to a substandard pre-finished melody." That would sound good.

Mom's entertainment dreams were a good topic change, though. Jason didn't have to talk about kissing Lindsey. He didn't have mention meeting Mullen. He didn't have to update his parents about not having written any of the compositions he was supposed to turn in.

After lunch, Jason and Dad went upstairs to get the

guest rooms Christmassed-up. The blue room and the green room, the lavender room and the peach room; the gold room on the top floor. Mom and Dad's suite was locked off from the guest areas, and that would stay plain. Dad said to Jason, "I've already decorated two Christmas trees, the one in the parlor and the one in the yard. I'm not decorating a third."

They started in the gold room, and Jason stopped dead in the doorway. The room smelled like vanilla. Lindsey.

It shouldn't keep coming back to him, that first furtive kiss followed by that second hungry one. Her hands in his hair, his hands on her waist, her lips and her breath and her body. The sensations had overwhelmed him, and even now they kept rushing back like Atlantic waves.

Desperate to clear the memory, Jason checked the message that had arrived, and that was a worse mistake. It wasn't his agent. It was Mullen.

"Mullen here. Is this still your number? Helena Sanderson is having a party and wants you to play."

The quartet had wall-to-wall performances this weekend. But still, Helena Sanderson? Actress, B-list celebrity, mother of an A-list celebrity? What was she doing in Maine? Well, for that matter, what was Jason doing in Maine?

Jason replied, "This is still my number. We're booked solid, so it depends."

For Helena Sanderson, he might be able to get Lindsey to dump whatever other gig they were playing.

Mullen replied, "Friday night. She had musicians, but she changed the venue and they cancelled."

Friday night was already taken.

Mullen added, "I told her about you, and she wants the quartet."

Jason texted, "We can do it. Have her reach out to me."

That meant, "Have her personal assistant reach out to me," but Mullen had bypassed Sanderson's staff just enough to drop Jason's name in conversation. Saying anything other than "Yes" would be perceived as a snub.

Mullen was helping Jason up the ladder. That was the language of how these things worked. Jason would rather face Lindsey's wrath than Mullen's scorn, and if he got her angry enough, maybe she'd kiss him again.

And here he was supposed to be forgetting about her.

Dad pointed at the phone. "Put that thing away and help me with the ladder," so Jason put that thing away and helped with the ladder. Dad wouldn't let Jason up there, though. Climbing ladders was Dad's job. Instead Jason hauled and fetched and moved, and it was in the middle of this that he realized he was thinking a series of notes. Thinking them about Lindsey.

He let them repeat in his head, listening rather than forcing. He and Dad moved on to the peach room with its fruity scent, and now the song's hook was assembled in Jason's mind. Okay, but where did it want to go?

Jason transposed it in his head, inverted it, played it backward. Not right. Back to the original. He changed key, humming it down a bit, humming it upward. Still not quite right.

Dad said, "I need a screwdriver," and Jason went downstairs to the toolbox.

He changed major to minor, and there it was.

He ran for his backpack and tore open the notebook, clicked the pen, and started writing. He got the hook down, then studied it for a minute and worked around it. Back up. Fill it with unresolved tension. Make it darker here. Give it a momentary brightness there, then back into the dark.

D minor: Mozart's key of death, the same key in which he'd written the Requiem. A song for a long-discarded lover, only Jason thought of Lindsey the whole time. His anger at her. Hers at him. Her kiss that meant nothing and at the same time filled him with the desire for everything.

He poured the outrage into the music. The unease. The yearning. The raw desire.

Abruptly he stopped, realizing he was breathing hard and his mother was standing behind his shoulder.

"Sorry." He shut the notebook even though Mom couldn't read music. "I just had a breakthrough."

"I figured that out when your father came down to get the screwdriver you were supposed to bring up thirty minutes ago."

He had? Jason gave a nervous laugh.

Mom set a violin case on the table. "This was in the attic when I got down the Christmas decorations, and I thought you might want it."

He shrugged. "I don't see why I would."

"What I meant was, I don't want it."

"Ah!" Jason touched the case. "Well, the case is worth something, at any rate."

Mom said, "You made it."

Yes, but Jason had made a lot of things. That didn't mean they were valuable. He pushed back his chair. "I should get back to Dad."

"There's no hurry. We were both pleased to see you so absorbed." Mom gave Jason a side-hug. "It's been too long since you looked happy."

CHAPTER FIVE

Lindsey hated logging into her bank account via the cell phone, but a payment notification had just come in—a full payment, based on the amount, not a deposit—and she had no idea what for.

They were in the music school basement, waiting for Jason's grand entrance so they could practice everything for the upcoming weekend. Hannah was still setting up, but Ashlyn had tuned and was poking around on her phone.

Whenever Lindsey handed out a contract, she specified an end date after which the contract was no longer valid. That was Mom's addition to Dad's standard contract, done twenty years ago after a bride turned in the deposit six days before her wedding—after the date had already been booked by another bride. But it was (according to the flaky bride) entirely Bob Castleton's fault that her wedding would be ruined.

No potential client had an outstanding quote. Lindsey couldn't even think of a client who'd asked about anything beyond New Year's Eve.

Lindsey said to Ashlyn, "Do you know a Helena Sanderson?"

"Gosh, that sounds familiar. Sanderson." Ashlyn's brows contracted. "There's an actress from like twenty years ago."

"Oh, that must be it. We're flying out to Hollywood for a soiree amongst the stars. She's just booked us." Lindsey tried to glean any other information from the bank portal. "This is bizarre. I'll need to call her to figure out what event she thinks we're playing, except I don't even have a phone number."

Ashlyn searched on her phone. "Helena Sanderson, Academy Award winner, mother of Florian DeMarco. Longtime actress in a soap opera."

Lindsey huffed. "Lovely for her. I still don't know who our client is."

Ashlyn kept scrolling. Then, "Um... She's got a house in Old Orchard Beach."

Hannah's head came up. "Wait, what?"

"Seriously?" Lindsey went back to the bank site. "The money didn't come from a local bank. You've got to be kidding me. I would remember talking to a Hollywood celebrity."

Jason. Bet her this was Jason.

Jason, who at that moment stepped into the room, his cheeks pink and his eyes bright. "Hey! Good news!"

Lindsey said, "Good news, you hand-sold a four-hour performance to one of your Hollywood name-in-lights friends?"

Jason drew back. "Oh, of course you'd steal my thunder."

That was rich, coming from the guy who had no idea what to do when the score said *subito piano*. "My phone let me know we got paid. When did this happen?"

"Oh, the deposit arrived? About two hours ago. That guy

we met Sunday night? He pitched us to her. She needs musicians for Friday night."

Lindsey's vision whited out.

On the grounds that they were a quartet and could read one another's minds, Ashlyn said it for Lindsey: "We're already booked Friday night."

Jason said, "I know, but this was too big to let it go."

Now Lindsey's ears were ringing too, and her hands were clenched so tight that the tendons hurt all the way up her arm. "You know..." It was a struggle not to scream. "I have one rule. One rule about scheduling."

Jason nodded. "That we can't be in two places at once. But I've worked it out."

Lindsey set her violin back in its case because no matter what happened next, she loved her instrument too much for it to get harmed.

Jason said, "We'll call in our subs. We get two subs out to Helena Sanderson, and two to whatever performance we already had on the schedule."

Lindsey's voice was thready. "Call in four subs? On a weekend in December? You want me to call in an entire substitute quartet?"

Jason nodded. "You and Ashlyn take one performance, and Hannah and I take the other. We can call—"

"I understand how phones work." Lindsey stood, glaring at Jason. "That's not the point. Four subs for one evening? Four subs for one evening a week before Christmas? You knew we were booked for Friday night. It's not even that you forgot—you just decided your friend was more important than our client."

Jason shrugged. "I don't even know Helena Sanderson."

"You don't even know her, and you're torpedoing both performances?" Lindsey stepped toward him. "How well is either group going to do with two subs who haven't practiced the material? How are the dynamics going to sound?"

Jason opened his hands. "What was I supposed to do?"

"You were supposed to tell her, 'I'm flattered, but I'm

afraid we can't be in two places at once'."

Jason gave a very subtle eye roll. "It wasn't me who offered us to her. Mullen was the one who put himself on the line."

"I never asked Mullen to put himself on the line. Did you? You wanted to hide under a table when he walked over to us, not beg him for a favor!" Lindsey's mouth had gone dry. "Did you forget what you told me about getting caught playing music for a living?"

Jason's eyes narrowed. "I did this for the group."

For the group. Lindsey should have fired him Sunday night. Two words, and this wouldn't have happened.

Jason said, "She'll have connections, and that's always good."

"Wait. Stop. I need to think." Lindsey closed her eyes. Focus.

This was not an unsolvable problem. It was an unnecessary problem, but not unsolvable. Her father's impending death was an unsolvable problem, but a double-booking she could handle.

"Okay. I hate this, but we'll go through with it." Lindsey steadied herself with a long breath. "Jason, the offer I made you on the phone this morning? You can forget I ever made it because as far as I'm concerned, I gave you an inch and you claimed a marathon."

Jason snorted. "Predictable enough."

How dare he? To belittle her after the tangle he'd just caused. She turned to him. "You are going to play first violin for your buddy Helena, and when you bollocks it up, you are going to be the one who sounds like a buffoon. Old Orchard Beach is far enough that those listeners weren't likely to become paying clients anyhow."

Jason waved a hand. "I assure you, they aren't there to listen to the music. Or know what they're listening to."

No excuse. Dad said you always play your best, even if there's only one person in the audience. Even if you're playing on a dirt road with your case open for people to throw change at you. Lindsey would hold that standard until the day she died. "I'm going to ask Ben to go with you because Ben had twenty years' experience playing cello with my father, and you played with him for three years." She held up her hand before Jason could talk. "Listen to me. You forged this red-hot mess, and this is how we cool it off enough to handle. You get Ashlyn and Ben. I just need to find you a second violinist." She turned to Hannah. "You and I are going to have to carry the other performance, and I'll track us down another second violinist and a violist."

Ashlyn breathed, "Do we even have two second violinist backups?"

"I'll find someone. If we're totally up a creek, my mother could pitch in," and she turned to Jason with a cold smile, "although I'd send her with you. She and Ben have played together off and on for years. Plus, I love hearing you call her Mrs. Castleton, as if you're ten years old and got sent to the principal's office."

Jason kept a patient glare trained on her. "That sounds like a plan."

A plan she shouldn't have had to stitch together in the first place. It was infuriating—beyond infuriating—how he made chaos and then acted as if she were unprofessional for calling it out when she solved his problems.

He added, "Can we get started? Since I'm going to need to get up to speed on the first violin line."

"You're going to need to come up to speed on your own." She went back to her seat and reached for her violin. "The thing we need to do now is figure out how to swap between first and second violin lines on the 'O Holy Night' part of Christmas Medley Two."

Everyone was dead silent. Lindsey's hand was shaking. She was flooded with adrenaline, and she longed to scream and hit something just to burn it off.

Ashlyn said, "So you and Jason are going to make it official?"

They needed something to do. She couldn't let Jason play first violin for the rest of the night while she sat around offering pointers he wouldn't listen to. But she also didn't want to send everyone home without playing anything. What she really needed to do was forge ahead and start calling all their backups, and she couldn't do that either because Jason would see that as giving up.

Jason said, "'Making it official' sounds like we're getting married."

Lindsey said, "I would rather be crushed to death in the dark by a two-ton pile driver, and I'm sure the feeling is mutual. But since Jason's ego requires at least two minutes of grandstanding per performance, I'll allow it."

Jason stood. "There's no call for your tone. I admit I created something of a problem, but I also walked in with a solution. I won us a high-end client with a high-end guest list, and she ponied up some serious high-end money because I doubled our rates for her. That's only going to help in the long run."

Lindsey looked up. "If you're flouncing out, I suggest you park yourself upstairs in the waiting room where the cell phone reception is best, and start calling our subs. Find me two second violinists and a violist. I'll call Ben myself."

Jason glared at her. "Today was actually a good day until about two minutes ago. I spent most of it writing music and landing an awesome client, and you're ungrateful."

Lindsey's voice was raspy, and she couldn't get any kind of volume behind it. "It's not a good day for me. You started the morning by harassing me over the phone, and then you ended it by torpedoing our Friday performance. You're exactly right: I'm feeling no gratitude."

Jason walked out, but he left his violin. He'd be coming back.

Lindsey doubled forward and put her face in her hands, her fingers pressed into her temples.

Hannah sounded tentative. "It's okay. You and I can hold down the fort on Friday."

So unnecessary. So ridiculous. Moreover, it made no sense. That guy Mullen had left Jason shivering in his own skin, so why would Jason ask him for a favor?

Ashlyn put a hand on her shoulder. "You all right? You didn't say Jason called you this morning."

"I was actually nice to him on the phone. I didn't blast him for Sunday night." She tried to draw breath. Crying over Jason would be stupid, but she wasn't about to cry, either. It was the anger, the frustration, the fury. She hated when anger threatened to come out as tears. Dad could have kept Jason under control, but Jason didn't respect Lindsey enough to control himself. Didn't respect the quartet—that was the real problem. The quartet itself wasn't something Jason thought worth his sacrifices.

Whether it was playing softer or playing more slowly, or not double-booking them, Jason wasn't thinking of the quartet as a team. It was always Jason thinking of Jason.

Hannah valued the group. Ashlyn valued the group. They considered the harmonies and dynamics. They looked to Lindsey for guidance and trusted her to advocate for what was best for everyone. Lindsey was constantly in everyone else's head, acting as their frontal lobes and managing everyone's playing in order to create the best possible sound for the whole.

Except for Jason, who did what Jason wanted and did it when he wanted, and usually the result was passable. The quartet wasn't even a secondary consideration because he never considered the group at all.

Ashlyn said, "He'll be back."

I halfway wish he wouldn't. But they had too many performances between now and Christmas. Again, the quartet had needs. The community of instruments and players had needs, and Lindsey had to safeguard them.

She shook it off. She had to. Instead, she pulled some sheet music from her backpack beneath her chair. "Jason and I are going to trade lines for 'O Holy Night', and I've rearranged the measures into the switch and the measures back out again. You two can practice the transition with me, and when he returns, we'll add him back as well."

At home, Lindsey didn't turn off the engine. Ashlyn said, "What's up?"

"I'm going to visit Dad." Lindsey didn't look at her. "Can you take my violin upstairs? I don't want to leave it in the car."

Ashlyn said, "I'm sorry. I thought it would get worse if I got in the middle."

"I don't expect you to get in the middle. Jason would just pull the superiority act on you as well." Lindsey flexed her hand on the steering wheel. "I'll be back soon."

Ashlyn said, "Do you want me to come with you?"

"I'll be fine."

It wasn't a long drive to the rehab hospital. The security guard buzzed Lindsey through without question, and Lindsey checked in with the nurses before proceeding to the corner room where her father was still awake.

"Hi, Dad." She poked her head around the corner. "It's Lindsey."

Dad was sitting up in bed, looking at the television. It was too loud, but lately he'd been having trouble with the buttons, either with finding the right ones or with pushing them the right number of times. Lindsey sat on the foot of the bed, and he fumbled momentarily with the remote before she leaned forward to take it from him. The remote also served as a nurse call button, and Mom had taped colors around the buttons Dad needed most often. Red for calling the nurse. Green for turning the TV on and off. "Should I shut it off, or just lower the volume?"

He said, "Off."

The noise ended. She handed back the remote, but when Dad set it down on the bed, it slipped off the side. It didn't hit the floor. Mom had solved that problem too by securing a six-inch-long safety pin around the cable so Dad would always be able to pull the cord back up.

The room glimmered with white lights. Sierra had strung them after Thanksgiving so Dad would have pretty things in his room, saying, "They're beautiful, and everyone can use a little beauty." Sierra had them on a timer to go off at eleven o'clock because Dad was usually up until then, and the nurses said he got agitated if the lights went off.

Lindsey said, "I looked at the guest book. Mom came earlier today, and so did Sierra."

Dad nodded. Lindsey said, "Did Mom bring lunch so she could have it with you?"

Dad gestured at the tray on the bedside table. The nurses had brought him a bedtime snack, but it lay mostly untouched. Pudding with a spoon. He'd eaten maybe two bites. There was also an apple juice with a straw poking out of the lid.

Dad's face looked gaunt, the skin too large for his body. He was losing weight, and there wasn't anything to do about it. Most days, Mom ate lunch with him because he'd eat more when she was there. The nurses didn't have the time to spoon-feed him, nor would he have tolerated it if they'd tried.

Dad was dying. A year ago, Dad would have been the one playing first violin for all these parties, and this year, Dad couldn't operate the remote control or reliably use a spoon.

Lindsey said, "Do you remember Jason Woodward? He's playing second violin, and he's being a pain."

Dad smiled. "A pain."

"He wasn't a pain like this for you, was he?" Lindsey looked for one of Jason's pictures on her phone. "Before he went to California, he didn't grandstand in front of you. He wouldn't have dared."

Dad shook his head.

Lindsey said, "If you want to know something cute, though, Jason borrowed the star violin."

Dad brightened. "The star is still there?"

He'd remembered! "It's definitely still there. I loan that violin to students who need a little extra boost, and I tell them the story. It helps them. Sometimes when it comes back to the school afterward, I play it myself, and it helps me too." She kept swiping through her photo albums. "It's funny that Jason would get it now."

Oh, here was the photo she wanted. Three years ago, right before Jason left, she'd taken a photo of the official quartet. Dad and Jason, Ben as the cellist, and a woman named Maureen as the violist. Maureen had left because of family commitments but still subbed for Ashlyn on occasion. Back then, Lindsey occasionally subbed for Jason, but she'd been working as a stringer and copy editor for a local newspaper.

She'd nearly gotten out. Nearly.

Lindsey expanded the photo so Dad could see Jason's face, but Dad slid it over so he could see Ben. Smiling, he said, "How is he?"

"Ben? He's doing great. I saw him a couple weeks ago." According to the guest book, Ben had visited Dad recently. "I'm going to call him to help the quartet on Friday."

Dad nodded. "A good man."

"He is. You picked a great friend." Ben was devastated. Lindsey had seen him break down in the parking lot, but he kept visiting. Dad had forgotten all of the kids at some point or another, and once he hadn't recognized Mom, but he'd never not recognized Ben.

Lindsey said, "Ben's daughter is going to have a baby."

Dad brightened. "Really? How wonderful!"

This news always brightened Dad up. Sometimes he already knew it, but lately he didn't remember it anymore so he kept getting to experience the joy for the first time. Lindsey said, "She's having a little girl. Ben's going to go out when she's born."

Dad smiled, and Lindsey's heart broke because Dad wasn't going to live long enough to see his own grandchildren.

Lindsey dragged the photo back to Jason. "Was Jason

really your best student?"

Her heart burned. Jason could disrespect her all he wanted, but it wasn't fair to tarnish Lindsey's relationship with her father. If Dad said that about Jason, then Dad was sidelining all three of his children. Well, all four, but Michael didn't count.

Dad paused, and Lindsey wondered if Dad even remembered Jason right now, let alone where Jason ranked in his list of students.

Dad had taught so many students in so many different fields. His students had ended up all across the country, plus several in Canada and a few in Europe. He taught them music theory and whatever instrument they arrived wanting to learn, and if he couldn't teach them, he contracted with someone who could. The school still operated that way. A recent student wanted to learn the bagpipes, so after Mom had taught her as far as she could with the chanter, she'd reached out to the local Knights of Columbus. Now the school had a bagpipe instructor who came on Thursdays.

On Saturday mornings during the fall, the bagpiper and his two students had gone out to a hill on the park. Lindsey had opened her window and listened to the mournful sound blowing through the leaves with their dying colors. Music was like that: make a beautiful sound, and it affected everybody.

Now she reached for the table alongside the bed where a visitor had left a ukulele. It was in tune, and she plucked the strings. You didn't tune a uke like a violin, and that always jolted her because if you showed her four strings, she wanted them to be G, D, A and E. Dad's room was full of little instruments, from the uke to a finger-piano to an ocarina to a harmonica. He used to play them all. Now, barely ever.

Lindsey had never added up all the alumni of the Castleton School of Music, but there had to be hundreds, maybe thousands. Twenty-five years of teaching, starting in the side wing of their rambling house (they'd bought the house because of that wing) and ending with the building on Granite Cross Road: so many students. Students had gone on to Broadway, to major metropolitan philharmonics, even to the Rock and Roll Hall of Fame. Every year, Mom would hang all the incoming Christmas cards and it was the roster of every New England music festival.

According to Jason, he'd bypassed all those: he was the best.

Lindsey went on. "I can't make Jason work with us. He does what he wants, and when I call him out, he shifts the blame back to me. It's not his problem that he played the wrong line, or that he won't lower the volume. Instead it's my problem for being unreasonable."

Dad shook his head. "You have to play together."

Lindsey said, "For someone who claims to have been your best student, he never learned that."

Dad shrugged. "Tell him you have to play together."

Lindsey fought frustration. She hadn't expected Dad to advise her. She just wanted to vent. "Jason doesn't listen."

"You make him listen." Dad paused. "What does he think he's doing?"

Lindsey said, "He's destroying the dynamics."

Dad shook his head. "What does he *think* he's doing?"

Lindsey said, "He thinks he's being the very best student you ever turned out from the music school."

Dad didn't answer.

Lindsey looked at her lap. "Did you ever play in two places at once? Jason booked us for two parties at the same time, a hundred miles apart."

Dad only looked sad. Lindsey continued, "I had Jason call in all our subs. I'm going to get Ben on the phone. Maybe Ben can rein him in."

Dad perked up. "You talked to Ben? How is Ben?"

She met his eyes. "Ben's doing great. Ben's a good guy."

Dad might have forgotten his best student, but at least he remembered his best friend.

CHAPTER SIX

Lindsey could go jump off a cliff for all Jason cared, and he only hoped he'd be around when it happened.

He got back into his apartment at nine thirty, still arguing with Lindsey in his head and coming up with great one-liners that would have nailed her to the wall. He'd provided a great opportunity, and she was fussing about the logistics. There was a lot of money involved, and Helena Sanderson's personal assistant had accepted without hesitation. There would be photographers at this event. There would be high-class individuals and prestige and anything Lindsey could have asked for, and instead she was hung up about the schedule.

Jason set his violin on the table, raised the lid on the laptop, and dealt with momentary vertigo.

What he really wanted to do was keep working on that song. It had been hard enough breaking away to get to practice at all, but now he was back here and all the longing twisted inside him. He wanted to keep working. He wanted to play it. He wanted to quiet the swirling in his head because as soon as he worked on Lindsey's song, he was going to be thinking again about Lindsey and how he hated everything about her.

A further complication was that he and the neighbor downstairs had an agreement: Jason wouldn't play his violin after nine at night. The week after Jason moved in, the neighbor had come upstairs with cookies and a sweet request to establish quiet hours. While it wasn't a legal obligation, Jason had accepted both the cookies and the restriction.

Even so, he wanted to play with Lindsey's song, recompose it, improvise with it. He'd have to mute the violin.

The obvious thing would have been to stay at the school and use a practice room, but that would have meant dealing with Lindsey for even one minute than he had to. She'd have been all over him about locking up and making sure to set the alarm, and by the end his jaw would have hurt from clenching it so hard. Then he'd have been too tense to work on the composition anyhow. The twenty-minute drive home had barely been enough to calm him down.

Jason opened his violin case, then frowned. He hated muting such a sweet instrument.

He did, however, have the loaner student violin. The loaner couldn't hold a candle to Jason's violin, plus it had a star carved on the rib near the base button. It wouldn't be a crime to mute that thing. Jason got it out of his closet, only then he found himself facing three violins on the table.

There was his real violin, the one he'd gotten after he'd signed with the L.A. Philharmonic. This one he loved and could see himself playing it for the rest of his life.

There was Lindsey's graffitied-up student violin. Not horrible to listen to, but without any magic. It would be an embarrassment to get caught playing it, but when they played on a yacht or in the cold, it would do.

Lastly, there was the violin he'd made himself.

Susan Castleton had introduced sixteen-year-old Jason to a luthier, and as a kid with his first car, Jason did what any sixteen-year-old would have done and drove out to the violin-maker's shop on every afternoon he could. He'd breathe the scent of the animal glue and wood shavings, watch the luthier microplaning violin bodies or softening strips of wood to inlay their purfling, and he'd listen to the man ramble about what makes a violin sing. A couple of summers later, the luthier asked if Jason wanted to apprentice with him. One summer, one thousand hours of menial work, and one violin. Except it was a bad violin, and it never sang.

Mom and Dad never understood what that meant. As with most of his musicianship, they listened to Jason, supported him, reassured him, and walked away mystified. "A violin needs a voice," Jason had explained. Another time he'd said, "It needs to resonate." They didn't get it. The luthier had said it wasn't unusual for early violins not to sing, and sometimes a dud still happened to him. The violin was perfect, except for the fact that it wasn't. It looked the same as every other violin hanging from the rafters, except that it never developed a voice and never rang out with the sounds a violin ought to make.

Jason had brought it home, looking splendid but otherwise good for nothing. Which, in retrospect, kind of hurt. No, actually, it burned. It felt like a foreshadowing of his own future that had slipped right under his radar on the first viewing of a film, but would have everyone cringing on the third or fourth viewing.

He took the mute from his real violin's case and fitted it to the student violin, but before he could play, his phone rang.

Jason braced himself for a barrage from Lindsey, but it might be one of their alternates getting back to him.

Only that was a Los Angeles number, and Jason stared at it through two more rings before forcing himself to answer. "Hello?"

"Woodward! Walt Ingram! Great to finally connect!"

Jason was sitting in the kitchen chair. He didn't remember getting there. "I didn't think you'd call tonight. Did Edward tell you it was a rush?"

That "finally connect" sounded as if they'd been leaving desperate voicemails for days, rather than, "Can you set up a call with Walt?"

Walt had enough enthusiasm to turn a windmill. "I figured I'd cut the red tape and just try you." It wasn't even seven o'clock on the left coast. Walt was driving back to Thousand Oaks and chatting it up while doing ninety-five on the 405, simultaneously tailgating and being tailgated, and to him that was Monday. Walt said, "Let's talk. I want to hear what you've come up with so far."

"Not until it's finished. We're not playing that game again." Send a demo and suddenly it's been pasted into the soundtrack and no one wants to change it afterward.

"Don't be so sensitive. Besides, has Edward talked to you yet?" No, Edward had not talked to him. "You're playing whatever you write."

Good thing he was sitting in the chair. "Even now?"

"Especially now. I know this blew up last year, but I told you it would pass, and it did."

Jason said, "After I got doxxed, had to delete all my social media, got dumped, and moved out of California."

"It would have passed anyhow, and the publicity was terrific. The movie is still making money, and we're about to start generating some serious buzz on the sequel."

Jason said, "When do you finish shooting Ultraviolet?"

"We're finalizing the dates and everything can still change, but we'd really like at least the first two songs by February first, and we want you out here to shoot in early March."

Jason said, "Gotcha." Numb, he glanced at the calendar to make sure it still said December.

The three violin cases sat, unsinging, on the table. Jason said, "Talk a bit about the movie. I've read the screenplay, but I want to crawl inside your head and get a better sense of what you're thinking before I finalize the pieces."

Walt launched into a sales pitch that went off the rails after two minutes, and then he was digging deep into the tone of the film, the themes, the undercurrents, the multiple interwoven threads. Jason asked about plans for a third movie if this one did as well as the first. (And what would you even call it? Violet Nights, Ultraviolet Dawn... Plum Meridian? Walt laughed hard at that title. Jason would have to wait two years to see how the third title turned out.) Jason tossed out different interpretations of a few ambiguities in the screenplay, and Walt got excited about those as well.

Violet Nights had left the audience with quite a few questions that were open to interpretation. Ultraviolet Dawn would have to answer some of those questions, meaning it needed to raise others. Keep this going and you could in effect have a thousand and one Arabian/Violet nights. Assuming the internet rage mob didn't just go ahead and cut off Scheherazade's head.

Walt said, "I don't know how you do your music witchery, but is that enough for you to move ahead on the compositions?"

"I think so." In retrospect, Jason ought to change Lindsey's song, but it would be a shame to lose its raw energy. "I think you'll like what I've come up with, but I don't want to settle for just liking it."

"Understood, man. Keep in touch. Walt, out," and Walt was out.

Jason didn't get up from the table. He didn't touch the muted violin, and he didn't reach for the sheet music. As for the voiceless violin, it just stayed there, lifeless.

Last February.

Mrs. Castleton? It's Jason Woodward. I was wondering if I could speak to Bob.

Unfortunately, right now, I'm afraid you can't. What do you need?

Jason paced a hotel room. He had his violin with him, a few days' worth of clothes, his computer, and some books. This wasn't a vacation. He'd vacated, but not for pleasure. For fear. For harassment.

I need Bob's advice. When will he be back?

He can't. I... It's really complicated, but I don't know when he'll be able to talk to you. You sound like a wreck. What's going on?

Jason felt wrecked. He was wrecked. His career was wrecked. His relationship was wrecked. His friendships were wrecked. He'd gotten slammed between an irresistible force and an immovable object, and without either one caring, he'd been crushed.

Have you heard of a movie called Violet Nights? It came out about a month ago.

No, I haven't been paying attention.

I wrote two songs for it, and I performed one of them in the film.

That's good.

No, it's not. The movie was amazing, but no one thought anything would happen—except it turned into a sleeper hit. And then it got controversial. Like, really controversial. The actors and the director are getting death threats.

Are you safe?

I am now. I'm in a hotel that's got security like you wouldn't believe. But—

Jason sat on the corner of a king-sized bed. That's just what the suite came with. He didn't need a king. He had no one to share it with, and he couldn't imagine sleeping anyhow.

But an internet mob went after me, and I made the mistake of answering them, and it only got worse. They found where I live, and now everything's on fire. I'd been shortlisted for an award, and that got yanked back. My agent was negotiating two different offers, one for an entire movie about a violinist, and both of those have gotten revoked.

What about the philharmonic?

I left six months ago, when my solo work started taking more of my time.

Are you financially secure for a while? Have you talked to the police? Are you in danger?

Everyone says it will blow over.

Everyone kept saying that, but then Jason had seen his own address up on Twitter with a link on how to dismember a human body...and that was the scariest moment of his life.

They're tearing me apart online. But it's not just online. No one reviewed the movie when it opened, but now that it's gotten attention, they're burning it to the ground.

It's all vindictive. Jason, take a deep breath. What about the other people this is happening to? What do they think?

They're all in a different part of their careers. This isn't going to sink them. But I'm just starting out, and they're going to sink me. The reviewers went after my playing. They said—

Breathe. It's okay.

They said it was banal and childish. I wrote those pieces. They were good. But they said the pieces were sentimental smarm. They said I'm good for nothing but fizzy pop music and cartoon theme songs, and I need to take a year off to learn to play.

You know how to play.

I don't know anything anymore. All this blew up so hard and so fast.

Then trust me that you're good. You got into the Los Angeles Philharmonic. You're one of Bob's best students. Bob's so proud of you.

My agent says to take some time out of the spotlight because these things happen all the time, but I'm not sure. The director thinks it's all part of the business, but he lives in a gated community. The actors don't even care because for every person attacking us, they say that's another ticket sold to the other side. But I'm getting slammed even by the reviewers who liked the movie. What they said about my playing—is it true? I don't know what to do.

Silence. Jason tried to get his breath back. He'd need to order room service for dinner, but he wasn't sure he'd even be able to eat. He'd need to figure out what he was doing all night if he wasn't going to sleep.

After a very long fermata, Susan spoke.

Let me tell you what's going on over here. And then I have a proposition for you.

Bob. Bob was dying. Susan laid it out much more steadily than Jason had poured out his crisis. She rolled out all the facts, one at a time. Gutted, Jason sat straddling the corner of the oversized bed, staring out the window over the freeway toward the Pacific.

Bob.

Bloodless, Jason whispered, "I'm so sorry."

He shouldn't have called. He should have realized when Susan answered Bob's phone, and he shouldn't have dumped all this on her. She wasn't going to know what he should do. Since early January, she'd been dealing with a crumbling family. How could she deal with a crumbling career? Why would she want to?

Instead, she had a suggestion for him, something to help them both.

If you want to take time off, you can rejoin the quartet. We need someone, and it doesn't have to be for very long. Your agent said to take some time off. Would you be willing to transplant for a year?

Jason had no one here. It was just his agent, plus all his contacts. His friends weren't talking to him. His apartment-mates wanted him gone, and he could make them find someone to take over his lease.

He could ask about returning to the philharmonic or even find another orchestra. He could stay buried in the second violins, surrounded by a hundred and seven other talented musicians. No one would care. No one would notice if Jason stayed or if he left, but disappearing in plain sight hadn't been why he'd come to California.

He wanted to escape. Get out. Go home.

"He needs to take a year off and learn to play."

Jason's eyes stung. He wanted to tell Susan he'd think about it. He didn't.

He could take over a quartet. He could select music and talk to clients and run rehearsals. He'd never be able to fill Bob's shoes, but he could take over Bob's role, and he could mentor Lindsey until she was able to do it. Clients wouldn't roast him over Twitter. Lindsey was a brat, but she wouldn't pretend to like him in order to make people talk about her.

Maine was the perfect place to crash-land. When Mimi broke up with him yesterday—well, Mitzy now—she'd said it was all about being seen with the right people in the right places to keep everyone talking about you, otherwise they'd forget. Now Jason needed to work the machinery to make them forget. They had to stop talking about him. Maine was the wrong place, and the Castletons were the wrong people.

What he said was, *Thank you. I'll take you up on that.*

CHAPTER SEVEN

Lindsey should have gone to Jason's swanky friend's party. For one thing, she wouldn't have been fielding this phone call from Ashlyn.

"Jason didn't want to say yes without consulting you." Ashlyn sounded unnerved. "It sounds like a great opportunity, but I guess after he double booked us, you put the fear of God into him."

Lindsey slumped in the driver's seat, eyes closed, battling a mounting static in her brain. "When does this producer need an answer?"

"Based on how he was talking? Five minutes ago." Of course. "Jason begged off on an immediate answer, but when he asked me to call you, he's...I don't know."

Lindsey watched the defroster doing its job on the windshield, wishing she had a device that would do similar work on her life. Push a button, keep the engine running, and when you opened your eyes, all the Christmas performances would have been done, and all the decisions made.

"Of course Helena Sanderson would have a TV producer in attendance at her party." Lindsey swallowed hard. "I'm confused about why they want us on their show."

"Jason seems to have a name with these people. I don't get it either, but Ms. Sanderson introduced Jason to this producer, and after about two minutes, Jason had the producer in contact with his agent or his publicist or something, and by the end of the party the producer wanted us on a network morning show on the 26th of December."

Lindsey rubbed her temples. "So we'd have to drive down to New York on Christmas night, sell our souls for a hotel room in Manhattan, film something at oh-dark-thirty, and then drive home? They'd never pay us enough to make that worthwhile, and there's no benefit for us in national exposure. Send Jason alone."

"After talking to Jason's agent, the producer says it's all four of us or it's a no-go, and everything is paid. The flight, the hotel, the car to the studio in the morning."

Lindsey sat up. "Flight?"

Ashlyn said, "Ah-yeah. Bangor to LaGuardia. Shuttle to the hotel. Shuttle from the hotel to the studio. We could tour Manhattan afterward if we want because they're also paying us."

Lindsey whistled. Then, "Ashlyn, who is he?"

"The producer?"

"Our second violinist. Why would a morning show want us on the air? Oh, and are we playing for them, or just sitting around talking?"

"Both. The timing stinks."

"Of course it stinks, but you don't get multiple opportunities for a national morning show. I'm talking to Hannah first, though, because she's not going to like this at all."

Ashlyn said, "Jason wants an answer before we go home."

Lindsey said, "She's already left. I'm guessing this means your performance went well?"

"It was by no means smooth, but we're okay, and the party is going overtime. Jason's soloing pieces by special request while I'm on the phone."

"Okay. I'll call Hannah." A minute later, she was texting Hannah, "Pull over and call me," and within two minutes the phone rang.

"Lindsey? Is everything okay?"

"What's your first impression if I said December 26th, all-expense-paid trip to New York City to appear on a national morning show? Jason's rich actress friend had a TV producer at her party."

Hannah went dead silent.

Lindsey said, "Would you consent? If all four of us don't consent, I'm telling Jason's high-powered friends they can pound sand."

Hannah sounded terrified. "Keep me from talking to them."

"They're not talking to either of us, trust me. Ashlyn and Jason are the beautiful ones."

Hannah laughed. "Are we performing for the show? Because that would be amazing."

"Apparently we are." Lindsey sighed. "Mom would keep Parker overnight. I just..."

Christmas was going to stink anyhow, probably Dad's last Christmas, and now this on top of it. But maybe it would be good to have so much work that she couldn't think about what her family was losing. Maybe she'd get through the holiday without shattering like a flawed champagne flute.

Hannah consented, so Lindsey texted Jason. "Answer is yes. Make sure that flight to New York isn't before 9 p.m., and get a fifth seat for Hannah's cello."

She texted similar to Ashlyn, then put the car in gear to head home. Tonight was too cold for road ghosts, too dry for black ice. By the time Lindsey reached their apartment, she had a reply from Jason. "Yes, ma'am."

And a second reply, also from Jason. "You're welcome."

Ashlyn wasn't back yet, so Lindsey did the bookkeeping and made a note to find out how much overtime Jason's group had played. It didn't matter how much Jason had overcharged from the start: she was going to bill the redoubted Ms. Sanderson for the extra minutes.

Uneasy, Lindsey flipped the switch on the electric kettle. It lit up blue. Then she positioned herself in front of her open laptop and typed into the search bar, "Jason Vanderbilt Woodward."

Fifteen minutes later, Lindsey looked up to see the electric kettle dim, its automatic shutoff long since tripped. She turned it on again.

Lindsey whispered, "What are you doing here?"

None of this was what she'd expected. None of it. Jason even had a Wikipedia page, for crying out loud. It had been defaced by people who hated him (a sentiment Lindsey could understand, though not the vitriol) and she reported the page for review. Then she went to Jason's personal website and attempted to construct a timeline.

Jason had quit the philharmonic about eighteen months ago. He'd written music for a children's show, and apparently that gave him an entree to write and perform the opening and closing themes of a Netflix series. That series had developed a cult following. Lindsey had heard of it but never watched an episode.

Last December, he'd recorded "Love Once More" with pop sensation Mitzy Maxwell, a song that had climbed to number two on the charts in February. They'd performed it at the Grammys.

Jason had performed at the Grammys? He'd had a number two pop song?

The Grammy performance video played for Lindsey, and that was definitely Jason. Jason with his perfect hair and incredible style, a tailored tuxedo, and just enough stage makeup to turn him into a cover model. Mitzy Maxwell, perfection itself, encouraged the crowd as she sang. She was lip-syncing. So, Lindsey realized, was Jason. Or rather, string-syncing. What he was playing on that violin wasn't the same sound playing through the speakers.

It made sense: during a performance this big, you didn't want to mess up. Especially not with the amount of movement going on. Mitzy Maxwell was dancing all over the place. Jason was in constant motion.

He'd criticized Lindsey over the summer: "You need to learn to dance." As if she could be in the same class as Mitzy Maxwell? Lindsey could have a personal trainer, a licensed dietitian, six wardrobe consultants, and a choreographer rehearsing with her nine hours a day, and she still couldn't set foot in the same class as Mitzy Maxwell.

Maxwell worked that crowd (and her body, and her vocal cords,) with a mastery Lindsey would never possess. Jason looked delighted. Lindsey had never seen him that happy either. Whenever he played with the quartet, he was grim.

At the bottom of the video, as Twitter comments streamed by in an endless scroll, Lindsey noticed a hashtag for the eighth time: #Mitson. It was hard to know where to focus: on the movement, on the comment feed, on the music, on the lyrics... Whenever the camera panned over the audience, though, Lindsey checked the comments. "Team #Mitson!" "They're so cute together!" "So jealous of #Mitson!"

You have got to be kidding me.

Like most pop songs, "Love Once More" featured a couple that hadn't been in love for longer than three days. The violin line was energetic with an awesome hook. Jason had a co-writing credit, but none of this seemed his style. Mitzy Maxwell dominated the stage in her glittery outfit and her well-styled hair, her light-lyric soprano voice and suggestive moves. More than once she'd come up behind Jason and wrapped her arms around him, triggering a stream of #Mitson comments and audience members with their hands over their mouths.

Then, at the end, Mitzy Maxwell kissed him. That resolved the #Mitson question. Not only had Jason gotten together with *the* Mitzy Maxwell, but they even had a 'ship name.

Lindsey Googled "#Mitson" and was not disappointed. Gushing fans had posted (and reposted) photos of the two at trendy Los Angeles locations. Some people thought Maxwell could do better, but most loved them as a couple. They looked breathtaking together when he accompanied Mitzy on her weekly trips to California children's hospitals, or when he wore a tux to stand in attendance as she donated twenty grand to a foundation to bring clean water to the world. Someone had gotten a photo of the pair asleep under an airline blanket in first class on a flight to Cabo San Lucas. The fans self-reported a tremendous death toll from sheer cuteness. Even Lindsey thought they were adorable.

After all this, what was Jason doing back in Maine?

The next thing on Jason's public timeline was a movie called Violet Nights. It had released last January with limited showings and exactly no critical acclaim until it had drawn word-of-mouth steam at the box office. Then it got a lot of attention. First good attention, and then a tsunami of negative attention.

Jason had actually appeared in the movie. As in, not only had he written two pieces for it, but he'd performed one in the film. At the time, he must have thought of it as a step upward, a film credit in a low-budget production that might get shown at a few artsy festivals, but at least it wasn't direct-to-Blu-ray. No, instead this thing blew up, and it blew up in the way of the Hindenburg.

Lindsey hadn't registered any of this. It all happened at the same time as her father's diagnosis and decline. For months she hadn't listened to pop radio and hadn't looked at social media because her family needed help. She'd been shutting down her fledgling journalism career and getting up to speed on how to run a quartet and a music school.

Trolls had lambasted Jason online, and he'd struck back. His attackers unearthed his personal information and posted it everywhere. His address. His birthday. Physical threats. Jason shut down his social media. Shortly afterward, Mitzy Maxwell posted a tearful #MitsonNoMore tweet that thrilled half her fans and broke the hearts of the other half. #TeamJason kept posting that Mitzy needed to get back with him. For her part, Maxwell hit all the right notes. She adored Jason and wished him the best, but a reluctant parting was what they both needed right now.

Lindsey checked the date. #Mitson died maybe eight days before Jason had moved back to Maine. Mitzy must not have wanted a long-distance romance—except that was ridiculous. A woman bedecked with as much money as Mitzy Maxwell could fly to Maine every Wednesday and Saturday if she wanted. It's hardly long-distance when you're flying first class and can marshal an airplane as your private office. Not to mention that whenever she went on tour, she'd perforce be long-distance with anyone.

Lindsey searched for clips of Violet Nights, and there were only a million. Eventually she tracked down the violin piece, and there was Jason on film.

Gosh, he was gorgeous. Hollywood had taken a work of art and perfected it, right there. He looked amazing, sounded amazing—just amazing all over. The violin sounded like his, but it looked more gold and had a greenish undertone. Lindsey got a vague idea of the movie's plot, that there was a controversial character named The Madrigal, and Jason's song served as her inspiration at the end of the second act.

Lindsey left the clip playing while she searched again. Violet Nights was going to have a sequel, Ultraviolet Dawn. Oh, and Jason was writing music for that movie too. Well, wouldn't Jason have fun?

She froze, nauseated. Hold the phone. This wasn't right.

Jason had gotten doxxed the first time. What would happen when this new movie dropped and everyone remembered him? Remembered him *and his quartet?* How much hate would the quartet get?

She looked for the date of the new movie. Five months from now.

The static in her head intensified. This TV interview was buzz-building for the second film.

Jason had just painted crosshairs on the quartet.

He'd put her and her father and her almost-sister and their lifelong friend right into a position where the internet, with its merciless fangs and claws, could shred them like newspaper. Every single one of them was easily found with a Google search. The music school was right out there, address and phone number. Mom's address? Discoverable. A troll could probably find Dad's hospital room if they searched enough in the deep web.

Jason knew what a mob could do. How dare he volunteer the rest of them like human shields without warning them of the danger?

Lindsey texted Mom. "How much of this did you know?"

A minute later, the reply appeared. "Depending on what we're talking about, somewhere between 0% and 100%."

Lindsey wrote, "Jason, Hollywood, internet mobs, Mitzy Maxwell, movies."

Mom texted, "About 75%."

Lindsey huffed. "You could have warned me. If the internet takes aim at the quartet, that's going to hurt."

Mom waited a bit before replying. "Internet rage runs hot and burns out fast. They didn't remember him after he disappeared. Why would they remember him now?"

Lindsey searched Twitter, and that at least seemed to be true. No mention of Jason at all in the past eleven months. But once the quartet got out there on the airwaves, everyone would remember again.

Hannah already had safety issues. Ashlyn was in a relatively new relationship with a man whose adoptive parents looked down on her. And Lindsey was about to lose her father. Did they really want to set a can opener to that particular can of worms?

Mom texted, "Has someone threatened him?"

Lindsey replied, "Not yet."

Lindsey texted Ben. "I hear things went all right tonight?"

He replied, "Wished you'd been there. Swanky party, nice tips."

She texted, "And you kept Jason in line?"

Ben's reply was, "It was good to play with him again. But he's not like he used to be."

That was curious. "Meaning?"

"He used to be warmer. His playing is very technical, but that might be because he wasn't familiar with the first violin part."

Lindsey had sat in on Jason's group's practice. Jason had done well getting up to speed on those pieces between Tuesday and Thursday. Unfamiliarity wasn't it.

Fortunately, Lindsey did have videos of the quartet before she was a part of it, and now she brought up one, a Haydn piece.

The first person she saw was Dad. Her eyes stung.

This lineup was Dad, Ben, Jason, and Maureen. Lindsey was supposed to be watching Jason, but she couldn't take her eyes off Dad.

Dad, with no clue what was to come in four years. Dad, carrying the time bomb in his genes that would atrophy his brain and take his words, his memory, his motor coordination, and his music. Would take his soul and leave the shell. Would take him.

She paused the video until she could breathe again, then went full-screen and enlarged the video so she could see only Jason. Otherwise she'd never stop watching her father.

She resumed play, pixelated but focused. And yeah, Ben was right. Lindsey hadn't paid attention to Jason because back when Jason had returned, life had been a bewildering array of pain and loose ends. Jason arrived, and Lindsey had been relieved to sign off on one more thing sorted. She'd never looked up what Jason had done in California. She'd meant to do that when she updated the website, but she'd never fully updated the website. She'd never looked back at what Jason had done in the past in her own quartet, especially not after he started gunning for her seat.

Jason played a lot freer back then. He moved more. He smiled. He looked comfortable. He wasn't upstaging Dad. In fact, his line was very emotional.

He just…looked happier.

He never looked happy now. He never seemed as if he were enjoying the music he played, or as if he enjoyed music at all. Was that because whenever Lindsey saw him, Lindsey was there and he hated Lindsey? Possibly, except Ben had seen it tonight when Jason ostensibly had what he wanted: first chair plus no Lindsey plus a bunch of impressive clients who could become similarly impressed with him.

Lindsey texted Ben. "I'm on it. And thanks again for filling in."

Ben replied, "No problem, sweetie. You know I'd do anything for your family."

He would. Ben would give her family seven hours on a Friday before Christmas. He'd sit with her father while her father raged at the nurses thinking one of them had stolen his keys. Ben would sit in the parking lot afterward, sobbing in his car. He'd do it for them.

What had Jason done for them? Had Jason given up a career and a rich girlfriend to help her father? If so, what did Lindsey owe him?

Lindsey killed the playback. She closed all the tabs in her browser. Eyes shut, she finished her herbal tea.

How could she tell Jason how to play when Jason had performed at the Grammys? He'd had his own fans and a girlfriend who could top the charts if she hummed "Happy Birthday to You" in the shower. No wonder Jason resented every time Lindsey told him what to do and when to do it.

Ordinary, predictable Lindsey had been facing down the demigod, and the demigod had taken umbrage.

Except demigodhood and burgeoning success and even name recognition hadn't left Jason fulfilled. If anything, it had made him less of a musician. Pre-recorded music, stage makeup, photo ops—and that naked fear when he'd heard a guy from California exclaim, "Woodward? Is that you?"

Ashlyn walked in the door. "Hey, you're still up." She dumped her coat and viola case on the couch. "Michael asked for the keys to our website. He wants us completely updated and streamlined before that TV interview goes live."

Lindsey shook her head. "We can't afford Michael."

"He offered to do it for free. You know, for love and family?" Ashlyn chuckled. "Go to bed. You're exhausted."

Lindsey met Ashlyn's eyes and was about to tell her everything when instead she stopped. None of this made sense, and they had a full weekend of performances still to come. Then Christmas Eve, Christmas Day, and if Jason got his way, a flight out on Christmas evening. Too many arrangements, too many questions.

All of it could wait. Jason's history would still be his history tomorrow, or Monday, or Boxing Day. Instead Lindsey wrote the website password on an index card for Ashlyn, then set her mug in the sink. "You're right. I'm exhausted. And there's still so much I need to figure out."

CHAPTER EIGHT

Christmas Eve used to be fun. Today, however, Jason had already worked a morning wedding, followed by an afternoon wedding, followed by a pre-service Christmas concert for a local church. Now everyone was killing time at the Castleton home until the quartet would play for an hour before a different church's midnight service. Enrique would sing at the service afterward, but at least the quartet could go home—and then be up again to play a Christmas gig at eight, followed by a Christmas party from noon until five.

After that, they'd head to the airport to fly to New York. Jason had offered that they could do what he always did to get to the airport (park at his parents' B&B and then take a shuttle). Instead, Lindsey in her wisdom had decreed they were driving to the Bangor airport in her father's former SUV, since it had nice traction and room in the back for four instruments. Jason didn't argue. At least it wasn't covered with Lindsey's ridiculous decals. *"Make some treble!"*

The place smelled of coffee, which was either a great idea or a terrible idea. Lindsey called from the kitchen, "Come fuel up. Sit anywhere."

Jason added his violin to the cluster of instruments hanging out in the foyer, then joined everyone in the kitchen.

The youngest Castleton, emo-edgelord Corwin, was balanced on two legs of his chair. "I have to say, right about now I feel super smart for not staying in classical music."

Lindsey said, "I've never had a beer bottle thrown at me in the middle of a set."

Corwin turned to Jason. "You've had a bottle or two thrown at you, right?"

Jason shot him a withering look, and Corwin chuckled.

The table was loaded with food: fruit, cookies, chocolates, potato chips. Every single one of those would grease up your fingertips. It didn't surprise Jason that no one else cared about it, but he wouldn't be eating anything.

Ashlyn came to the table with her mug of coffee. "The L.A. Philharmonic is known for its brawls. Last year, the concertmaster even loosened his bow tie."

Jason took a seat. "The concertmaster is female, so she asked the conductor to hold her earrings."

Hannah laughed out loud, then smothered it. Enrique, who had inexplicably attached himself to Hannah in the last couple of months, put his arm around her. "Smooth."

"Thanks." Jason glanced at the coffee maker. "The real question is, do I want to be exhausted during the performance, or unable to sleep afterward?"

Hannah said, "It's waking up for tomorrow's eight a.m. performance that worries me."

Mrs. Castleton said, "Jason, if you want to stay overnight, that will save you a lot of driving."

Hannah's kid brother Parker said, "It turns out random

sleepovers here are a thing."

Lindsey deposited a mug of coffee in front of Jason, almost as if he'd asked for it, except he hadn't. She said, "Jason has parents. They probably want to see him on Christmas, even if it's only for five minutes."

Jason chuckled. "I'm the last person they want to see tomorrow! The bed and breakfast is full up. My mother's starting the day with a Christmas breakfast for everyone, followed by a magical Christmas day for the guests, including an open house and sleigh rides. At the end, there's a dinner for thirty people. My mother would prefer I keep my distance until at least December 28th."

Lindsey went back behind the counter. "You can stay here without worrying about cooties, then. I'll be going home."

Jason didn't look at her. "Thanks. I'll keep that in mind."

Corwin said, "So when you're doing that interview, you're totally going to plug my band, right?"

Lindsey gave him a thumbs up. "I'll plug your work as much as you promote mine, baby brother."

Corwin rolled his eyes. "You could just say no."

"But it sounds so rude when I do it that way."

Jason muttered, "That's never stopped you before."

Ashlyn choked on her coffee, but instead of clapping back, Lindsey nodded. "You're right. Corwin, no."

Corwin raised his eyebrows at her, and she giggled.

Jason closed his eyes. No wonder Bob spent so much time at the school.

Lindsey returned to Jason with a bowl. "Eat whatever you want, pretty boy. We've got a long night."

She was just trying to get under his skin, so Jason said, "I'm fine."

She handed him a pair of chopsticks. "If you change your mind." Wow, she was in rare form tonight. Jason used the chopsticks to snag a blueberry off the serving platter, and he extended it to her. She plucked it free in her fingertips. "Thanks! That hits the spot."

As Lindsey settled back in front of her own coffee, she

turned to Jason. "Speaking about the interview, we're not going to get any time to make a game plan ahead of then, so let's do it now. How do we get out of this with your reputation enhanced and our safety intact?"

Everyone went quiet. Jason looked around. "Me? Why am I planning this?"

Lindsey cocked her head. "We're building buzz for you, aren't we? Because it in no way benefits us. If you haven't already contacted your publicity people or whoever we're doing this for, you need to do it tonight to work out what impression we're supposed to leave."

Jason's stomach clenched. "How does a public appearance not benefit you? There's money, and you'll get to advertise the quartet as nationally recognized."

"We're in Maine. No one cares if we're nationally recognized. You didn't disclose what this was about before we all stepped into the crosshairs, but I have the whole group to look after. Not just you."

Hannah sat up. "What's going on? How are we going to be in the crosshairs?"

Jason waved dismissively. "No one's going to take a shot at the quartet."

Lindsey wove her fingers together. "I Googled you last week, and I'm hearing guns cocked all around us."

He realized then that she looked livid.

The internet was forever. She'd found everything.

Last March, when Jason had walked in at the first practice, Lindsey had pretended his solo career never happened, as if he were on a leave of absence from the philharmonic. She'd offered to find him a part-time job to pay the bills as if he weren't receiving residuals from any number of income streams. It was frankly insulting, and then she'd forced him into the second violin role to complete the snub.

Only now—

All the hair stood up on Jason's arms. "What did you find?"

She hadn't been pretending. She *had* thought he was on

leave of absence from the Philharmonic. She *had* been concerned that the quartet wouldn't keep his rent paid. She hadn't been snubbing him. With her own life in flames, she'd never looked him up, never found him out.

Lindsey lowered her voice. "Tell us how you want that interview to go and what they're most likely to ask. You've always wanted to lead a quartet, right? Well, now you're sitting in the first interviewee chair, and the rest of us provide the supporting lines. Top priority is keeping Hannah and Ashlyn safe, and as for myself, I'd prefer not to deal with an internet conflagration while we're rehabbing you to the world."

He'd better drink that coffee. This was about to become a much longer night. "My agent thinks it will go fine, and there won't be any kind of conflagration."

Hannah leaned forward. "I'm really confused. What's going on?"

Enrique kept a hand on Hannah's back. "Rehabbing what?"

Ashlyn said, "Who'd attack us? Slighted Tchaikovsky fans?"

No one had looked him up. To them, Jason was just Jason. He'd left and come back home, and none of them questioned it. None of them had been in his target audience from the start—except possibly Corwin, who was staring right at Jason with a steady patience.

So Jason told them. He told them about Violet Nights and the chaos afterward, about the threats and the character assassination pieces.

He didn't tell them about his reviews. That still hurt. *Take a year off and learn to play.* At least Lindsey hadn't found those. If she had, she'd have dangled a flyer for the Castleton School of Music, reminding him the first three lessons were free.

Emotionally spent, Jason sat back in his chair and waited for the mockery, the accusations. The insults.

Instead, Lindsey pushed a small bowl of potato chips in front of him. What was that supposed to mean?

Ashlyn said, "Back up. For real, you dated *Mitzy Maxwell?*"

Of everything he'd just said, Mitzy was what they were going to latch onto?

Hannah whispered, "This is bonkers."

Corwin huffed. "You guys all live under a rock. Last January, you couldn't turn on the radio without hearing Jason blowing up that violin on 'Love Once More'."

Lindsey side-eyed Corwin. "You never mentioned it."

"I didn't think I had to, the same way I didn't mention that you breathe oxygen."

Parker's eyes were huge. "I had no idea that was you."

Jason picked up the chopsticks and nabbed a potato chip. The night was definitely getting longer.

Ashlyn breathed, "Mitzy Maxwell."

Lindsey said to her, "Brace yourself for the cuteness. They even had an adorable 'ship name."

Jason's stomach tightened. Why did everything have to be one-upmanship with her?

Ashlyn frowned. "Jayzee?"

"Mitson."

Ashlyn shook her head. "'Jayzee' sounds cuter."

Lindsey opened her hands. "When I'm in charge of the internet, I'll fix that."

Jason rolled his eyes. "Either way, it wasn't a big deal, and it's over. People out there are getting together and breaking up all the time for the fans."

It stung, but he'd make the breakup sound like a decision of convenience, tactics to generate numbers and social media followers.

Corwin smirked that irritating smirk. "California isn't some kind of special dating pool. You say that as if all the musicians around here haven't gotten together and broken up a dozen times. Remember the mess with Declan and Rose and Travis and Mia? Even at this table, Lindsey dated Enrique, and she tried to set me up with Ashlyn."

Ashlyn blurted out, "Thank goodness for standards!"

Corwin mimed relief. "I know, right?"

Jason caught Enrique's eye. "You've upgraded."

Lindsey high-fived Hannah. "Sorry for wasting your time, Enrique."

"Not that much time." Enrique was laughing. "It was over after like three dates."

Lindsey made big eyes. "Full disclosure: four dates because we needed to even up who paid for what. And for your information, Corwin, I've kissed Jason more often than I kissed Enrique."

Jason started. "Lindsey!"

Enrique recoiled. "So—twice?"

Jason set his coffee mug on the table with a louder bang than he intended. "Thank you for that. Here's the thing: you love to pull out these uncomfortable or embarrassing revelations and then hide behind your posse, and that's not your most attractive feature."

Mrs. Castleton was fighting laughter. Lindsey merely raised her eyebrows. "You think I have any attractive features? I'm flattered."

"You figured out how to improve your kissing technique after you flubbed the first one. Commitment to self-improvement is always attractive." Jason stared into her eyes. "It's far less attractive when you hide behind your family to blurt things out of context in order to one-up the person you're talking about."

Mrs. Castleton was suppressing the most amused grin Jason had ever seen. Arms folded, Corwin snickered as he balanced back on his chair.

They were well past #Mitson. Lindsey had furrowed open the wound in his heart and then done a slash-and-burn on his soul—and now this? As if she could replace Mimi? As if he'd want her to?

Jason leaned into the table. "You leverage your audience to get what you want. You use Ashlyn as a springboard or your family as a hedgerow, but it's only a bunch of cheap shots at everyone else's expense. Just now, you made it sound like I put the moves on you, and you rejected me."

Lindsey opened her hands. "Now hear this. I kissed

Jason to get his attention, and he declared me a lousy kisser, so I kissed him again. He conceded I had improved, and we haven't kissed a third time."

Lindsey: standing in a hole, digging it deeper. "You're still framing everything so it sounds like something it wasn't. And, I'll add, you're doing this *after* you ambushed me about a history you could have discussed with me beforehand. You made my past sound like I was running drugs instead of writing music and getting crucified on the internet. If you're ever curious about why you're so irritating, you've just identified one of those things. Congratulations."

He pushed the bowl of potato chips back in front of her. At this point, he'd rather starve.

Hannah shifted uneasily. "Guys, we still need to play together tonight."

Lindsey's shoulders dropped. "I'm sorry. You're right, that was a cheap shot. But we do need to pre-plan the interview. Are they going to ask about Mitson? Are they going to ask about the work you're doing for the upcoming movie? Should we hear those pieces ahead of time so I don't embarrass you on the air by saying something completely inappropriate?"

Then she sent the potato chips back to him. This was beyond annoying.

Hannah said, "More to the point, should we try to smooth over the more controversial parts of Violet Nights? We could each mimic the opposite of one of the things they accused you of, to show that you're not a monster."

Enrique whistled. "Whoa. That would be a trick."

Hannah shrugged. "A quartet is used to playing complementary parts."

Jason glanced at the ceiling. "You assume the average person understands nuance. As of last February, I don't."

Corwin snorted. "Dude, ride the wave. The more the people start hating you on one side, the more people start adoring you on the other." Corwin, of course, was wearing a "Season's Greetings!" hoodie emblazoned with a mushroom cloud. "Remember last year, Twitter trended for thirty-six hours with 'Edgar Chantz Is Over,' and guess who released an album, got three number one hits, and went platinum? Edgar Chantz is not 'over,' and neither are you."

Jason rubbed his temples. "Edgar Chantz has a fifteen-year career behind him."

Corwin waved a hand. "If you know what's in this second movie, get ahead of it and declare it as your personal anthem."

Eyes closed, Jason tried to imagine how that would look. "I've read the screenplay. The first movie was a lot more nuanced than people gave it credit for. The internet got ahold of one character and assumed everyone involved in production agreed with the way that character felt at her worst."

Lindsey said, "The Madrigal?"

Jason rested his forehead in his fingertips and rubbed his temples. "I couldn't stop thinking about that screenplay the moment I set eyes on it, and it only improved in the filming."

Lindsey said, "Maybe we should watch it? I only saw the clip where you appeared."

Hannah slumped back into Enrique. "You were actually in the movie? I'm so out of touch."

Ashlyn shook her head. "There's no time left to watch a whole film, but it doesn't matter. If the point is to rehab Jason's public image, then we can't sound even a little controversial. Soft-pedal everything. He's merely appearing on a talk show with his three quartet members, all of whom are totally gorgeous and think the world of him."

Lindsey said, "Two of whom."

Ashlyn elbowed her. "You can pretend to like him for fifteen minutes."

Corwin said, "She can't pretend to be gorgeous."

Jason snickered, and Lindsey nodded. "That's exactly what I mean. It'll only boost Jason's standing in the teen girls' eyes if he's nice to the ugly one." She arched her eyebrows at him. No, Jason would not correct her. He would leave that humblebrag right where she dropped it. Without missing a beat, Lindsey turned to Ashlyn. "Are you suggesting we play up how amazing he was to walk away from a star-struck career to help our family?"

Ashlyn gave a thumbs-up. "Exactly. He got a call from home, and without hesitation, he walked out of L.A. to repay an old debt."

Lindsey looked back at Jason. "Regardless, there are things we will not mention. As much as possible, we do not mention Hannah's family. We do not mention Ashlyn's."

Ashlyn raised a hand. "For the love of all that's holy, please do not say anything that will lead my mother to the ice cream stand."

Jason took another potato chip with the chopsticks. He was hungry after all. "Similarly, don't under any circumstances mention my parents' bed and breakfast. If the mob had found it last year, they'd have detonated their reviews."

Lindsey said, "Consider it done. Also off-limits is Michael. I assume we'll have to mention Dad. I'll handle that."

Across the table, Susan Castleton was studying Jason in a way that made his spine tingle. She was darn near telepathic, and he took another potato chip so he had something else to pay attention to. "Say whatever you want. I appreciate the boost."

Lindsey patted Jason's hand. "I'm not doing any of this for you. It's my responsibility to make sure Hannah and Ashlyn don't get pilloried, since the possibility never concerned you. Also, I need to make sure you're really gone in March when your lease is up."

"No worries. March comes, and I'm out of here." Jason couldn't ignore Mrs. Castleton's gaze, so he finally looked back at her. "It's not that I'm unconcerned about Hannah and Ashlyn—or Lindsey. I don't think anything terrible will happen."

Christmas night. Jason unlocked the hotel room to confirm it was a suite, which was nice, but then it turned out to have one bedroom, which was not. Then they found the solitary bedroom had two full sized beds crammed almost next to one another, which was a disaster.

Lindsey stopped in the bedroom doorway. "Of course." She turned to Ashlyn and Hannah, both of whom looked as exhausted as she did. "You two, sleep in this one. Jason, you get the bed by the wall. I'm camping out on the floor in the main room."

With that, she went into the common area of the suite. Jason followed her. "You can take the bed."

"No, I cannot take the bed. Hannah and Ashlyn deserve a decent night's rest, and you need to sleep because you're the one we're doing this for." Lindsey dropped onto the reading chair and started unlacing her boots. "Despite my reputation as a lousy kisser, there is no way I'm sharing a bed with you, hence I'm taking the floor. I will claim one of the pillows."

Ashlyn rounded the corner. "You and me and Hannah can try to fit."

Lindsey waved her off. "We all need rest, not elbows and jostling. I'm exhausted enough to sleep on a rock wall. But we should set alarms and decide who gets which shower time."

Jason sighed. "Fine. I'll get up for the first shower. We need to be out of here by five thirty."

"Then quit arguing and get to bed, otherwise you're not getting even four hours' sleep."

In the common area, they pushed all the furniture to the walls, which cleared enough space for an adult to lie down. Lindsey pulled both comforters off the beds and flattened them into something like a sleeping bag, and before Ashlyn and Hannah had finished changing into pajamas, she'd opened all the drawers and closets to locate the spare blankets. One went on her makeshift pallet, and the others went on the hotel beds.

Jason had figured this overnight would be awkward, but already in his career he'd done dozens of awkward things. When the philharmonic had traveled, he'd roomed in hotels with plenty of people he'd never wanted to. That wasn't even to mention the travel orchestra during college. Plus, he'd trained himself to sleep on an airplane. He'd get through this.

By the time he was ready for bed, Hannah was already asleep and Ashlyn was programming an alarm on her phone. "I'll take second shift. Let Lindsey sleep as long as she can."

That might have been a bid to make Jason feel guilty, but Lindsey had other options, so he shut the lamp and flipped over to face away from the light in the common area.

He never saw Lindsey's light go off, but then his alarm was chiming and it was far too early in the a.m. If he'd wondered why the producer had been able to find them a slot so soon, it was this: no one wanted to pull an all-nighter on Christmas Eve and then a second between Christmas and Boxing Day. Jason hoped the shower would wake him up, but it didn't really.

The setup, at least, was convenient. The shower was separate from the toilet, which was also separate from the sinks. Everyone could get ready at once if they just planned it well. Which, they hadn't. Coordination should have been Lindsey's gig, but she'd been as overwhelmed as the rest of them.

Ashlyn took the second shower, and by the time Jason was done dressing, Lindsey was ready for her turn. "Next time," she said, her voice raspy, "we get multiple rooms."

Jason said, "It's a Manhattan hotel over Christmas. Not a lot of square footage to share."

Ashlyn took over the mirrors, so Jason parked himself in one of the reading chairs. Lindsey had re-folded all the blankets into a stack. Of course she had.

Lindsey was out of the shower. Hannah went in. Jason took over at the sink to shave and make sure everything looked good.

Between Ashlyn and Lindsey, one had used citrus-scented products, and the other vanilla. Their apartment must smell perpetually of creamsicles. His lips tingled momentarily as he remembered the vanilla scent of Lindsey's kiss, and he closed his eyes. She'd jumped him in an elevator, played him with an emotionless kiss, and he'd enjoyed it. Now he burned with humiliation.

It blew through him, then: he couldn't do this. Emotionless kisses. Cameras. Artificial smiles. Laughing as though no one were passing judgment. His life on display as entertainment, and then the questions, the questions, the questions.

"Don't pass out on us, pretty boy. We need you for this interview." Lindsey nipped around behind him to plug in the hair dryer, but then she stopped. "Whoa. You're not okay. Did you get any sleep?"

"I'm fine." Jason tried to draw a deep breath, but his throat kept catching. *I'm not fine. I'm dying.* He leaned into the sink and struggled to stay upright, but his lips were numb and his heart raced so fast it hurt his chest. He was having a heart attack. Everything was about to end. He was dying.

The smell of vanilla rushed him. It was Lindsey with her arms around his chest. "You're okay," she breathed against his neck. "We're doing this together. There are four of us."

With a crushing pain around his heart, he stared down the sink drain. He was going to throw up. He hadn't eaten a meal since the lukewarm vendor meal at yesterday's Christmas party.

Lindsey surrounded him. Warmth. "Breathe," she hushed in his ear. "I promise you're okay. Breathe with me. Count. Five things you can see."

Sink. Faucet. Counter. Soap. Toothpaste.

"Four things you can hear," Lindsey prompted.

Lindsey's words. Hannah's shower. His own breath. And…nothing. No fourth thing. He couldn't do this.

"Three things you can feel." Lindsey was getting ahead of him. He couldn't keep up.

Try. The pressure of her arms around him. The porcelain under his fingers. Nothing else. He couldn't even feel three things. No, wait. Her wet hair against his cheek. The cuff of his dress shirt against his wrist. That was three things, right? Oh, and he could hear Lindsey. That would be the fourth thing he heard. Okay. He could do this.

"Two things you can smell."

Vanilla and citrus. Lindsey always smelled like vanilla. Back in the elevator and now and any time he'd gotten close enough to catch her scent, it had been vanilla.

"One thing you can taste."

He wanted to taste her kiss again. Instead his mouth still tingled of mouthwash, and he concentrated on that.

Behind him, the shower went off. Lindsey whispered, "Breathe in. And out."

"I'm okay." He closed his eyes, but the sense of doom returned. He focused again on the sink.

"You're very not okay." She let him lean into her. "Do you get panic attacks often?"

He shook his head.

"Was this your first?"

He screwed his eyes shut. "Is that what this is?"

"Ashlyn gets them, so I've learned to talk her down." When Lindsey released him, the dizziness rushed back like a wave. Jason clutched the counter so he wouldn't reach for her. "I didn't realize the interview would be this bad for you. Did you get any sleep?"

"I slept. I'll be fine." He pushed away from the sink and stood straight, but that meant he got a look at himself. His skin was colorless. "I wasn't supposed to do any of this stuff until March. I had time."

Lindsey hugged him again, and he fought the urge to

collapse onto her. "We're never prepared for what's coming down the pike. We'll get you through this. I promise."

We. Jason kept considering that "we" as they went downstairs to get the car to the studio, then as they arrived at the studio, and then again as they got settled in the studio's green room. *We.*

CHAPTER NINE

Jason seemed human in the green room, with coffee and a continental breakfast laid out. Starving, Lindsey grabbed a cinnamon roll. The makeup people came in, and so did Cass Camden, who'd be the network interviewer. Everyone seemed friendly and excited, even though obviously they did this every morning with multiple guests.

Gorgeous in black pants and a cranberry dress shirt, Jason was sitting with his hands between his knees, and Lindsey couldn't lose the image of Jason mid-panic.

She'd held him, and it wasn't her imagination that he'd leaned into her. Not at first. At first, he'd been rigid like a flagpole. Midway through the sensory exercise, he'd angled toward her. When she'd gotten to scents and he'd inhaled, she'd feared for a moment he was trying to smell her shampoo. Whatever he'd smelled, he'd relaxed.

They'd never mention it to each other again. He wouldn't want to tell her about his anxiety. She didn't want to bring up that he really was a fine specimen of a man if you ignored how he loathed her. She wouldn't consider how good his body felt against hers, or how for just a moment, she wished she could make him as happy as he'd seemed in any of those videos before last year.

Jason looked up from his coffee. "A few rules. TV producers love sound bites, so keep your sentences short. If you have something you want viewers to remember, repeat it. Don't say anything you don't want taken out of context. If they ask a question you don't want to answer, answer something they didn't ask. Assume every mic is a live mic. If you're wired and you want to use the toilet, physically take the mic off and leave it outside."

Ashlyn laughed, but Hannah's cheeks turned pink. "That would be awful."

Jason said, "And it happens. See a mic? It's on."

Lindsey said, "You sound like Corwin. He says to assume every gun is loaded."

"Same thing, except the live mic is more dangerous. No one is your friend, least of all the electronics. The only thing anyone wants is more viewers, and if they step over your dead body to get them, it's all the same."

Hannah shuddered. Lindsey put a hand on her shoulder. "No one wants to assassinate us. We're handy to fill a vacant slot in their lineup."

A producer entered the room. "We'd like to do a sound check."

Lindsey straightened her black leather skirt, then slung the strap of her violin case over her shoulder. "Ash, you're with me. Jason and Hannah, hang out and eat plenty of muffins."

Jason stood, but Lindsey shook her head because he still looked shaken. "It's a sound check. They can check my sound the same as yours."

The music school's recording studio wasn't even a tenth as complicated as this beauty. Lindsey would love to stick around afterward to get a tour of all the equipment.

She and Ashlyn double-checked their tuning, then went

out in front of the cameras. Wearing a cream and gold sheath dress and with her hair in a fantastic up-do, Ashlyn looked amazing under the lights—but she always did. By contrast, Lindsey was wearing boots and a skirt and a copper-colored blouse.

The sound guy said, "Play some scales. Warm up. Do whatever you want."

Ashlyn did a three-octave C scale, and while she was on her way back down, Lindsey started playing a C scale going in the upward direction. Ashlyn hit the bottom note and then started back up again, so Lindsey pivoted into a G scale. Ashlyn rolled her eyes, then started messing around.

Lindsey said, "Is this enough?"

"Keep playing," said the sound guy.

Lindsey spun out the G scale into the beginning of the Ode to Joy, the first song every Castleton played on any instrument. At age two, Corwin had gotten a kazoo at a birthday party, and on the drive home, from his car seat, he'd begun buzzing out the Ode to Joy.

Ashlyn, who of course knew the Ode to Joy, started the harmony, and then because she was bored, she syncopated it.

Laughing, Lindsey took off on her own. Her father spent ages talking about Beethoven—the symphonies, the quartets, the solos. You could spend a lifetime studying the man's work and never finish learning, but better still was that once it clicked what Beethoven was doing, you could improvise using his methods. It wouldn't be a master work, but you'd lay down hints of what was to come, that way when you went ahead and did it, your surprise felt like a fulfillment rather than a jolt.

She and Ashlyn faced one another, moving with the rhythm but embedding in those movements the cues to feed the improvised melody back and forth. Dad and Mom stressed the improv classes, so no Castleton gathering was complete until someone picked up an instrument they'd never handled, started mucking around, and abruptly had an accompaniment of five other players.

It was early. They'd slept so little and performed so much. There had been scant time just to play with their instruments, play with their music—play. Have fun. Set it free and remember why you got into this in the first place.

Jason didn't usually improv with them. If the other three got off on a tangent when a quartet practice went wildly wrong, he'd wait it out while they got a little crazy.

Even if Jason wouldn't improv with them, for now Lindsey could include him. She transitioned to an instrumental version of Mitzy Maxwell's lyrics from "Love Once More." Ashlyn's eyebrows went up, and Lindsey signaled her to keep going.

Jason had been overwrought. He must have buried the feelings deep so he wouldn't have to think about last year's internet inferno, but here he was, about to step into the line of fire. And for what? For a movie?

If he wanted this as a career, that's what he had to do. It was a shame that made the music no longer fun.

Not even "no fun." Actually frightening.

Lindsey messed up mid-play and laughed at herself, but Ash forged on with the violin line from "Love Once More." Lindsey struggled to remember the vocals, but because she knew the key and could predict the chord progressions, it wasn't hard to keep pace. After thirty seconds recreating the Maxwell-Woodward Grammy performance, they started trading the violin line from one to the other, until finally both ended up near the same set of notes. Lindsey cued Ashlyn, and they got into sync before ending together.

Grinning, Lindsey tucked her violin under her elbow, flipped the bow up to rest on her shoulder, and bowed.

Ashlyn had her viola and bow in the same hand, and she resettled her dress. "Well? Was that enough of a sound check?"

The producer walked in, clapping. "That was a fantastic sound check. Thank you!"

Back in the green room, a very stressed Hannah was texting, but Jason was back to sitting on a chair at the breakfast table, elbows on knees, paper cup of coffee in his hands. A wave of concern rushed through Lindsey, but she forced herself to look over the breakfast items as though nothing were wrong.

Nothing was wrong. Just keep telling herself that: nothing was wrong. Jason would have his feet under him during the interview. Still, it was hard not to put her hand on his shoulder. She wanted to touch him and be touched. She wanted to ground him and be grounded. For once, just once, she wanted to smile at him and have him smile back.

With delight, Cass Camden addressed Jason. "It's a thrill to have you on the show today."

Lindsey gave her performance smile, the one she and Ashlyn had practiced in front of mirrors because audiences and clients required it. Doubtless Cass Camden had practiced her "delight smile" with a delight coach and periodic refresher courses. This was an entertainment segment, not news. Ergo, everyone was a hero.

Jason also wore a performance smile. "Thank you, Cass. It's great to be here."

Cass said, "Tell me, what's been going on with you? You wowed audiences at the Grammys, and then you disappeared."

Jason delivered a well-rehearsed narrative about an impassioned call from home regarding his violin mentor, the man most formative in his musical career. Cass looked appropriately compassionate. She gestured to the group of them. "And these ladies are the rest of your quartet?"

Good for Cass, counting to four! They'd been arranged so Ashlyn sat closest to Cass, with Jason on her other side. Totally expected: put the most beautiful people together where the camera will catch them most often. On the adjacent couch sat Lindsey, with Hannah furthest from their interviewer. Hannah had wanted it that way, and right before the interview, she'd begun looking like the world's worst attack of stage fright.

Cass gave a puzzled expression. "Tell me how a string quartet works. Why are there two violins?"

After answering this question so many times, Lindsey replied without thinking. "Imagine a human chorus, with sopranos, altos, tenors, and basses. Since the strings are the instruments that most closely approximate the human voice, we do the same. Soprano," she said, pointing to herself, and then in turn to Jason, Ashlyn, and Hannah, "alto, tenor, and bass."

As the words left her lips, Lindsey felt a frisson of terror: national TV. And she was talking on it.

Cass exclaimed, "Oh! I thought first violin meant you were better than second violin."

Lindsey laughed. "Please, no. Jason will be the first person to tell you I'm utterly ordinary."

Jason fired Lindsey a dark look. Cass gasped at him, "You wouldn't!"

Jason arched his eyebrows. "Would I dare contradict my immediate supervisor?"

Lindsey tilted her head. "Jason says I'm playing first violin because I called shotgun."

Jason glared daggers. Missing Jason's expression, Cass laughed. "If you were better than him, I'd have to wonder how good you are."

Lindsey opened her hands. "The man can play. You can *hear* he can play. Plus, he has the world's sweetest instrument."

Cass said, "Have you played it?"

Lindsey recoiled. "I would never touch his instrument."

Ashlyn choked back a laugh, and Jason straightened. "Excuse me? If you ever require my *violin*, just let me know."

Lindsey leaned around to talk to Cass directly. "His violin is a work of art, and he takes better care of it than most people take care of their health."

Jason folded his arms. "As if you don't love your violin?"

Lindsey looked him in the face. "I love my violin, but I know how you virtuosos bond with your violins. You tuck them in with blankets. You wipe them down with a soft cloth. You talk to them and give them names."

Jason raised a hand. "Your father named his violin. I haven't named mine."

Lindsey recoiled. "You haven't? Really?"

He smiled at her, and the effect was glorious. "O shotgun, my shotgun—yes, really."

Cass turned back to Jason. "How is it being back in Maine after your years in California?"

Lindsey crossed her legs, wishing she could cue Hannah to untense herself. Ashlyn looked perfectly relaxed while she and Jason bantered with Maine jokes, and then Ashlyn faked up a Maine accent that made everyone laugh. "We thought about interviewing in flannel shirts and work boots," Ashlyn added, "but that would wicked scare *yah viewahs.*"

So far Cass was following the outline Jason had predicted—following it to the letter. An introduction. Two questions about nothing at all. Next would come the heaviest stuff, and last, she'd ask about the future. They'd cut for a commercial break, and the group would play for five minutes.

With the fluff questions finished, Cass said, "Jason, let's talk about Violet Nights. There was a lot of controversy when the film made it big, and you were right at the center."

What Jason had said last year on his social media was, "It doesn't surprise me that ignorant trolls can't understand a film written for adults. You might try expanding your vocabulary and maybe exploring the world outside your bubble."

What Jason said this year was, "The film raised multiple perspectives on an important topic, and it was a much-needed public conversation about the issue."

Had his agent crafted that sentence? It was as gorgeous

as Jason was.

Cass said, "You left L.A. right after the firestorm, and people speculated that's why. Not to mention your breakup with Mitzy Maxwell. You two looked so happy! Why the split?"

How did interviewers get away with asking things like that? Friendships had boundaries, but sit in a studio and suddenly your heartbreak was everyone's entertainment.

Jason gave a measured smile. "Mitzy would be the first to agree the film's questions are important enough to warrant public conversation. A complex problem requires a complex answer."

Nice pivot. Also nice to rebrand getting flamed and doxxed as "conversation." As if either side were listening to the other.

Cass prompted, "Then why the breakup?"

Enough. Lindsey said, "They wouldn't break up over a film. The Madrigal is an important character precisely because she's on both sides of the question. Her indecision allows the audience to step into her perspective to re-examine what they already know." Lindsey leaned forward, hands clasped on her knee. "The violinist's song resonates at that moment precisely because the film refuses to provide a definitive answer."

Jason's eyebrows went up, and Lindsey steeled herself. It wasn't fair for Cass to goad him about last year's internet battle or an interrupted romance. Let the viewers get their blood sport some other way.

Lindsey went for an academic tone. "Jason's song used a Lydian mode to emphasize the tension in the Madrigal's conscience, a technique that I find frankly brilliant."

Cass gave a nervous laugh. "You just went beyond the limits of my music theory." She didn't ask what a Lydian mode was, unfortunately. Lindsey could have killed the rest of their time with a music lesson. "I hear you're doing three songs for Ultraviolet Dawn, Jason. Tell us what they're like."

Jason raised his hands. "Spoilers! I had to sign a

nondisclosure agreement so strong that if I violate it, my grandkids will be paying off the penalties."

Cass laughed. "No, no, no—not the plot twists, but you can tell us a bit about the songs."

Jason shook his head. "Lindsey just said songs are revelation. If I were to tell you one of them is a tortured love song, the kind you play when you're not going to be with the woman you want, that would give you a hint of what's in the movie."

Cass winked at him. "And I bet we would all know who you wrote that for."

Jason looked coy. "Whether you guess right or wrong, the NDA says I'm not allowed to tell you even one note of the songs or one word of the script."

Cass gave a camera-ready pout. "Lindsey, he said you're his immediate supervisor. Make him tell us."

Lindsey snickered. "Come on, pretty boy—give us the no-spoiler version."

The audience woo-hooed, and Cass sat up. "Pretty boy?"

Jason turned to her. "Nice going, shotgun," and Lindsey laughed while her cheeks burned.

Cass was enjoying this. "He *is* a pretty boy, isn't he?"

Lindsey raised her eyebrows. "Let's just say it's obvious why Walt Ingram wanted Jason in his film. Intriguing music in a Lydian mode, a classic violin, and *all* the looks."

Jason rolled his eyes. "Yes, those are the established requirements for perfection."

Lindsey grinned. "I wouldn't know. I'm nothing but an ordinary violinist."

Cass was laughing. "You guys have been great! Thank you to Jason Woodward and his quartet, and we all look forward to hearing from you again in Ultraviolet Dawn! We'll be back after the break to hear the Castleton String Quartet doing what they do best, and afterwards, what is up with those hemlines?"

The cameras went off, and Jason pointedly stripped off his mic.

Lindsey handed hers to one of the assistants. "I'm sorry.

That slipped out."

Jason side-eyed her. "For the rest of my life, I'm calling you 'shotgun'."

In the studio area, they double-checked their tuning, then took their places.

Lindsey leaned close to Hannah. "Breathe. You look rattled."

Hannah quivered. "Rattled" would have been a step up.

Since it was Boxing Day, Lindsey and Jason had arranged an extremely truncated Christmas medley. Lindsey would lead them in a version of "Carol of the Bells" that would pass the main line from first violin to viola to cello, and finally to second violin. Jason would transition "O Holy Night", and they would end with an ensemble take on "Angels from the Realms of Glory". The sound guy cued them to start

So weird. So weird playing for five minutes for people they'd never see, and who would never see them again. Getting paid for it, too. Although the hassle of traveling cost more than the token payment.

The playing was flawless but unmemorable. Hannah concerned Lindsey most, nervous as she was, but none of them needed to jump in and cover for her.

Then their five minutes of fame was over. Everyone went back into the green room except for Jason, who stayed in the hall to text his agent. Looking anguished, Hannah rushed for her cello case to check her phone.

Ashlyn stretched. "Well, guys, we made it. We're now the as-seen-on-TV Castleton String Quartet."

Lindsey hadn't taken her eyes off their cellist. "You okay, Hannah?"

Pale, Hannah gathered herself to talk, but then Jason burst into the room. "Good news and bad news!"

Hannah's eyes widened. "Good news?"

She was way too freaked out. Something was up.

Jason of course didn't notice. "The network has another show that wants us tonight, since we're already in New York on the network's dime. They'll change our plane tickets for us, but the bad news is, we'll be in the same hotel overnight."

Hannah blurted out, "We can't! We have to go home!"

Jason recoiled. "Why?"

Lindsey turned to her. "Talk to me. What's going on?"

Hannah bit her lip. "Your dad."

Lindsey's heart bottomed out.

"He's lost. He escaped his unit at the hospital, and they don't know where he is. They've called a silver alert because they believe he got out of the building."

Ears ringing, Lindsey stood immobilized.

Ashlyn went up next to her. "When did this happen? Why didn't they tell me or Lindsey?"

Hannah had tears in her eyes. "I wasn't supposed to find out either. Parker's with your mom this morning, and they went to the hospital so they could watch the show with your dad, only when they got there, he was missing. They think it happened at shift change. Parker texted me before your mom told him not to."

Jason guided Lindsey to a seat, which was good because she wasn't sure she could still feel her lower extremities. She needed to get home. She needed to find Dad.

Ashlyn said, "Can we get an earlier flight? Maybe send you home standby?"

"Wait." Lindsey closed her eyes. "Give me five minutes. Let me think."

Jason said, "I can call the producer—"

"I said give me five minutes!" She glared at him. "Five minutes isn't going to affect whether we get an earlier flight. But five minutes' thought last year would have saved you a metric ton of suffering, so let me think."

If she left now, the earliest she could be home would be one o'clock. By then, Dad would have been missing at a minimum six hours. A silver alert meant the police were looking for him, plus Mom, plus Parker, plus Corwin, plus Sierra. Anyone Mom didn't know in Hartwell, Corwin did.

It stank. One more person looking six hours from now wasn't going to be any help.

Hannah said, "They're not sure how far he could have gone, but they're pulling all the security footage to at least figure out when he left and which direction he went."

Jason huffed. "How could they let him leave?"

Lindsey struggled to find her voice. "I'm going to call my mother and get the story directly."

In the hallway she found an alcove where no one was rushing about. Mom answered on the second ring. "I'm so sorry, honey. I didn't think to tell Parker not to text his sister."

Lindsey fought the urge to scream. "I needed to know."

"You didn't need to know. You needed to do your interview. We've got everyone looking for him, and by the time you get back, he'll likely be returned."

Lindsey lowered her voice. "Oh, and you're not worried?"

"I'm scared out of my mind, but he has his coat, and it's in the upper forties. We've got people checking the most likely spots." Mom's voice broke. "Pray or send good vibes or something, but don't rush home."

"Yeah, but if Hannah hadn't told me, we'd have taken an offer for a second show tonight."

"Take it." Mom's voice was flat. "Your father's going to be found, and it's not as if you have radar. We don't need one more person."

"And I get to be the heartless daughter of the year?"

"Then let me lose Mother of the Year right now: I can't be strong for everyone. I've already talked Corwin off the ledge when he wanted to go postal on the nurses for letting Bob elope, and I've talked Sierra back into sanity because she was too shattered to think. I can't be your frontal lobe too. Do the second show. Tour Manhattan. I will let you know the minute anything happens."

Lindsey slumped against the wall, eyes closed.

"Honey, I love you, but you're doing something important for Jason, and you can't help here. If you walked onto a plane and it took off now, you'd still be four hours away. Stay there." Mom's voice trembled. "Please."

Lindsey didn't reply.

Mom said, "I'm getting another call. I'll talk to you as soon as I know anything. I love you."

Lindsey whispered, "I love you too."

Dad.

Where are you?

CHAPTER TEN

Lindsey walked back into the green room like the Ice Queen. "New plan." She pointed to Ashlyn. "You, go home. Mom needs someone to be strong for her, and I'm nominating you." She pointed to Hannah. "You, go home. Parker must be freaking out, and you hate the TV stuff anyhow."

Jason bristled. "And your father...? You don't go home and help find him?"

She pointed to him. "You, shut up." She turned back to Ashlyn. "My mother has all of Hartwell on the streets looking for Dad. Unless he hitched a ride, he's indoors somewhere in town, which means he's got to be safe. It's four hours home even if the air travel works perfectly, and it won't work perfectly. By the time you get home, he'll have been found, and Mom will need a pair of fresh hands to hold everything together. Unfortunately, that means you get to deal with Corwin, whom I'm given to understand is volcanic."

Jason snorted. "I wonder why?"

"You're not shutting up." She turned to Jason. "You and I will do the second show."

Jason folded his arms. "How about this? I do the second show solo, and you go home with the other two?"

Lindsey met his eyes, and her glare was like firing a nail gun through his skull.

How long had they played together? Long enough for him to read that cue: she wasn't going to say it unless he argued, but he'd freaked out this morning. She thought he couldn't handle the second show alone.

Shame burned from Jason's throat to his cheeks.

Instead, Lindsey said, "It was important to your agent that you appear with other people. We'll keep the agent happy."

Ashlyn put a hand on Lindsey's arm. "Then you go back and let me stay." She forced a smile. "You're the one who keeps saying that if we're ever on a magazine cover, it'll be me and Jason in the foreground."

The hair stood on Jason's neck. What on earth?

Lindsey only shook her head. "My mother wants me to stay away, but she needs you." She turned to Jason. "Can you have your people do that? Hold just us over until tomorrow, but bump these two up to the first flight they can catch?"

Jason pulled out his phone. "Without talking?"

"Fine. You can un-shut-up." Lindsey handed Ashlyn the car key. "We'll figure out later how Jason and I get back from the airport."

Hannah murmured, "I don't like this."

"I don't like it either!" For the first time, Lindsey lost composure. At least she was a human being, not a robot. "For crying out loud, do you think I want this? But my mother doesn't want me home, and going off half-cocked isn't going to help anyone. This is the best I can come up with."

Jason hadn't dialed out yet. "Maybe you don't need the

best. Maybe you need to do what you want to do."

Eyes closed, Lindsey stood with her fists clenched and her shoulders tense. Ashlyn hugged her, and after a moment, Lindsey's head dropped.

She wasn't the Ice Queen. If anything, she'd turned into a slushy.

Ashlyn murmured, "We'll do whatever you decide, but you don't have anyone here for you."

Jason's hands tightened. Good to know he wasn't anybody.

Lindsey huffed. "What are you talking about? I have Jason."

Even with her life in pieces, Lindsey could throw shade. It was a talent.

Five minutes later, a very competent assistant had her instructions and would be sending Jason all the updated arrangements. He also had a text from his agent: "I wish you'd been in the promo clip."

Awesome of the network to pull a clip without him in it to promo his interview. Edward would be on the phone with the show's publicity people to get that changed, so Jason let him handle it.

Fifteen minutes later, a car dropped them off at the hotel, and Jason had new information. Lousy information.

"Hannah and Ashlyn and Hannah's cello are booked on a flight at eleven." He fought nausea. "And you guys did a jam session in front of the cameras?"

Ashlyn nodded. "We messed around with some tunes for the sound guy."

Jason said, "Did you not know they were recording you? Had I not just told you to treat every mic as a hot mic?"

Lindsey snapped, "Who cares? The mics had to be live because they were sound-checking us."

Jason said, "They used a clip from that to promo the segment."

Lindsey halted in front of the elevator and didn't push the up button, so Jason stalked past and jabbed it for her.

Her voice was thin. "I hope they didn't air the part where

I blew the transition."

Ashlyn said, "Or when I thought we were playing an entirely different song."

Jason said, "So now we look like idiots?"

Lindsey shook her head. "At least it's my corpse they kicked to get viewers, not yours."

By the time they were back at the room, he had a text from the producer's assistant that in fifteen minutes, Hannah and Ashlyn would have an airport shuttle waiting. Ten minutes later, both were out of the room, and Jason was alone with a tense and irritated Lindsey.

Perfect. Just perfect.

Jason spent time coordinating with Edward and the evening show's producer, but then a text came in from Michael Knolwood, the jack-in-the-box Castleton. After Michael confirmed he had the right person, he sent, "You need to get your social media accounts up again."

Jason stared at his phone. "Why?"

"The quartet website is getting a ton of hits. Based on the search terms, they want your Twitter and your Instagram."

He replied, "I shut them down last year after I got torched."

"Deleted or just locked down?"

Jason fought the urge to hurl his phone against the wall. "Locked down. I needed to save the death threats for law enforcement."

Michael texted, "If you give me your password, I'll bring them live and clean them up."

Jason stalked to the window. He could throw the phone and wait for it to crash onto 34th Street. But with his luck it would survive and someone would figure out how to revive the accounts anyhow.

He couldn't do this. Couldn't.

Michael texted, "I'll delete the three hundred most recent followers, since those are most likely to be trolls. But you're getting enough attention now that you need your social media public, especially if you're on air again tonight."

Blast it. Jason hit the button to call.

Michael sounded pleased. "Ashlyn said it went really well, and website traffic agrees with her."

"And the hate mail?"

"Hasn't started yet, but I'll delete anything that's merely insulting and not legally actionable."

Jason said, "What are your rates? And what qualifies you to do this?"

"Nothing for today. You don't want me handling your social media over the long term, but I'll suffice for twenty-four hours."

Lindsey appeared in the bedroom doorway, looking exhausted now that she'd washed off the stage makeup and changed out of dress clothes. Jason figured he didn't look any better. He told her, "It's your brother. He wants to turn on my social media."

She recoiled. "Is that wise?"

"He says it's wise."

Michael said, "Is Lindsey there? Tell her my parents started a prayer chain with their church to help find Bob."

"I will." Given what he'd overheard about Michael's parents, Jason wasn't sure he should tell Lindsey anything of the sort. "If you think this is worth doing, then fine. Give me fifteen minutes to turn it on again, and I'll change my password to MichaelCastleton."

Lindsey's eyebrows went up.

Michael said, "I like that. I'll be in touch."

Jason hung up and logged back into Twitter.

Lindsey said, "Michael? If someone's starting a fight on Twitter, my money was on Corwin."

"Michael's getting website hits saying people are looking

for me." Jason logged into a dormant Twitter account with almost a thousand notifications. He was about to make it un-private when he thought better, then went into his tweets and his replies.

He'd said these things. He'd said all these, and he'd as good as doused himself in gasoline.

His fingers hovered over the button to make his timeline public again, but then he went back to the Violet Nights tweets. One at a time, he deleted them all.

When he looked up, Lindsey sat slumped in a chair, watching him with a dark sadness. He snapped, "What?"

She shook her head.

Jason changed his password, then made the timeline public. He texted Michael. "Ready."

Michael replied, "Thanks. On it."

Then, "Ashlyn's sent some photos. I'm going to post as if I'm you. Nothing controversial."

Michael could hardly do worse than Jason had.

Jason should have had two more months until all this happened. He texted Edward, "I have a social media guru reviving my social media."

Edward replied, "Excellent."

A minute later, Edward sent a link to a clip. "Post the network promo with how lucky you are to be working with these women."

The non-Jason promo? Odd.

Jason clicked on the link, and Lindsey and Ashlyn flared to life in their typical facing-one-another jam session stances. Lindsey looked great in that copper and black blouse, but she couldn't dance to save her life. Ashlyn at least moved with ease. Then Jason realized what he was hearing.

They were playing "Love Once More," and mocking the ever-loving stars out of it.

Heat fired up his throat, and his arms tensed. Sure, Lindsey talked sweet about protecting the group and rehabbing him to the world, but without remorse she'd taken his song and ridiculed it to everyone. Nice. Don't believe the protective act and the gentle touch. Believe what she did. Always believe what people did.

Dear heaven, please don't let Mitzy find this.

Ashlyn had slid into Jason's violin part, modulated to a key where the viola could handle it. Meanwhile Lindsey was almost doing Mitzy's part. Not exactly, but it was recognizable as the vocals, especially when Lindsey syncopated it the second time around. That was exactly how he and Mitzy had performed it at the Grammys.

Lindsey was fighting laughter, but Ashlyn was focusing hard to make the viola respond as quickly as it needed to. Ashlyn had learned it fast. As of Christmas Eve, she hadn't even known the song existed. Lindsey must have been awake all night figuring out how to parody it.

The clip lasted fifteen seconds. Jason stopped it and glared up at Lindsey.

She was looking at him without expression. Busted.

This was what the network was using for their promo in the later markets? *This?* Why on earth would Edward want him to post a clip of Lindsey lampooning his song?

Jason hit the play button again, struggling to put into words just exactly how much he hated Lindsey and how quickly and painfully she could go to the devil. What did Edward see in this?

Lindsey looked fabulous, but she'd have looked fabulous playing an A scale. Her clothing choice for today was on point. The makeup artist had glitzed her up and fixed her hair, and when she moved, she looked hot. Ashlyn looked astounding as well, her gold hair in an updo and her makeup brilliant. It made sense the network would want footage of these two for their promo, but why this clip?

When Lindsey faced Ashlyn, she grinned, and Jason paused the video.

Oh. Of course.

That wasn't mockery. Lindsey was thoroughly enjoying herself. She was hunting for Mitzy's lyrics in the key, and she was having a blast. That's why the advertisers chose this: Lindsey at play was joy itself. That's why Lindsey hadn't taken the violin line: invert the piece. Invite the listener to experience the song all over again. Do it because it's fun. Experiment with it because you love music.

He continued playback, eyes glued to onscreen-Lindsey.

When had Jason last had this much fun playing? When had he let his violin tell him what it wanted? His fingers curled as though he had the neck in his hands, and he fingered his phone as though following Ashlyn's notes.

The tension built too much in his throat for him not to say something. He re-paused the video. "Any news from home?"

Lindsey shook her head.

Blast it. "Do you want to wallow in misery, or should I distract you?"

She gave a startled laugh. "I guess distract me?"

Jason said, "You gave a great defense of Violet Nights for someone who never saw the movie."

She shrugged. "I read five critiques in case I needed to say something. And I did like the Lydian mode."

As if he were Cass doing the interview, Jason shifted from the easy topic to the harder one. "Why did you play 'Love Once More' for the sound check?"

Lindsey sighed. "I'm so over the Christmas music, and your song was in my head. Ashlyn and I had watched the video a few times. What made you write it?"

Ah, now it was her turn to play Cass. "I met Mitzy at a party, and she was fun to talk to. I'd written music for a show she likes, so she asked me back to her place. We stayed up all night writing a song together."

Lindsey's half-closed her eyes. "That's sweet."

"After that, she offered me a deal: if I co-wrote a second song with a violin line that worked around her voice, I could have twenty-five seconds of violin solo."

"A *cadenza*," Lindsey drawled, eyes half-closed.

"Mimi's classically trained. She would recognize if I called it a cadenza." Jason lowered the phone, Lindsey's face frozen mid-playback. She looked ebullient. Before him on the chair, she seemed lost. "She said we looked too cute not to do anything about it, and within a week we had a 'ship name and a romantic thing."

Lindsey smiled. "She's right. You were adorable together. And the song did well by you."

Jason said, "I can't stand to hear it anymore."

Lindsey opened her eyes. "I'm sorry."

His shoulders sagged. "Well, you didn't know."

"Why'd you break up with her?"

Jason stared at the carpet. "She broke up with me. I was bad for her reputation. If she'd stuck by me, I'd still be in California."

Lindsey nodded. "You'd have married her?"

Fighting irritation, Jason said, "She never loved me. That's not how things work out there. It's about being seen with the right people at the right places and giving the public something to talk about. They don't talk about you if you're happily married, and if they're not talking about you, they're forgetting you."

Lindsey sighed. "Which is completely awful. I couldn't live that way. But since we're asking invasive questions, why do you always call my mother Mrs. Castleton?"

Surely Lindsey knew she'd done a key-transposition from gouging out his heart with a grapefruit spoon to slathering on sweetness with a butter knife. He said, "You'll find this hard to believe, but I was a total jerk when I was thirteen." Lindsey mimed shock. "Your mother was giving advice during a performance class, and I called her Suzie Q. Your father escorted me out of the class and into one of the practice rooms. He told me he didn't care if I was his best student, or if I went on to be the next Wolfgang Amadeus Mozart—I would either treat his wife with respect or I'd be out."

Lindsey's eyebrows shot up. "Whoa."

"Very whoa. I apologized to her, and after that, I took no chances. I'm not sure I'm capable of calling her anything else after this many years." Jason stretched. "Look, we should get out of the hotel. The second show gave us some spending money, and we both need new clothes."

Lindsey flinched. "Good grief. That's going to get expensive."

Jason shook his head. "Not necessarily. Plus, you should see Manhattan. When was the last time you were here?"

"Five years ago. I don't suppose we can bust into Carnegie Hall and hang out until dinner?"

They hit the street. Lindsey kept checking her phone as if she could find her father that way, until Jason took it from her hands. "How about I keep this in my pocket to save your sanity?"

She didn't take it back. "Where are we going?"

They checked out Saks Fifth Avenue, but after two minutes in the women's section, Jason decided it was the wrong vibe. "Tonight's interview is low-key. You could show up in jeans, but you can't look like you're closing a real estate deal."

Lindsey frowned at a price tag. "There's also the fact that I'd rather not declare bankruptcy."

Jason chuckled. "It's covered."

They took the subway to 59th and Lexington, but when they emerged on the street, Lindsey looked wasted. She hadn't slept well, and neither of them had slept much. It was almost lunchtime, so Jason suggested a Moroccan restaurant. Mute, Lindsey trailed him inside.

They were being seated when her phone buzzed in his pocket, so he handed it to her. Her eyes widened, and she sighed.

"Good news?"

"Great news." She started typing a reply, but then another message came in, and she stopped, wide-eyed, with a painful laugh. "My father is such an idiot."

Jason found himself laughing too. They hadn't even looked at the menu. "What did he do?"

"He was camped out in the waiting room at the car dealership. Everyone assumed he was waiting for a repair. I think he assumed it too. I have no idea how he got there, but he was safely drinking coffee and watching TV."

Jason said, "Any idea what channel?"

Lindsey slumped forward, face in her hands. "Oh, that would be rich, if he saw us."

Rich or terrible. If Bob was wandering Hartwell and waiting for an oil change on a car he didn't have, who even knew whether he'd recognize his own daughter on a talk show?

Demurring that she had no idea what any of the food was, Lindsey let Jason order for both. Jason asked the waitress about shellfish. Lindsey seemed grateful that he'd remembered.

Jason itched to reach for her hand, but she had her palms clasped in her lap. He said, "See? We got you through this."

That was the same thing she'd said to him this morning. "We'll get you through this." But it wasn't "we." "We" hadn't slept on the floor so everyone else could get a good night's rest. "We" hadn't laid out guidelines to protect Ashlyn and Hannah from internet attacks. In Lindsey's mind, it wasn't "we" doing it at all. It was her.

Or rather, the group was "we," but she was protecting it. She was the one putting herself on the line.

While she texted her mother, Jason studied her hands, her face, her posture. She'd done the same about deciding who should go home: she'd looked at the "we" and sacrificed herself. Her mother needed Ashlyn. Hannah wasn't comfortable in front of the cameras. Jason needed someone with him. What Lindsey wanted went by the wayside, and her decisions became about what everyone else needed...except as Ashlyn said, no one was looking out for Lindsey.

Even something as small as remembering her shellfish allergy was something to her. He hadn't realized.

She'd researched everything about him, and while he kept expecting her to use it against him, she hadn't. Instead she was using it to protect him. She'd listened to his Grammy performance so often it unconsciously came up during a sound check. But then she'd said to Cass—

Oh. What she'd said to Cass.

Lindsey had found those reviews. She'd come across the smears of his composition and the attacks on his performance.

He should take a year off and learn to play.

It would have been so easy to have humiliated him on national television. "Jason found out my father was dying, so he decided to take a year off and learn to play." Instead she'd told Cass, "The man can play. You can *hear* he can play."

The internet had handed her a weapon, and she'd turned it back at his critics.

None of that was mockery. She wasn't undermining the foundation of her own quartet. In everything she'd done so far, it was the opposite. No wonder she thought Jason was trying to destroy it.

Therefore, while Lindsey was still communicating with home, Jason sent the promo clip to Michael to tweet it out. Michael replied, "Thanks. BTW, Bob is back in custody."

Jason replied, "Lindsey told me."

Michael sent, "Also, you'll be glad to know you and Lindsey are a thing."

Jason stared at the phone, glanced up at Lindsey, then back at the phone. "How?"

"Your 'smoldering look' at her. I'm handling it."

Calling him "pretty boy" during the interview must also have something to do with the buzz. People wouldn't hear the nuance, that she was teasing him for caring what he looked like.

The waitress returned with their meals, and Lindsey smiled as she thanked her. What were the odds Lindsey would find their "being a thing" hilarious? Probably less than the odds she'd be disgusted and want to fly home right now.

They ate in silence, although Lindsey did ask what the entrees were supposed to be. Afterward, with Lindsey looking revived, they entered Bloomingdale's.

He directed her straight to the cocktail dress section,

and there they played. Short dresses, long dresses, glittery dresses, formal dresses, dresses no more concealing than a bath towel, dresses with more fabric than a textile mill. He'd hold one up to her and she'd run away, or she'd point to one and he'd flinch.

After Lindsey stopped blanching at the price tags ("It's covered," Jason kept assuring her) she selected two subdued sheath dresses in solid colors.

No, no, no. He went right for a thigh-high dress with a dramatic neckline and a frilly skirt. "This," he said, holding it against her. "No, let's go darker. This one too. And..." A navy dress with a flouncy skirt caught his eye. "That's five. Try them on."

If he could go into the fitting room with her, it would make this part so much easier. He'd done that with Mitzy, although usually she had her assistant bring home twenty dresses so she could try them on. There'd been no hanky-panky when he and Mitzy shopped because you don't do that when everyone can hear over the top of the door, but it had been efficient. Mitzy would try something on, and they'd laugh or cringe, but then he'd be out of there with the dress on a hanger to fetch a different size or color while she tried on the next. Mitzy had always been fun. Here, Jason had to wait while Lindsey called out the results. "This one's a disaster." "I'd show you number two because it's funny, but I can't reach the zipper." Then, an outraged, "Did this designer ever *see* a human body?"

But then she emerged wearing the navy-blue dress with the deep V neckline, and Jason's eyebrows went up like an elevator en route to the penthouse. The high-low skirt had a cascading flounce that brushed her knees, and champagne-toned godets flared out the skirt whenever she moved.

Catching his expression, she sighed. "Yeah, I was afraid of that."

"No, it's stunning." He walked around her. The cut maximized her figure, although it didn't form-fit. "Raise your arms as if you're playing." It still looked good. No, it looked great. Lindsey looked great.

She gave a weak smile. "Can we say this is the one? I need a nap."

She would have fit right into his arms if he'd stepped forward. A changing room wasn't that different from an elevator, was it? Lindsey was doing all this for the "we" that was the quartet, except none of these appearances benefitted anyone except Jason. That meant he shouldn't harass her—much as he'd like to.

Jason nodded. "Change back, and meet me in the men's section. I'll pick out something to coordinate."

They grabbed a cab on Third Avenue, but Jason stopped a couple of blocks from the hotel when he realized Lindsey needed shoes. She browsed the silver open-toed sandals. Had she no sense of style? Jason put his arm around her waist to guide her toward a pair of platform heels in glossy beige, no straps. "This matches the inner pleats, and straps would only interrupt the line of your legs."

Lindsey tried them on. "I'll have to trust you on this, pretty boy, but they're not cute."

"They're not supposed to be cute. Heels are supposed to make you look tall and sexy."

She stood. They fit. "Pig." He grinned at her, and she handed him the box.

Next door, he bought her a pendant on a bronze choker over layered chains, and he let the jeweler talk him into coordinating earrings. Then, finally, back to the hotel. Jason carried the shopping bags. Mitzy's fans always thought that was cute. Lindsey didn't seem to notice.

He'd way blown the per-diem. Fortunately, he hadn't told Lindsey what the "spending money" actually was.

In the room, Lindsey stripped off her boots and coat, but before she collapsed on the bed, she stopped, staring at the carpet. "Thank you. I would still be finding things to wear, and I wouldn't have realized until after dinner that I needed shoes. I'm too exhausted to think."

Jason burned to put his hand into her hair and draw her near. Her emotions were spent, her body exhausted, her brain tired out. He could pull her up against him and ask if she'd consider continuing what they'd started in the elevator. She was worn thin enough that she might consent. She'd hate him even more afterward, but he'd win a few minutes now.

Jason held his ground. "Not a big deal. I may follow you."

Lindsey's eyes narrowed. "Not in my bed."

He raised his hands. "Two beds, two bodies. That's the correct proportion of beds to bodies."

She vanished into the bedroom.

None of this was fair to her. A dress and a necklace couldn't pay back for her entire soul screaming to be with her family. Instead she'd helped Jason breathe sparks onto a career that was cold charcoal. She'd answered humiliating questions on national television and had volunteered to do it again for the quartet.

No, be honest. She'd done it for Jason. She didn't like him, but she'd sacrificed for him.

Jason sat at the table to check his texts, and his eye landed on his open backpack and the corner of his music notebook.

He reached for the spiral binding, then opened to a blank page. His awesome gel pen warmed to his hand.

Bob, missing. Susan, frantic. Lindsey, separated from her clan when she wanted most to be with them. Jason, gripping the sink in case he collapsed.

Jason was standing on the shore, staring into the tidal wave of the loss that was to come. Bob. Bob, missing forever. It was approaching. They couldn't stop it, couldn't avoid it, couldn't mitigate it.

Jason clicked the pen, and he wrote for an hour.

CHAPTER ELEVEN

For the second time today, Lindsey was standing in a prep room while Jason looked faint. This time they'd done their sound check together, and Jason had kept it to a violin duet they'd both played repeatedly as students. Tonight, they were following his playbook. Following hers had resulted in chaos.

The makeup artist came in, looked Lindsey over, and said, "I'll be right back."

Lindsey turned to a startled Jason. "Take that as a good sign: no matter what happens tonight, you're going to look fabulous compared to me."

He did look fabulous. A shirt and pants picked almost at random off the rack coordinated perfectly with her outfit and left him looking dreamy. This must be Hollywood stuff because he knew things about fashion that left her blinking. That detail about strappy sandals cutting off the line of her leg? She'd never heard that before. (Not to mention that crack about making her legs long and sexy.)

The makeup artist returned with another woman, who got a look at Lindsey and said, "Yep, you're coming with me," and two minutes later, Lindsey was in a different room with, it turned out, the wardrobe consultant. The wardrobe lady set a bunch of pins around Lindsey's waist, then had her raise her arms to shoot a few more pins beneath. It was only when the wardrobe lady uncapped a seam ripper that Lindsey exclaimed, "Wait! What are you doing?"

"I'm going to tack it up. Take it to your tailor when you get home." Sure, because everyone had a personal tailor. The woman ripped out the side seams, and Lindsey could only stress about the price tag. It took five minutes for the woman to tack up a new waistline, then fix the gap under the arms. "Exhale," she said, and abruptly Lindsey was zippered in a dress that fit like a glove. "Nope, still not right." Off came the dress, and then Lindsey was standing braless while the wardrobe guru was asking her size. "Wrong. You're not a 36 C." She handed Lindsey a pair of plastic cups. "You're a 32 DD. You got measured in a department store, and they sold you what they had. Stick those to you." Lindsey was momentarily glued into a plastic bra with no straps and no back. It was scary to think she was one strong breeze away from nakedness. The dress went on again ("Exhale!"—zip!) and the wardrobe consultant gave a grim nod.

Lindsey, who would have thought herself fine the way she was at the start, stood in front of the three-way mirror wondering how any dress could look this good on her—or be that much improved, considering how much it had cost to begin with. She whispered, "Thank you."

"I didn't do it for you." The woman huffed. "I did it so I wouldn't get fired."

That must be New Yorker for, "You're welcome."

Jason's jaw actually dropped when Lindsey returned. "Well."

"Yeah. Don't ask me to go clubbing afterward. It's held

together with two threads." She turned, and the skirt flared. "I'd say you look good too, but stage makeup is just weird."

"Yeah, it takes some getting used to." He gestured to the chair. "Your turn," and then the makeup artist did Lindsey, creating weird contours and shading effects for appearing under the stage lights.

Then it was more waiting. Jason took a selfie with Lindsey and sent it to Michael.

"Michael didn't realize how much you were going to take him up on that offer," Lindsey mused. Jason looked great in the picture. Of course he did. In addition to his other blessings, the muses had bestowed on him a mega dose of "insanely photogenic." He'd gotten up close for the picture, and the air of his cologne lingered about her.

He was such an amazing male and such a selfish man. The way he'd been so thoughtful to her this afternoon— shopping, of all things—only made it worse. He could treat people well when he wanted to. He just chose not to.

Ten minutes later, Lindsey and Jason and their violins were onstage with their hosts, seated on a pair of couches. This set was less like a news studio and more like what Corwin had done to the basement: bluer lighting, a grunge feel, and a faux living room on a circular stage. Lindsey didn't breathe too deeply, afraid her tacked-together side seams would surrender in front of the studio audience.

The male host, Will, leaned closer to Jason, "Feel free to put your arm around her or snuggle up together. Keep a relaxed body language. We'll take breaks at ten-minute intervals."

Lindsey huffed. "Maybe you could wedge a pillow between us instead?"

Shifting toward her, Jason covered his mic with his hand. "Social media is trying to make us a thing."

Lindsey's eyebrows shot up. "By all means, feel free to discourage that with the truth."

He glowered at her. "You set us up for it this morning, and everyone ran with it."

They began. Will and Dana chatted almost exclusively with Jason, which was exactly how Lindsey preferred it. One evening's service as arm candy for a gorgeous guy wasn't too much to repay him for helping out her father.

"But giving all that up for Maine...?" Dana said. "I'm sure it's beautiful up there, but it's frigid!"

Jason laughed. "I have to admit, I miss it being sixty-eight and sunny every single day."

Lindsey said, "Not me. I love having seasons."

"Green Christmas," Jason said. "Palm trees."

"Killer traffic," Lindsey said. "An entire population that has no idea how to drive in the rain."

Will and Dana groaned, and Jason said, "The 405 doesn't have traffic jams. It has disasters! People tailgating with no clue whatsoever about stopping distance. Chain-reaction accidents."

Lindsey flashed a thumbs-up. "I'll keep my winter coat, thanks."

Jason said, "As if Maine doesn't get black ice."

Lindsey said, "I know how to pull out of a skid. I know how to increase my following distance in bad weather."

Dana said to Jason, "Still, something brought you out of Brentwood to the back woods."

A subtle change in tone was the only clue that Jason had slipped from chatting into a prepared statement. "Lindsey's father was the most influential music teacher I ever had. When Robert Castleton was diagnosed with a terminal condition, his wife Susan asked if I could stand in for a year until the quartet could get back on its feet."

Lindsey's head shot up because even flattened out, Jason's voice belied every single word of the sentence. "Wait, I thought my mother called you to come back."

Jason looked startled. Will laughed. "That's what he said."

No, that wasn't what Jason had said. He'd said the words, but his voice and tone had said the opposite.

Dana said, "Still, despite the reason, it must have been good going home."

119

Jason shrugged. "I don't know that I've ever fully considered myself a Mainer. Lindsey was born there, but I wasn't."

Lindsey huffed. "Dude, you're a Mainer. You may have gotten rid of the accent, but you're a Mainer."

Jason rolled his eyes. "I'm an *outsider.*"

"There are people in town who consider *me* the weird outsider because my father grew up in Lewiston!" Lindsey fought irritation as she forced herself to laugh. "Like, I was only born in that town, but we're still those weird newcomers."

Will said to Jason, "Where'd you come from?"

"Greenwich, Connecticut. My father was CFO of some Fortune 500 company. When they restructured, they offered him a golden parachute, and he and my mother leaped. They bought a restaurant supply company for a change of pace, so I spent a significant portion of my childhood hearing about table linens and delivery trucks."

Lindsey nudged his arm. "Wherever we go, Jason knows all the best hole-in-the-wall restaurants. He'll direct you down five dirt roads to this shed you can barely even see through the trees. It looks condemned, but then he greets the waitstaff by name and recommends the minestrone, and it's wicked awesome."

Dana laughed as Jason's cheeks turned pink. If Lindsey tortured him a bit on national TV, a restaurant fetish was harmless enough. Dana said, "That's a handy skill."

Lindsey added, "You should see him fold a tablecloth. It's savage."

Jason arched his gorgeous eyebrows at her, and she went warm. The audience oohed.

Will said, "Robert Castleton must have meant a lot for you to return to the land of the napkin delivery."

Jason leaned back and crossed his legs at the ankle. Suddenly he was back in "prepared statement" territory. "I can't overstate Robert Castleton's expertise or the novel approach to teaching. Lessons weren't just a matter of showing up for half an hour and going home. He and his wife fostered a community among the students, and Castleton-trained musicians have ended up all over the world."

Lindsey mindlessly plucked an A on her instrument. She should grab this clip of Jason for the school website as an endorsement.

Dana turned to Lindsey. "That must have been wonderful for you, growing up surrounded by music."

Suffused with guilt, Lindsey said, "It was. It really was."

An imbalance the universe was righting, taking her father by stages.

Dana prompted, "Go on."

A glance at Jason didn't let her off the hook. Lindsey braced herself. "My father gave everything to his music. He had the school, but he also formed a quartet with his best friend. When Jason left for the L.A. Philharmonic, I stepped into his slot. Dad didn't want him to go, but it was time."

Jason snickered. "You made him clear out that slot for you."

She shook her head. "Not at all. I was happy being your sub."

Jason turned to her with an anger that came out of nowhere. "You needed a job, and you're his daughter."

That was odd—and wrong. "I was convenient! You were ready to fly, and the world needed to hear from you. I heard him and Mom arguing about it. Heck, I argued with him about it, and I have the emails. Joining the quartet meant I needed to back off on the newspaper work because I couldn't cover stories on the weekends—but he insisted you wouldn't leave unless I agreed to come onboard full time."

Still irritated, Jason went totally silent.

Lindsey recoiled. "Did you really think Dad considered you the seat-warmer for the rightful heir?"

Well, then. Yet another reason for Jason to hate her. Except this one wasn't true.

The audience oohed, and Jason recovered. "You have to admit, it didn't look good."

"Then you weren't paying attention. He bragged about you like crazy." Lindsey folded her hands on her knee and looked at Dana. "My father is the most successful musician I know. He was offered two different concertmaster positions when he graduated from the Royal Academy of London. He could have gone to Vienna or to Paris, and instead he went back to Maine because of my mother. But Jason wasn't tied to Maine. Dad knew that if he left before he put down roots here, he could do even more." She turned back to Jason. "He wanted you unfettered."

Jason looked shocked. "That I didn't realize."

She nodded. "My father didn't get to do that. He took a job as a church musician so he could marry my mother and make a home."

Dana said, "Couldn't he have married your mother and gone to Vienna then?"

Without thinking, Lindsey said, "She wouldn't have left."

No. Of course Mom couldn't have left Maine. Dalton-become-Michael was in Maine, and if Susan wanted any chance of finding her son, she had to be where he was.

Oh!

It had never made sense that with orchestras asking for him, Dad still went back to Maine. Not until now—now, when Lindsey knew the rest of the story: *Dad already loved Mom.* Without that piece, Dad's coming home had seemed provincial. With that piece of the puzzle...whoa.

Dad had sacrificed everything.

Reeling, Lindsey breathed, "Dad gave up everything for Mom because love was more important than status. Then he wove that love into the way he taught his students. My parents taught us—not just their kids, but all their students—to work together, to think together, to anticipate one another's choices. We had classes in one another's preferred music styles, and they'd have us teach each other. We had intensive improv classes and hours-long jam sessions where you could step in and out of the playing. Instead of recording a few albums and headlining a few concerts, Robert Castleton created a thousand musicians and scattered them across the world like constellations." Lindsey forced a smile because her eyes were watering. She was going to ruin that stage makeup. "That's the best success there is."

Dana said to Lindsey, "That must be terrible for you, then. Your father's illness." When she nodded, Dana said, "How do you feel?"

Lindsey sat up. "Did you just ask if I'm sad about my father's impending death?"

Jason said in a warning tone, "Lindsey."

"Is that the current state of journalism?" She looked right at Dana and hammered her fingers against the neckboard of the violin, sounding a warning note. "Because I find that offensive."

Jason turned to her, eyes piercing. "Lindsey!"

The audience hooted. Dana waved him down. "It's okay, Jason. It was a dumb question." She turned to Lindsey. "I should have asked, is it disconcerting having to fill all those roles at once? It sounds like everything went topsy-turvy, and without warning you ended up first violin and Jason as the second."

Jason was looking right at Lindsey, his eyes alight, his posture one intent warning.

This was not a thing to discuss on the air.

Continuing this conversation was not going to rehab Jason to the world.

Lindsey folded her arms and dropped her head. "I'm sorry. Yes, it's very hard. In a just and fair world, Jason should be in the spotlight, and I should be writing for a newspaper. My father should be in this seat. And as for Jason, on his celebrated—and brief—trips home to Maine, Jason should be doing electric violin cameos with Clear Enigma, my brother's alternative rock band."

She blinked, then swallowed hard. The audience made sad sounds.

Jason put his arm around her. She shook her head. "Don't."

He let her go.

Will said, "We'll take a break for a few minutes, and when we come back, we'll talk a bit about Ultraviolet Dawn."

Every mic is a live mic. Lindsey said nothing to Jason while the tech people adjusted everyone's equipment and the makeup artist touched up her face. The wardrobe lady straightened Lindsey's waterfall necklace, then shifted the skirt's cascading flounce. "Cross your legs, for Pete's sake," she muttered. "Show off your shoes."

Jason alternated between glancing away and studying her, but Lindsey couldn't look at him.

Her father could have traveled the world. He'd come home for Mom. They'd both stayed in case they could find Michael. Every time Lindsey thought about that, her soul rang like a bell.

Jason leaned toward her, and again with the mic covered, said, "Remember what I said about answering the question they should have asked."

"I'm sorry," she whispered back. "I lost it."

His eyes were piercing, but he didn't look angry. "It's fine, but next time."

The interview resumed. Dana wanted to know more about musicians naming their instruments, which gave Lindsey and Jason a chance to argue about the fact that Jason had yet to name his. "A pretty piece like that needs a name!" she exclaimed.

Jason said, "You haven't named yours."

Lindsey said, "I named my first violin, but this one hasn't spoken to me yet."

Dana exclaimed, "Wait, violins speak to you? Why didn't I know this?"

Jason said, "Lindsey's father's violin is named

Frederika."

"That's just a joke." Lindsey said to Will and Dana, "My father bought the German violin at a time when he and Mom didn't have much money. He was just starting the music school, and she'd taken over his position as music director at the church. Whenever they couldn't afford something, my mother would say, 'Oh, right, you spent that on your German girlfriend.' A lady at church was scandalized when she overheard, so they stopped calling it his German mistress and started calling her Frederika."

Jason was laughing. "Your poor mother! I never knew that violin as anything other than Frederika."

"Now you know." She arched her eyebrows. "But that church lady should have realized: if you buy an expensive enough violin, you can't afford to have an affair."

Dana said to Jason, "Your violin didn't prevent you from dating Mitzy Maxwell."

Jason drew breath, but Lindsey took Jason's advice about answering the question they should have asked. "Speaking of which, why didn't you play your own violin in Violet Nights?"

Jason looked like he had whiplash. Will said, "How can you tell which violin is which?"

"Usually by tone, but this time it was the finish." Lindsey gestured to the violin in Jason's lap. "The one in the film had a greenish gold shine."

Jason recovered. "That was my unnamed violin. They CGI'd it to resemble sea water."

It really was all about the appearance, wasn't it? Take something perfect and change it. Keep people talking.

The conversation was exhausting though. After enough small talk to punch Lindsey's card until next April, Dana said to the audience, "Did you guys all catch Lindsey and her violist playing this morning for Cass Camden?" Everyone applauded and whistled. "Lindsey, what *was* that?"

Although most of the interview was unscripted, Dana and Will had prepared this part with them. Lindsey clicked into performance mode. "Ashlyn and I jam together all the time, and we were having fun with Jason's number two hit song."

The audience roared approval.

Will said, "Which I'm told actually shot up the charts again today and briefly trended on Twitter."

Jason looked startled. Dana said in a teasing voice, "Lindsey...? Are you competing with Mitzy Maxwell?"

"Me, compete with the classiest woman in America?" Lindsey opened her hands. "Let's see: pop sensation Mitzy Maxwell, versus a flannel-and-jeans-wearing music teacher from the frozen north. I know who my money would be on, and it's not me."

Will leaned in. "So you weren't throwing down the gauntlet?"

Lindsey sat back. "Ms. Maxwell can relax on her throne as queen of America's musical heart. In two months, I'll still be shoveling my driveway, and Jason will be back in Los Angeles."

Dana said to Jason, "What do you think?"

Jason gave an adorable sigh. "We've got the opposite of a love triangle. Neither woman's pursuing me." The audience laughed, but some people booed. Lindsey started, but Jason put a hand on her shoulder.

Dana said, "So if we asked the two of you to play it again here...? Right now?"

Jason sat back. "We'd actually planned something else, but if you insist..."

Wild applause. That was their cue, so Lindsey and Jason headed to the performance circle where their bows were waiting.

Lindsey said to him, "You really should give your instrument a name."

The mics were live, but audiences always loved musician banter.

Jason replied in a low tone, "I would, but you'd never let me live it down." The audience laughed.

They faced one another, and Lindsey waited. When he

didn't cue her, she realized he was waiting on her. Even though this was Jason's gig...even though it was Jason's song...he was waiting on her cue.

That was odd, coming from a man who always jumped his cue. She started them.

They'd worked on the violin parts since the afternoon, then rehearsed it with the studio's keyboardist and drummer. Lindsey hoped this version would hold together better than the tacked-up halves of her dress.

She leaned hard into the tune of Mitzy Maxwell's vocals to evoke all the emotion that Mitzy got when she sang. *The violin is the closest approximation to the human voice,* she'd told Cass, the same thing she told her violin students. Anything the human voice can do, the violin can do just as well—and tonight Lindsey unleashed it to sing.

Jason had crafted his violin part to wrap around Mitzy's voice, and with Lindsey's violin fully engaged in the vocals, wrap around it did. Supporting, enhancing, at times overwhelming, Jason was again too strident—but someone in the sound booth was compensating. Jason was also incredibly technical, which only freed up Lindsey to make her instrument cheer and sigh and teeter on the verge of tears and then surge with relief that the one she loved... loved her too.

They reached the chorus, and Jason raised his bow over his head. Suddenly the audience was singing the chorus, and Lindsey laughed as she played along, dancing as much as she could while Jason moved about the front of the stage, encouraging them to keep singing.

The audience stopped singing while they went through the verse, but for the second chorus they were all back again. Then the bridge.

Jason shot into the solo part (ahem, his cadenza) while Lindsey played softer, lower, slower notes in the correct key. He blew through every trick he knew on a violin, as if he were Paganini himself. The radio edit of this song gave him twenty-five seconds to show off; the live version, right now, let him loose for a full five minutes.

Gosh, he was great. There was nothing Jason couldn't do on that violin, except right now it was all energy and showmanship with none of the heart. Every so often he passed the music back to her, and she played for a few measures before giving it back to him. Every time, the audience cheered him. Every time, his eyes brightened so he looked ferocious.

This was what he'd been born to do. This moment, this recognition, this moment of domination over the sound.

Jason cued her, and Lindsey re-entered the chorus. They flowed back into the standard performance of the song and crescendoed to a close.

The audience was cheering. Jason raised his hands, violin in one and bow in the other. Lindsey kept her violin and bow in her right hand, tucked under her arm. Then Jason turned to her, so she stepped toward him for a hug.

It wasn't the post-performance Grammy kiss he'd shared with Mitzy Maxwell. This should make it clear: they were colleagues.

When Jason put his arm around her waist, though, and they faced the crowd, Lindsey shivered. Their truce was about to end. The night was over.

When they returned to the hotel at eleven o'clock, Lindsey felt too revved up to sleep, and Jason was by turns delighted and unnerved. They ought to celebrate the moment, but Lindsey couldn't think of how. The studio had provided plenty of food, and it didn't seem wise to go clubbing or even to pick up a bottle of champagne. They'd been awake since four, and they were sleeping in the same room. Best just to call it a day.

Jason fumbled the key card, which only went to show how tired they both were. He muttered, "Set a backup alarm. I could sleep through a bomb."

Lindsey held up the doorknob card. "Room service breakfast?"

He shook his head. "It's always lousy. We'll hunt something down before we head to the airport."

If the texts were any judge, Jason's agent was pleased, and the movie producer was beside himself. The only one who hadn't checked in, and please may she never check in, was Mitzy Maxwell. Lindsey had talked up the woman to the moon trying to get ahead of the internet matchmakers, but she'd pass out if Maxwell ever spoke to her. Best if Lindsey never got noticed.

Jason brought his pajamas into the bathroom while Lindsey debated changing in the bedroom at the same time. Too risky. She removed the gorgeous shoes and the necklace, then studied herself in the mirror. Form-fitted as it was, the dress looked so stylish. She'd need to find a tailor to seam it up.

No wonder Jason wanted to return to this lifestyle. Everyone and everything was geared toward pampering. The only thing truly real tonight had been the music.

Lindsey silenced her alerts. She'd gotten a couple dozen congratulatory texts, including from her mother: "That was astonishing, and I love what you said about your father. I'm so glad you stayed, sweetie."

Lindsey wasn't glad. It was a fabulous experience, but she should have been with her family.

She was washing off her stage makeup when Jason emerged from the bathroom in a black undershirt and blue flannel pants. "All yours." His makeup was gone but his hair was still amazing. Lindsey's skin tingled as he stepped around her. She locked herself in the bathroom to change.

She reached for the back of her dress...and couldn't get the zipper.

She twisted harder, but the dress wouldn't give. What was going on? She'd gotten herself into it.

No...she hadn't gotten herself into it. The wardrobe consultant had sewn her into it. Or rather, had sewn up the side seams and then zipped Lindsey into it from the back.

Stay calm. The best thing to do was gain as much room as she could by breathing all the way out like the wardrobe lady said, and then try again. Except she still couldn't grip the zipper. The tab was locked beneath a hook and eyelet, and the clasp only slipped beneath her fingertips. She couldn't pull the dress up over her ribs. There would be no way to get out through the neck. She was trapped.

Maybe she could find a fork and use that to push the zipper down? Only she still wouldn't be able to unfasten the hook.

Lindsey closed her eyes. The best option was to rip out the tacked stitches on one side of the dress and slither out. The best option—except the dress was so perfect, and so expensive.

Face burning, she found Jason sitting on the edge of his bed with his phone. She must be pink all the way to her navel, and when she spoke, her voice trembled. "I need some help."

Jason looked up. "A mission to Duane Reade for emergency tampons? I'm in. Tell me the brand name and the box color."

"I wish." Lindsey turned around. "Can you unzip the top of the dress?"

Jason burst out laughing, and she spun back. "Jason!"

He dropped his phone on the bed. "Lindsey—shotgun, my shotgun—this is the best thing that has ever happened. For once in your life, you need me."

She folded her arms. "I can sleep in this thing if I have to."

"Not when you have a knight in shining armor here to assist. Turn around."

"Forget it, pretty boy." She walked to the room phone. "I'm going to call housekeeping."

"Housekeeping isn't going to come until tomorrow. I think this is wonderful." Jason came up behind her, and she tensed in case he rested his hands on her shoulders.

"Please don't be mad. I only laughed because it's ridiculously funny. Let me."

She bent her head and lifted her hair, and Jason leaned toward her but didn't touch. "You know..." His breath tingled against her neck. "You're putting me in an interesting position."

She felt him move the back of the dress, but not the zipper. That must have been the hook.

He touched the nape of her neck. "So many options."

Her hair stood on end. "If you choose the wrong one, I swear I'll end you."

He snickered. "Well, something's going to kill me. This works as well as anything else."

"Open it about five inches. I can get the rest."

"This is such a shame in so many ways." In slow motion, Jason eased the zipper between her shoulder blades. "For one thing, you look astounding in this, and for another, I'm sure you'd look good out of it too, only I'll never have another chance to see you either way."

"Pig." She reached around to make sure she could get it the rest of the way. She couldn't.

Jason's voice went sultry, and it sent shivers through her. "Remember how you told everyone I kissed you? The perfect revenge would be telling everyone we spent the night together, and you begged me to undress you." Jason slid the zipper toward her waist, and his breath caught. "You're not even wearing a bra? Lindsey, you're killing me!"

"You're the epitome of a gentleman." Lindsey turned so she could back out of the room, but she kept her arms folded in front of her chest. "They glued me up and braced me with molded plastic and then informed me I don't know how to dress myself."

Jason gave a roll of his eyes as he went back to his half of the room. "Yeah, wardrobe people will do that. Also, I tie my shoes incorrectly."

She stepped backward. "Well, thank you."

Jason looked over his shoulder with a hopeful smile. "If

wardrobe left you in doubt about how to get into your pajamas, I'm still here to assist."

"Pig," she snapped again as she fled to the bathroom.

"Shotgun," he called after her.

When Lindsey returned, Jason was in his bed, and she slipped into the other one. The door was bolted and every light off except the lamp between the beds. Lindsey made a nest of pillows and snuggled down, walled in by fluffiness and weary to her core.

Jason leaned over to get the light, but with his hand on the switch he hesitated. His face was a battleground, his eyes not directed at her, his brow tight. "Thank you for doing this for me."

"Hey." She tried to meet his eyes, but he wouldn't look up. "Thank you too."

"Yeah. Good night," and the light went off.

Cuddling the closest pillow, Lindsey expected to fall asleep instantaneously, but instead she found herself awake for a while, listening to Jason's breaths and improvising Mitzy's song all around that rhythm.

CHAPTER TWELVE

Edward's text beat the phone call by thirty seconds: "Incoming."

That was not enlightening, but it probably had something to do with the looming deadline for Ultraviolet Nights. Jason had only wasted three weeks since New York with no third song to show for it. Wouldn't this be a joy?

In his kitchen, Jason answered the Los Angeles number anyhow, but he kept it professional. "Woodward."

"Jason Woodward! So glad to connect with you. Lansing Burke, Ledgewood Studios!"

Jason straightened. "Burke! Good to hear from you! We met at Mitzy's birthday party?"

He'd met two hundred people at Mitzy's birthday party, so that was a safe guess.

"Absolutely." While Jason rummaged in his brain for any detail he could remember about the guy, Burke went on. "I hope you don't mind that I hit up your agent for your phone number, but I needed to get ahead of something here."

Jason already had the laptop lid up and was mere seconds from typing "Lansing Burke" into the search bar. That phrasing bothered him. In L.A., you usually wanted to preempt good things, but you wanted to get ahead of bad things. "What can I do for you?"

"My daughter adores you." Jason fought a snicker: Hollywood kids were not immune to the glitter just because they grew up surrounded by it. It wouldn't be the first time someone had approached Jason for a signature on an album cover. *If I mail you the CD insert, can you sign it for my precious? It would mean the world to her.*

That wasn't worth a phone call, though. That was worth a text. A text to his agent, in fact.

Burke's face came up on the screen, and then Jason remembered. Lansing Burke was an awesome guy who'd kept trying to look down Mitzy's cleavage after he'd had too many drinks, but he was big into philanthropy and made things happen in pop music. He'd managed three successful boy bands. If his daughter adored Jason, she'd been trained up into the practice.

Burke continued, "Kylee's out of her mind about seeing you next week at music camp, so I need a favor. The kid switched from cello to violin because of 'Love Once More,' and she'd love to play it for you. I was hoping you could maybe give her some pointers and then encourage her to practice. I've shelled out a lot for lessons, but she'd rather post pictures of her violin on Instagram than practice the thing."

Jason closed his eyes tight to figure out how to reply, but under time pressure, the only thing that emerged was, "You mean the Northern Maine Music Academy's string orchestra camp?"

Bob Castleton had founded that event along with the owners of three other music schools: a winter camp for elite children whose parents pulled them and their high-end instruments from their private schools for a week's intensive instruction. This year, instead of Bob teaching, it was Lindsey. Note that. Not Jason: Lindsey.

Burke chuckled. "How many orchestra camps are you teaching at? No, wait, don't tell me. She won't stop until she attends them all."

"None," Jason said. "Our first violinist will teach there, but I won't. I've never been a music teacher. Does their website name me as an instructor?"

"Oh, this is awkward. Hang on." Burke must be doing on his end what Jason was doing in the kitchen: Googling the camp roster. "You're right. It doesn't look like you're there."

Good to know that Jason was right about where Jason was working next week. "You had me worried that they were advertising me."

"No, my daughter must just have hoped for the best. She's going to be devastated. Is there any way you could put in an appearance for her? She's talked about nothing else since she signed up, and I'll never forget it."

Jason couldn't tell if that was a threat or straight-up manipulation. Jason wasn't entirely heartless, and also, he wasn't entirely an idiot. "Don't devastate her. Let me see what I can do."

"Thanks. This is everything to her." And the call was over.

Everything? First off, if Jason were to die tomorrow in a freak meteor crash, that girl's life would not cease. She'd dust herself off and find some other musician to crush on.

Secondly, the longer Jason thought about it, the more he realized he was being played like a dime store fiddle. Lansing Burke wouldn't have pulled his daughter out of school for a week-long violin camp across the country without researching the living daylights out of it, or having his assistants do so. Lansing Burke made things happen, and he was making something happen now. If Jason didn't appear at the camp, Jason was the monster who crushed his daughter's violin vocation. If Jason did, there was an "attaboy" in his future, along with the theoretical (and highly remote) possibility that Burke would remember him and grease some wheels.

The "camp" would take place at a ski lodge that appreciated having a guaranteed full house for an entire week that was neither Christmas break nor February break. It was a ninety-minute drive from Juniper, and the region was gorgeous. Maybe the view would inspire Jason's final song for Ultraviolet Dawn—the one he'd spun his wheels on ever since New York City. The song that was, you know, due soon. On deadline. Of which he'd written exactly zero notes.

Well, written many notes and kept none.

He should have that song finished, for crying out loud. The quartet was in its dead season because no one wanted to get married in Maine in late January. He'd done a couple of interviews, but of the variety where an interviewer set up cameras and collected a series of sound bites that would total thirty seconds in someone else's news segment. Jason was well on his way to becoming a C-list celebrity, but at least no one bothered to dox the C-list for sitting in an office with music posters at his back, saying, "I'm really excited about the developments for season three."

Lindsey, though... Every time Jason's career got her attention, her tone changed. Since New York, whenever he'd mentioned anything to do with California, she'd treated him like an injured kitten. Did he have to do an interview? She'd volunteer the school office, and she would be upstairs if they needed anything. Did he want to record something? Feel free to use the school's studio while she would stay in the music library reshelving books.

He hated—still hated—that she'd seen him melt down the morning of the Cass Camden show. Lindsey had talked him through the panic and never mentioned it again, but she hadn't forgotten. She'd defended him to the TV audience. She'd dealt with the media trying to pit her against Mitzy Maxwell, and she'd made his return as easy for him as she could.

It was the "we" thing.

"We." It wasn't as if he and she were a "we." All along, her "we" had been her quartet, her family, and her friends. Lindsey hated him, but still she wanted things to turn out well for him. He was the biggest irritant in her life, but when she saw him foundering on the brink of failure, she extended a hand.

If he asked about the camp, she'd fit him into it. Once she got over the irritation at changing plans to accommodate, she'd figure out how to make it happen. Which was, in effect, what Lansing Burke was doing, too. Only Lansing Burke didn't care one whit about Jason, and somehow, Lindsey did.

The other three were already setting up when Jason arrived for quartet practice. Lindsey exclaimed, "How nice of you to show up!" and he gave her a tolerant nod.

Hannah said, "We're getting a mountain of snow tomorrow. Maybe we should stay late tonight and cancel Thursday's practice?"

"That'll be up to you because you're driving furthest. If the roads get you from Brighthead to Hartwell without too much pain, I have to assume you can get across town and Jason can get here from Juniper." Lindsey gave Jason an A to tune to, but his violin was still in the case. Yes, Lindsey with her "we" who always thought Jason shouldn't be there last—conveniently ignoring that someone had to be last. If Jason showed up early, then he just transferred the target to Hannah, and how rude was that?

Jason unclasped the case. "Before we begin, I have a question. A friend of a friend has a daughter who's going to be at the string orchestra camp."

Lindsey closed her eyes. "Wait, don't tell me. This

darling girl is arriving with her Stradivarius violin, which I need to make sure doesn't get exposed to the cold even though the camp paperwork specifically talks about playing outdoors?"

Jason paused. "You have the most vibrant fantasies." None of which involved him, he hoped.

Lindsey flashed him a smile. "That's not it? Because I'd love to play a Strad—I mean, *protect* her Strad by standing guard over it in the ski lodge lobby—at least once before I die."

Jason winked at Lindsey. "I've played a Strad."

Lindsey perked up. "Does that mean I can kill you?"

Hannah said, "Who do you know that owns a Stradivarius?"

They were all watching, meaning Jason was performing for an audience of three. "A guy from the Philharmonic is friends with someone at a museum that has two Strads in their collection, a violin and a viola. That guy gets paid to keep the instruments in playable condition because they lose their voices if they go dormant. One night he let me in after hours, and he let me play them."

Hannah sighed. "That must have been awesome."

Jason tightened his bow. "It was."

Lindsey gave him a wicked grin. "Get me into that locked room with the Strads, and maybe I'll help your friend of a friend with whatever they want."

Jason snorted. "If you and I are ever in a locked room together, I strongly suspect I'm not emerging alive. I was hoping you'd help the kid even without the involvement of a Stradivarius."

Lindsey said, "Shall I promise her I have no interest in you, that way she can feel free not to hate me? Or does she already hate me because I'm the live body standing in between you and Mitzy Maxwell?"

Jason's heart shrank. Mitzy was the live body who'd stood between him and Mitzy.

Ashlyn said, "I think it's hilarious that the media put you and Jason together."

Lindsey beamed. "No one recognizes true love better than entertainment reporters and a pining throng of tweens."

Jason mimed nausea, and Lindsey gave him an A again while smirking. "Stay classy, pretty boy."

Jason said, "It's not my fault, shotgun. Or have you forgotten who blurted that out on the air?"

Lindsey turned to Ashlyn. "I owe you five bucks. Didn't we have a bet that if our quartet was ever on a magazine cover, it would be you and Jason in the foreground?"

Jason hesitated mid-tune. "Yeah, you did say that during one of the interviews. What gives?"

Ashlyn rolled her eyes. "Because you and I are beautiful."

Jason said, "And Hannah isn't?"

Lindsey laughed so hard that Jason actually had to roll that back in his mind until he realized what he'd said. Hannah gave only a demure, "That's not nice. Lindsey's pretty."

"Please." Lindsey was gasping. "Stick Ashlyn on Jason's arm and the world will swoon."

Ashlyn shook her head sadly. "More likely the world would take note at Jason's instinctive flinch."

Jason said, "Remember what I said about the general public: they don't get nuance. You and Hannah are both taken, so that leaves exactly one option for the universe: Lindsey and I must couple up. It's a requirement, plus it gets clicks, and clicks drive ad revenue."

Lindsey said, "When I find true love, I'm putting clicks and views on my bridal registry."

Jason frowned at her. "You can't get married." When she looked annoyed, he added, "You said there's always going to be a Castleton heading the Castleton String Quartet. If you get married, there won't be a Castleton."

Lindsey offered a tolerant sigh. "If only there were a workaround for that. Or do you assume that if you'd married Mitzy Maxwell, she'd have become Mitzy Woodward?"

Jason paid close attention to his violin. "She doesn't want to marry me, so we'll never find out."

Hannah said to Lindsey, "Whatever happened to that guy you were dating last winter?"

Since returning, Jason hadn't seen Lindsey with a boyfriend. She shrugged. "I have no idea what happened to him. He was so eager to spend time with me and attend to me during every waking moment. Then my father got sick, and *poof*! No more attentive guy."

Jason's hand tightened on his violin.

Hannah looked down. "Oh. That's awful."

Jason glowered as he tuned. "More like spineless."

Lindsey seemed in no hurry to start practice. "It was the best thing he could have done for me. Much better to find out he's a total manbaby now than after five years. You have a fight and he runs to his mommy to have her do his laundry and feed him, and surprise, it turns out you have one more child than you thought."

Jason rolled his eyes. "Speaking of children, I'll go you one better than that. A guy back in California had the gall to whine that there was no food in his house because his wife was staying with their premature baby in the NICU. I suggested grocery delivery if he had no time to shop. No, no, no. He had plenty of time. It was, *she always does the shopping,* and, *I don't know what she wants.*" Jason lowered his voice. "I'll tell you what she wants. She wants to come home to a fridge full of groceries she didn't have to buy herself."

Lindsey beamed. "Thank you for that. You'll make someone a good husband."

"And you deserved better than to have some toad ghost you when you needed him to be strong."

Who was ever strong for Lindsey?

Lindsey averted her eyes. "The world's already given me quite a few things I don't deserve. Best not to keep count." She reached for her music. "By the way, I'm going to put together a medley of patriotic songs for our President's Day appearance, so if you guys have something that brings a tear to your eye, let me know."

Jason prompted, "The orchestra camp...?"

Lindsey paused. "Oh, right. Lay it out there. What does my pretty boy desire of me?"

Desire was...an interesting word to use. The sensation of her kiss flitted through his head. The shape of her in that dress. The scent of vanilla. "A music producer is sending his daughter, who's eleven. She switched from cello to violin because of 'Love Once More,' and she wants me to give her a lesson on how to perform it."

Violin in her lap, Lindsey sat as if listening to a dial tone. Finally, she said, "Is she a princess, requiring a private lesson from Sir Jason Vanderbilt Woodward the Gorgeous? Is her father the king?"

Jason sighed. "It feels that way, doesn't it?"

At least Lindsey wasn't freaking out about the inconvenience. She hadn't even made a crack about having to endure Jason's presence during her one peaceful week away from him. "Sure. I'll give you the camp director's number. The students have time off every day to practice. You can work it in then."

That was too easy. Jason felt almost disappointed that she didn't push back harder.

A minute later, Lindsey had texted him a contact. "If you're driving all the way out there, you can't just give one kid a lesson and then vanish. The director will have you talk about careers and preach the virtues of hiring someone phlegmatic to handle your social media."

Jason dropped his phone into the empty violin case. "That would be fine. Thanks."

"No problem." Lindsey snickered. "But let me know if King Music Producer the Third bought his princess a Stradivarius or a Guarneri. I'll volunteer to babysit it inside the warm lodge for a couple of hours."

Jason got off the phone with the camp director, convinced he should just have flown to Los Angeles and taken Lansing Burke's little violinist to Disneyland.

Nevertheless, it was settled. The director had gotten back to Jason within three hours with a plan for Jason to visit on the camp's last day. Ah, but then the director extracted his pound of flesh. "The string orchestra as a whole is going to put together a piece for their recital. Is there something you'd like to solo?"

At least that would break up the suffering of having to listen.

No, this was an elite group. It wouldn't be as bad as Lindsey having her first- and second-year students stumble through Suzuki Method Two. Jason offered, "Vivaldi's *Grosso mogul?*" to which the director responded like a five-year-old getting a puppy for Christmas. Arrangements (hah) would be made. Lindsey would be aghast.

The piece was exquisite, and Jason had headlined it before with a professional orchestra in Portland. Why not repeat it with an orchestra of string prodigies? He'd have to practice, but he'd only have spent that time staring at his unwritten music anyhow. Plus, a lot of influential people sent their kids to this camp.

Jason had ten days to prepare. He'd be fine.

Lindsey would be there. He'd show her what he really could do.

That drew Jason up short, and he stood with his eyes closed, trying to figure out who he was and why showing off for Lindsey felt simultaneously more important and more unnerving than showing off for Lansing Burke. Why he wanted to prove a point to Lindsey. Why he wanted to see her applauding and then hear her critiquing his performance.

It wasn't that he had feelings for her. Well, he did have feelings. Negative feelings. They were spending so much time together and so many sparks were flying that it only made sense he'd think about her judgmental glare. Who knew? He might end up with performance anxiety about soloing in front of her and never actually end up getting the bow to the strings.

As for playing outdoors—Lindsey was right that there would be plenty of outdoor playing. "Saturday is the acoustic playday," the director had explained. "Cold acoustics, warm acoustics, indoor acoustics, outdoor acoustics." That was nicer than Lindsey's explanation had been: "Why bring the kids to Maine if you can't threaten the misbehaving ones with frostbite?"

It would be cosmic payback for every time Jason had griped about how hot it was in the philharmonic, where you were only allowed to remove your tuxedo jacket as a concession if the temperature got over a certain threshold. Otherwise, you were under the stage lights in multiple layers, and you shut up about it.

His violin had never complained about the heat, but the cold and the low humidity might harm it. As Jason walked into his kitchen, he called out, "Star-studded student violin, you're coming with me."

Wait, no. There would be photographs. Specifically, the glitter-eyed Burkeling was going to want selfies with her celebrity crush. All it would take was a shot from the wrong angle and that star would get immortalized on social media. How totally cute. The tween fans would never forget it while the critics would never stop laughing. He'd need his real violin.

Except for the cold. Ninety minutes in a heated car, followed by time outside, followed by time inside, followed by more time outside... It was just wood. Thin wood, at that. Different types of thin wood. Old wood. Sudden expansions and contractions weren't the recipe for a healthy violin.

Blast it. Could he borrow one of Bob's violins? Not Frederika. Frederika was just as temperamental as Jason's unnamed beauty, and the one he'd borrowed when he went out to Los Angeles was just as likely to react badly to sudden changes in temperature.

Jason lifted the student instrument and flipped it over to get a good view of the star near the base button. It had gold flecks in the gouges, so maybe the vandal's parent had gone in with a marker to minimize the damage.

Some people had no right to a violin. This was a full size, not a sixteenth. This wasn't a case of a five-year-old gluing stickers all over his bright blue machine-made violin. Someone did this who darned well should have known better.

Lindsey knew about the star, but she had no time to fix it, no energy, and maybe not the money. She was constantly thinking about everyone else, so maybe it was time someone thought about her. Jason could do that. During his summer with the luthier, he'd smoothed out a deep scratch. He could erase the star.

Jason angled the violin in the light and then changed position again. In a stroke of luck, the vandal had penetrated the varnish but hadn't gouged the wood. While scratch repair was a bit beyond DIY violin care, it wasn't as difficult as rejoining gaps in the seams or sealing a crack.

He'd return the violin to the school in better shape than he'd taken it out. Lindsey had done so much for him. He could repay her that much at least.

CHAPTER THIRTEEN

No eleven-year-old girl had ever been as thrilled as Kylee Burke, who kept staring wide-eyed at Jason with her mouth agape. Lindsey periodically sneaked glances across the room, and the girl's adoration had continued unabated for forty-five minutes.

Although Jason was a prat to Lindsey, he behaved like a gentleman with the kids. He'd shown up this morning after breakfast and was going to take Kylee for an individual lesson as soon as Lindsey was done with the music theory class—but he'd helped co-teach it, which was cool. He'd even argued with her about the uses of certain keys to create specific moods, which would help the kids learn to question their own assumptions. The acoustics play would happen later, and she was glad to see he'd brought the star violin instead of his unnamed beauty. It wasn't the first time the star violin had come to this camp, so maybe it felt at home.

"Any questions?" Lindsey prompted.

One of the kids raised a hand. "I don't understand that thing you said about the beehive. Like, is that about drone notes?"

"Forget drone notes. Imagine an actual beehive with actual bees, where ninety-eight percent of the bees are worker bees." She sat on the edge of the desk. "There are a few dozen drone bees, and then one queen. When you're composing or improvising, you want about the same proportion of easy to difficult passages. You'll need a lot of notes that get stuff done. You'll have a few measures that are ornamentation and trickery. Finally, you'll have one section that's sheer virtuosity, reigning as the queen bee of the piece."

The student frowned. "But why only one?"

"Because the virtuosity builds on everything that came before. If you just put it out there, the piece goes splat because there's no foundation. That's when musicologists turn up their noses to sneer that it's *violinistic.* Worker passages build the foundation. Drone passages build the emotion." She turned to Jason. "Play a game with me. Give me the notes of the Schubert '*Ave Maria'*, but do it as flat and technical as you can."

Jason gave a few perfect but emotionless measures. He was good at that. Lindsey said to the student, "That's exactly as written. But the string family has a warmth about all of them that can fill the heart. Show off if you like, but what you want is to evoke emotion."

She played the same passage, but she emoted the living daylights out of it.

Jason said, "Of course, in a real performance, you don't want to go over the top quite that much. It sounds juvenile."

Lindsey shook her head. "While I was hyping it up, emotions aren't juvenile."

Jason grimaced. "Of course they are. The trick is to evoke the emotions by involving the intellect."

Lindsey turned to him, brows furrowed. "I don't care

what they taught you in the conservatory. Listeners want feelings. They want stories. They want to *want*. The academics may pontificate about intellectual engagement, but think about that movie script you loved. It was the characters and their struggle that hooked you, not the intellectual game."

Jason glowered at her. "And then you can have the critics beating you to death with an iron bar because you sold out your talent."

Lindsey said, "Meanwhile, the general public continues to ignore the critics because they remember what they love, and they go back to what they remember. It's not selling out to create something people want to buy." She turned back to the kids. "There are academics and critics who want nothing more than to take music out of the hands of the people and keep it carefully contained in concert halls with high-priced tickets serving as velvet-covered museum ropes." She pointed at them. "Get right in there and get dirty with it. Experiment and muck things up. Create sounds that break hearts. Forge music that gives hope. Shine out there. Parlor tricks are awesome, but in the end, what matters is the love."

Jason performed on stage with the little kid.

Lindsey sat on the aisle near the front, watching as Kylee played a simplified version of Jason's line from "Love Once More" while Jason played the vocal line.

It had to hurt him. He'd said he couldn't stand to hear the song any longer, and now not only was he playing it, but he was playing the part of the woman he used to love. Despite it, though, he was smiling and encouraging, and Kylee looked by combinations terrified and thrilled.

He was being nice. Even considering Jason might want

this girl's father to owe him a favor, performing with Kylee surpassed the requirements. The kid had wanted to meet him, talk to him, and take a selfie. He'd done all that and then praised her and performed with her. Jason even looked like he was enjoying himself.

He'd actually handed Kaylee a photocopy of a page he and Mitzy had scrawled notes on during the composition process. Then, as if that wasn't enough, he'd worked with a few other kids during the afternoon's free practice periods.

He could be nice when he wanted to, and he'd picked a good time to want it. The kids didn't care about having any number of conservatory-trained PhDs at their disposal when they could also have the guy who'd shared a 'ship name with Mitzy Maxwell.

When the piece finished, Kylee was beaming, and Jason walked with her off the stage so the orchestra could set up for the Vivaldi piece they'd learned all week. Sixteen minutes left until freedom. After that, the kids and their parents would enjoy the afterparty, and Lindsey would head home to sleep in her own bed for the first time since last Friday. She might even stop by the hospital to see Dad. She'd already changed into travel clothes, and her violin and suitcase were waiting to check out of her hotel room.

For the next sixteen minutes, Jason could upstage everyone during the *Grosso mogul* concerto because that's what concerti were for. Lindsey sat back to enjoy the performance—so lively, so brilliant. The kids were fantastic, considering their ages and that they'd only worked together for a week.

Jason went full bore on the solo part. He was so talented. If Dad really said Jason was his best student, then it was understandable. Jason could do anything on that violin, and he did it with style, looking great and sounding great. He was taking this as seriously as if he were playing at the Hollywood Bowl, so Lindsey let the sound wrap through her.

It was a shame. Just a few differences in the world, and

he could have been amazing. If he were a little less perfect, a little more relaxed, a little better humored, a little less strident, he was the kind of guy she could have loved. A guy who could give a weekend to a child with a bossy father...a guy who could pull himself together after a panic attack and then pamper her for a day in Manhattan...a guy who could do the hard work when the going got tough...

Regardless, Jason didn't like her either, so it was just as well. When Jason paired off, he'd find a self-assured woman who'd sacrifice for his career, who'd look without flinching into his soul, and then inspire all his best compositions.

Everyone stood to applaud, and the director leaned close to Lindsey. "He's phenomenal!"

Lindsey masked the smirk that struggled to break through. "He's definitely one-of-a-kind."

During the afterparty, Kylee came up to Lindsey with a huge smile, her mother at her back. Lindsey shook her hand. "Congratulations on your performance! You did great!"

"Thank you!" Her cheeks were pink. "We're leaving now to go to the airport, but I wanted to tell you that you were a great teacher. I'm glad Mr. Woodward loves you."

Lindsey glanced at Kylee's mom, unnerved. "You're welcome, but we're just good friends."

"Oh." Kylee seemed sad, then looked past Lindsey.

Before Lindsey could turn, she felt Jason's arm around her shoulders, and she glared at him. *Thanks. Thanks so much.*

Jason said, "Great playing, sport! Now, what are you going to do when you get home?"

Kylee beamed. "Post our selfies on Instagram!"

Kylee's mother laughed, and Jason groaned. "Kylee, I'm dying here!"

Kylee frowned, then perked up. "Oh! And practice every day without watching the clock."

Her mother mouthed at Lindsey, "Thank you," and

Lindsey suppressed a snicker.

Jason held out his hand for a high-five. "Exactly! And give that music sheet to your teacher so she can help you with the rest of it."

Kylee left with her mom, and Jason guided Lindsey away from the other party-goers. He breathed in her ear, "How long until we can escape? The weather looks lousy."

Her hair stood on end at the contact. Lindsey murmured, "How about now? Now seems fine."

Lindsey and Jason slipped out to the prep room to grab his instrument. Jason opened his case to retrieve his phone, and Lindsey glanced at the violin. "Oh, I thought you'd brought the star violin."

Jason checked his messages. "I did."

"Dude, no star."

He shut the case. "Oh, that. I removed it."

Lindsey grabbed his arm. "You did what?"

He yanked away from her. "It wasn't deep, just a surface scratch. It came right off."

"Why?" Her voice pitched up. "No one asked you to do that!"

He turned, wide-eyed, as if he'd just noticed she was in the room. "What's wrong?"

Her breath was too fast. "You erased it? You *erased* it? You're thinking about yourself all the time, and not once did it occur to you—"

Jason pointed to the case. "It was vandalized! And it was small. No one could even see it."

"Right, the great Jason Vanderbilt Woodward couldn't deal with a couple of scrapes no one could even see on a violin that wasn't his!"

Looking disgusted, Jason folded his arms. "Lindsey, huge overreaction here. Someone graffitied a random violin, and I fixed it."

"It's not a random violin!" Lindsey's voice broke. "I told you that was my violin!"

Jason shrugged. "The school's violin."

"*My* violin! My first full-size."

Jason recoiled. "And you scraped a star on it?"

"My father did that!"

Jason went pale.

"It never matters to you!" Lindsey advanced on him, eyes burning. "It never matters how small something is—you'll just erase it when it suits your convenience. You're erasing everything about my father, one bit at a time. You'll destroy his quartet. You'll get rid of a star on a violin that no one's ever going to see—a violin that I let you borrow for free."

Jason backed up to the table, ashen. "I had no idea."

"Because you never listen! You never think about anyone other than yourself. You resent my father, and you hate me, and it's not fair. It's not fair that he's dying instead of —"

Lindsey cut herself off and closed her eyes as tightly as she could. Stop. Stop it. Stop talking.

Gripping the table at his back, Jason managed, "Instead of me?"

"Instead of *me*." Lindsey couldn't fight back the tears. Stupid anger, coming out her eyes. "You said it yourself. I'm no one special."

Jason was as colorless now as when he'd had a panic attack, and everything just burst out of her. "My father's the one with the talent and the skill and the specialness, but he's going to be dead in six months, and because of you there's one less bit of him in the world. If the world had to take someone to right the balance, why didn't it just take me?"

Jason choked out, "It doesn't... It doesn't work that way."

"I know it doesn't work that way!" She wiped her eyes with her sleeve. "But why is he the one leaving instead of me? Why can't I just trade with him?"

Jason raised his hands. "Lindsey—please. I made a mistake. No one wants you dead."

"You said yourself you'll feel a burst of joy the day I die. No one's going to feel that for him." Lindsey stalked past and snatched the star violin. Well, not anymore. Now it was just a violin. "You've been trying for a year to destroy his legacy, and you just wiped out one bit more of him. Congratulations."

He grabbed the handle.

"Let it go." Her voice was a hiss, a balance on the knife-edge between screams and tears. "You've done enough."

Jason let go of the case. Vision blurred, she fled upstairs.

Jerk.

He was such a jerk. He'd do anything to hurt her, anything at all. He'd be nice to a kid, and then he'd treat Lindsey like garbage. He'd pretend to help her father, and then he'd do even the pettiest things to wipe out the man's memory.

Dad, I'm sorry. She shouldn't have let Jason take her violin. Last summer, she should have said, "Figure out the instrument situation or I'll call a replacement." She should have fired him any of a dozen times.

Jason didn't pursue her up the stairs to her hotel room. She yanked on her coat and grabbed her bag and both violins. No Jason in the lobby. Maybe he'd already gone. Maybe he'd drive off a cliff and she'd never see him again. Let the world forget him instead of Dad.

Except Dad was going to die no matter what. Wherever Lindsey went, there was death.

When she checked out, the woman at the desk sounded concerned. "Are you all right? You can stay longer if you need to."

Lindsey hadn't looked in the mirror before abandoning the room, but her eyes must be red and her face strained. "I'm fine. It's a long drive home."

"Be careful." The receptionist handed Lindsey a receipt for $0.00. "It rained this morning, and it'll freeze overnight."

It was a touch above freezing as Lindsey set her bag and her professional violin into the trunk, then stood hugging the case of her childhood violin, belly to her belly, head pressed to the head. *I'm sorry, Dad. I'm so sorry.*

Feeling ridiculous, Lindsey put her childhood violin in the passenger seat and buckled it through the handle. Jason was a jerk, and she needed to be able to touch the case. Needed the proof that everything wasn't going to vanish between one second and the next.

Her high beams didn't catch any ghosts. There were no storm drains, no town sewers to breathe into the night. For a long stretch she saw no headlights or taillights, but eventually she got tailgated by a truck driver who'd never heard of following distance. With one lane in either direction, he'd never be able to pass, so Lindsey kept her eyes open for a place she could pull over. Let the driver aim his blinding headlights into someone else's mirrors.

This was the same thing Jason had been doing ever since last March, expecting Lindsey to get out of his way, looking right over the top of her and seeing nothing but his eventual destination. Well, nuts to that. Jason could sit tight in the second violin seat, and the truck driver could sit tight at the speed Lindsey felt comfortable driving. She wasn't a lousy first violinist, and she wasn't a slow driver. Everyone should just get a grip on themselves.

Karma struck: now an even slower minivan hogged the road in front of Lindsey. She debated pulling off at any random fast-food place and giving both the truck and the slowpoke sedan a ten-minute lead. Why was this so hard? She only wanted to get home. Get home, get a shower, get in bed. Maybe by the time she got home, she wouldn't feel like crying anymore.

She touched the violin and knew that was a pipe dream.

Jason had been so close to convincing her he wasn't a total jackwallop, and then he'd done this. And that was the kicker: he hadn't just breezed it off. He'd made it out like he'd done something nice.

That's why you ask, idiot. You ask before you fix something that's not broken. You ask why the music school owners never bothered to fix it themselves. You ask why the top-notch luthier who services the school's instruments never got permission to fix it.

Except you only ask if you care. You only ask if you think other people have reasons for what they do. You only ask if you think other people exist.

The temperature was dropping, and Lindsey longed for herbal tea and the familiar smells of her apartment. She'd get home by eleven. Shower. Bundle up in bed and read. She could see Dad tomorrow. At home, she could cook her own food. She could forget about Jason. She could calculate the number of days until the arrogant prat flew back to California and never again set foot in Maine.

She could do that now, in fact. Twenty-eight days in February, ten more in January...but when in March would he leave?

The slowpoke minivan turned on its blinker to exit, and Lindsey eased off on the gas to give it room. The minivan pulled into the exit lane...and then slid.

Black ice.

By reflex, Lindsey hit the brakes and swung into the left lane to avoid the minivan, now in a flat skid. It did a full 180 so it was sliding backward with its wheels locked. Then it kept spinning, sliding perpendicular across the lane. Lindsey's antilock brakes kicked under her foot, and she yanked the wheel into the direction of her own skid to regain traction. Her car got a grip on the road, and she yanked the wheel to avoid broadsiding the minivan.

Like thunder, the truck smashed into Lindsey's trunk and hammered her, engine-first, into the minivan.

CHAPTER FOURTEEN

For ten full minutes after Lindsey fled, Jason couldn't breathe. He couldn't name the things he could feel and couldn't remember what the five senses even were or how many details he should list for each one of them or if it counted that he could feel his chest pounding or his skin beading with sweat.

Sight, sound, taste, touch, balance...but wasn't intuition also a sense? How do you find five things for balance? He couldn't do the trick to get out of this. Lindsey knew the trick, but Lindsey was gone.

He was going to die. Lindsey said she ought to die instead of her father, but it was Jason who was about to die of a heart attack.

She'd freaked on him. He'd screwed up. He hadn't asked. He'd repaired it and thought she should feel grateful. Now he was going to die.

Tonight's program caught his eye: Vivaldi. Jason started

reciting the notes of the cadenza. Get control. Name the notes to himself in rhythm, the sixteenth notes, the double stops on the beats. Breathe. Work one note at a time through the next few measures. Jason fingered the notes on the table in front of him, and slowly he got on top of his own rapid breathing. His chest stopped burning, and the crushing sensation ebbed. The world wasn't going to end. He wasn't having a heart attack.

He was going to get kicked out of the quartet. Everything was happening sooner than he'd anticipated. He'd end up back in Los Angeles before March, and it would all be over.

The pain on Lindsey's face kept knifing through him.

After a week away from her, he'd walked into her classroom this morning and remembered the kiss, remembered teasing her in the hotel room, remembered the fun they'd had dress-shopping and her amusement mixed with toleration as she'd let him pick out her shoes and her necklace. Then he'd hung out watching her teach because it felt good to be near her, and he'd never watched her teach before. Whenever he'd had a pause during the Vivaldi, he'd looked at her in the audience.

Every time he'd caught her expression, she was smiling. Smiling at him.

That would never happen again. He was erasing her father and destroying her father's legacy, and the worst was that right now, Jason couldn't deny it. She'd taken her violin with her, so he couldn't even fix what he'd done. Although fix wasn't the right word. He hadn't broken anything.

He'd broken her heart.

Voices passed in the hallway. Jason didn't want to get caught here, didn't want to talk to anyone, didn't want to get pressed for an autograph or a conversation about how wonderful it was that he used to date Mitzy Maxwell. He wanted to get home and call Lindsey once they were both out of their cars. He'd explain if she'd listen. He hadn't thought it through. She was right. He'd decided on a course of action for his own benefit and then convinced himself she'd benefit from it. Lindsey hadn't factored into the decision at all.

Jason retrieved his coat and had no violin to take. He left.

Lindsey had a half-hour lead. She'd had to check out, so maybe she was fifteen minutes ahead? Juniper was twenty minutes closer than Hartwell, so he might reach his apartment at around the same time she did, meaning he could call before she went to sleep. He'd hope the ninety-minute drive had cooled Lindsey to a dull burn, and he'd try to straighten it out tonight.

Jason fought the urge to speed. The roads looked clear, but years of driving in his dad's delivery truck had taught him never to trust mountain roads, unlighted and curving and with constant changes in elevation.

Erasing Bob was the last thing Jason wanted. When everything had fallen apart, it had been Bob's voice Jason craved. Even when it felt like Bob had played him dirty, Jason trusted the man's musicianship. Jason wouldn't destroy Bob's legacy. If he'd known what the star was, he'd not only have kept it but would probably have shown it off to Burke's daughter. "We all have teachers we admire. This is from the man I admire the most."

Kylee aside, Jason would never be someone's most-admired violinist. Jason would perform for thousands of people. He would appear in movies and headline as a soloist, but that future felt entirely empty right now. Bob had picked up human souls and breathed music into them. Watching Lindsey teach, Jason had remembered Bob teaching, and it struck him how much grace Bob had given the world, how much joy, how much of a grounding. If music was about emotion, then Bob had been about the love.

He'd given love, and he'd created love. But he hadn't headlined, and Jason had called that failure.

Jason could create sounds, and those sounds could create money. Jason had called that success.

Bob had created stars. Music stars and little carved stars. He'd scattered them through the world like constellations. That's what Lindsey had said during the interview.

Jason hadn't created any stars, not even himself. Instead, he'd created fire. He'd scorched his own future and then burned out Lindsey's heart, and he had no idea how to restore it.

That wasn't success. You could call it a lot of things, but not success.

Red and blue lights flashed a mile ahead, and Jason slowed. Some wretch was having a worse day than he was. Flares dotted the road, and three ambulances plus a fire truck lined the shoulder with their lights in a steady whirl.

Jason edged into the single lane to pass, and by reflex he looked. There was a delivery truck with the front staved in, and with a sudden nausea, he thought of his father's delivery truck. Lindsey was losing her father. Jason still had his.

The delivery truck had t-boned a minivan, and between them was a sedan crushed like an accordion.

"Make some treble!"

Jason's numb brain didn't process until he'd passed the trio of wrecks, the ambulances, the flares. Then he yanked the wheel to put his Audi in the drainage ditch. He hit the blinkers—dashed from his car back to the accident scene—ran as hard as he could despite the darkness—ran until he reached the tangle of cars.

An emergency worker shouted, "Hey!"

"Lindsey!" He staggered to his knees at the door that they'd already cut off its hinges. She lay slack, skin colorless except for the blood on her face, on her neck. The car was crumpled around her like an empty beer can crushed under a booted heel. "Lindsey, talk to me!" He reached for her seatbelt, but someone yanked him back. A police officer, hauling Jason to his feet. "Let me go. I know her! Is she okay? Is she dead?"

"She's alive," the officer said. "She's got a head injury, so you can't touch her. They've got to take her out on a spinal board."

Jason struggled. "You've got to help her!"

"She's being helped!" The officer let Jason go, but Jason only stood with his chest heaving, vapor shooting up with every breath. The officer said, "You can't jerk her neck around. The EMTs will get her out of there as soon as possible."

The airbag had detonated. She was limp, head back, bleeding from her nose and over her eyebrow. Jason took another step toward her. "Let me go to her."

The officer said, "Don't try to move her, but since you're here, what's her name?"

Jason knelt alongside the accordioned car holding Lindsey's hand. The ground was rough under his knees, and she was cold, so cold. He answered questions, rubbing her hand to warm it. Her name. Her address. Her age. Her physical condition. "Can you get her a blanket? It's freezing." The EMTs arrived then, and Jason had to back away while they unfolded an entire human being out of that crumpled can of a vehicle.

Lindsey. Lindsey.

"Where are you taking her?" A minute later, Jason was entering a hospital name into his phone. The officer was telling him not to try following the ambulance, and then Jason found himself holding a yellow copy of a form with license plate numbers and addresses and names he couldn't read.

The ambulance doors slammed. Numb from the cold and the shock and the fear, Jason would have done anything to hear her snap, "Quit standing around, pretty boy." She hadn't even called him that yelling in the lodge.

She could die. She could die, and he'd never be able to make it up to her.

The officer lowered his voice. "Are you okay to drive?"

Jason gestured with his phone. "I've got the directions."

The officer huffed. "GPS isn't going to make good decisions on the road. Keep your head together and take it slow. GPS'll direct you to the hospital garage, but follow around to the back of the hospital and there's a parking lot closer to the ER. And for heaven's sake be careful. The roads are a nightmare."

The ambulance blared its siren once and pulled onto the state route, heading downhill along a straightaway.

As Jason turned, he caught a glint in Lindsey car. "Let me take her violin. The cold isn't good for it."

She'd buckled it into the passenger seat. The door was staved in, a shower of glass across the case, making Jason glad for his leather gloves. With the trunk crushed into the back seat, her bag and her other violin weren't in evidence. Someone would have to retrieve those tomorrow, once the truck was off the back of the car. Then, wondering how he'd function enough to drive, Jason walked up the road with the unstarred violin.

A security guard ushered Jason through a metal detector before escorting him to an ER cubicle. A nurse was exiting, so Jason stepped to the side, then slipped behind the curtain where Lindsey lay on a gurney.

"Sir, we need you to leave." A nurse was cutting Lindsey out of her sport bra. Someone else was inserting an IV.

A different nurse took him by the arm. "Are you her husband?"

They were back in the hallway. Jason fumbled for an explanation. "I'm her second. I mean, her co-worker."

Lindsey had looked dead. Colorless, motionless, with monitors everywhere—she looked dead.

"Well, we can't really talk to you, but we're going to examine her for internal injuries, check her neck and spine, and then get her a CT scan the minute the machine opens up." The nurse's voice was straightforward, just how Lindsey sounded when she was triaging a situation that had escaped control. "Can you contact her family?"

Jason kept trying to see around the curtain. "They're in Hartwell. Is she going to be okay?"

"We have no idea how bad the head trauma was. We don't think there are internals, but we haven't finished examining her." Someone left the room, and the nurse said to him, "Can I bring him in?"

"Not now."

Jason's voice was raspy. "I'll call her mother. Where's a good place to use a cell phone?"

The nurse pointed toward a waiting room, but someone was already in there. Jason went further, through a long hallway with alcoves and branching corridors. He'd never been in this hospital, but they had signs everywhere. He'd be able to navigate back to the ER.

He called Ashlyn first. She sounded confused. "Jason? What's up?"

"Are you driving? I'll wait until you pull over."

"No, I'm home. What's wrong?"

Jason leaned against the wall. "Lindsey... I'm at the ER with Lindsey. She got in a car wreck." He was talking over Ashlyn's exclamation, but he couldn't get the sentences together in his head. "They won't let me in the room. I don't know how bad it is."

"Oh, no, please." Ashlyn's voice picked up. "Which hospital are you at? Are you okay?"

"It's—" Jason's brain blanked on the hospital name for a moment, and then he remembered. "Saint Rita's Hospital. The nurse told me to get her family here."

"That doesn't sound good."

"It doesn't look good, either. I need you to get her mother."

"I'm getting my shoes on. Listen, it's going to take like five minutes to get to Mom. You call her because she's going to ask questions it never even occurred to me to ask. What's wrong with Lindsey?"

What's wrong? Other than everything? "I don't know.

161

They won't tell me. They're looking for internals. She's unconscious. They're going to do a CT scan."

Ashlyn breathed out a few words Jason didn't catch, and then, "Okay. I'll do my best to get us there in one piece. Stay with Lindsey. Don't leave her."

"I'm not leaving her." Jason's voice broke. "Ashlyn, just —"

"I'm nearly out the door. Call her mother. Bye."

Ashlyn hung up, and Jason clicked through his contacts to find Susan Castleton.

They'd be here in an hour.

Don't leave her.

Don't leave her, except they wouldn't even let him near her.

And then...then he did get near. When Jason returned to Lindsey's room, he ducked to the other side of the curtain and oriented himself in the narrow space. No one stopped him. Lindsey's room was empty except for Lindsey.

She had monitors on the back wall, a thin blanket covering her, and tubes running beneath the blanket. There wasn't an oxygen mask or a canula, so she must be breathing okay. A whiteboard had a bunch of information Jason didn't try to process. He pulled a chair alongside the bed but didn't sit.

Then, as if he'd failed to notice the moment sunrise turned into dawn, he realized Lindsey was looking at him.

"Hey." He couldn't get his voice much louder than the surrounding sounds, as if his brain had unconsciously clicked into an orchestral mentality. "How do you feel?"

Just because he could talk didn't mean he could say anything worthwhile. Lindsey didn't answer.

A nurse entered, followed by an orderly. Jason said,

"She's awake."

The nurse nodded. "She spoke to us before." She got in Lindsey's field of view. "Are the nausea meds helping, honey?"

Lindsey nodded.

"That's good. We're going to take you for your scan." The nurse turned to Jason. "Did you talk to her family?"

"They're coming." Susan had sounded by turns stunned and scared. Ashlyn had arrived while Jason was on the phone, long after he'd run out of information to give. "Lindsey, did you hear me?" He bent closer. "Your mom's coming. So is Ashlyn. It'll take a while, but they're on their way."

The nurse said in a low voice, "We're getting a lot of car accidents tonight. Tell them to take their time."

Jason said, "Is Lindsey going to be okay?" *Tell them to take their time* meant it wasn't time critical—but that worked in both directions. "Did you find internal injuries?"

"It looks like just the head trauma, but the doctor will be in shortly." The nurse patted Lindsey's ankle. "Honey, we're taking you for a ride."

Lindsey reached for Jason, then flinched with her eyes screwed shut. "Don't go."

"I'm staying." He grasped her fingers, but they wheeled her away so her fingers slipped through his, and she was the one who left him.

It took another couple of minutes of sitting in a curtained-off room for Jason to remember he should text Mrs. Castleton.

"Lindsey woke up. She's groggy. They took her for the CT scan. They think no internals."

Mrs. Castleton replied, "Thanks. We've just left Hartwell."

Jason sent, "The nurse says the roads are awful and they're getting a lot of accidents. Drive carefully."

"Will tell Ashlyn."

After that, with no reason to continue the conversation and no one else behind the curtain, Jason was fully alone.

Pacing, Jason couldn't stay still in the little ER chamber, but then the curtain parted and they wheeled Lindsey back in. They'd cleaned the blood from her face, but her eyes were shadowed with what must be the start of two black eyes, or maybe the airbag had broken her nose. The nurse got Lindsey hooked back up to the IV, and while Jason watched, a hand rested on his on the bed rail. He wrapped his other hand over Lindsey's.

"She's cold," he told the nurse.

"Oh, let's fix that." The nurse returned momentarily with a heated blanket for him to tuck around Lindsey. It was white, like everything else in the hospital. Sterile. White sheets, white pillow, white blanket.

"Hey," Lindsey breathed.

He said, "You did okay in the scanner machine?"

"I fell asleep." She was practically asleep right now. "Wasn't supposed to."

If the ER cared about keeping her awake, surely they'd come in and check every so often...? "Ashlyn and your mom are on their way."

She held his hand tighter. "I'm queasy."

One nurse call later and there was more anti-nausea drug in the IV. "Does she need to stay awake?" Jason said.

The nurse patted Lindsey's shoulder. "Keeping you awake was the old concussion protocol. Sleep if you need to."

"Okay." Her voice was a whisper. "Thank you."

She didn't relinquish Jason's hand, and finally he hooked the nearest chair with his ankle and pulled it close enough to sit.

She gave a soft sigh. "My head hurts."

Unnerved, Jason said, "Do you want me to get the

nurse?"

"Not that bad." She half-opened her eyes. "I pulled out. You know, of the skid. It just... Couldn't."

"Some accidents can't be avoided. That was a box truck behind you. Those get a lot of momentum." Jason fought to keep the images out of his head. Her car, crushed. The moment he recognized the musician decal. The denial. The way he'd overshot her car and then run back up the side of the road.

He said, "Were you scared?"

That was the wrong question. *He'd* been scared. He was still scared. He'd gotten here from the accident scene, but he was going to have to drive again to get home, and the whole way, he'd have those images behind his eyes.

She murmured, "No time."

It was dark and quiet. When would Ashlyn get here? Lindsey needed her mother. She needed anyone.

She said to Jason, "I'm sorry."

He used his free arm to cushion the bed rail and laid down his head on it. "You didn't wreck the car to hurt me."

"I'm sorry I yelled."

It didn't seem like such a big deal right now. In a soft voice, he breathed, "Tell me about the star."

Their heads were twelve inches apart, hers on a pillow, his on the rail. Their hands were joined, their fingers interlocked. It was pillow talk in the worst way possible.

"I'm sorry about the star." Jason's low tones melted into the sounds of the monitors and the muffled talking from the hallway. "I'll try to fix it."

Lindsey murmured, "You erased it."

Jason wished the air weren't so dry, the lights so dim. The walls pressed all around them. "Why did your dad carve a star into your violin?"

She rubbed her thumb over the outside of his hand. "It doesn't matter."

"It mattered a lot before. We're both here, and I'm not leaving for a while."

She was quiet for long enough that he thought she

wasn't going to answer.

"I was twelve." Her brow was tight. She must be in pain. "A kid. You know."

He offered a smile even though her eyes were closed. "I know how people grow up."

She went on, "I failed an audition. I was so upset. I didn't want to do it anymore. I'd never be good at anything."

Jason's stomach clenched. "But that's not true."

"I was twelve. Dad carved the star with his pen knife. Mom had a metallic marker. He inlaid the gold." Her face stayed tight. "He said, 'Even if no one else sees it, you're a star.'"

Lindsey could have been erased tonight with less thought and less time than it had taken Jason to erase that star. Five miles per hour faster and that truck could have pulverized her. If she hadn't been wearing her seat belt, or if the airbag hadn't deployed...

Lindsey said, "I told you it was dumb."

Cold, Jason choked out, "It's not dumb. I'll fix it."

"I give that violin to...you know...students who need something. Confidence."

When was the last time Jason felt confident? How had that instrument ended up with him, the one who most needed reassurance? And then he'd obliterated it with his arrogance the same way he'd cindered his own career. "It's not dumb at all. Your dad made it for you."

"It didn't change anything. I'm not special."

Jason pressed his forehead against the bed rail until his eyes hurt. "For goodness sakes, Lindsey, let it go. I was angry. I said that because I wanted to hurt you. I'm sorry."

She sounded so floaty, like a butterfly on air currents over a pond with nowhere to rest her exhausted wings. "Doesn't mean you were wrong."

Jason's eyes burned. "Of course it means I was wrong."

"I'd thought it already. I don't deserve this life." She stayed limp as his hand reflexively clenched hers. "I was given too much. I'm destroying my father's legacy because I'm not good enough. I can't make us harmonize. You're the special one, and I can't make you bend. My father's dying, and I'm failing him."

Jason shuddered. "Lindsey, stop. That's not true."

"We were too small for you. You left. Now you're back and you can see." Lindsey opened her eyes. "None of us made it big."

Nausea engulfed Jason. "What if I was wrong? I've been thinking about what you said. About your father and about success. How he has a better perspective on success than I'll ever have."

They were looking at one another, face to face, darkness to darkness. Jason felt his soul wide open, his fear and frustration and failure all burgeoning in his heart like a chord in the key of death. He'd never understood Lindsey as well as he understood her in this moment, and she was seeing right into her second violinist and getting a good view of everything he'd ever been made of.

Lindsey held his gaze. "I was trying to hurt you when I said that, too."

Jason put his head down at last, breaking eye contact. "I guess we both succeeded. We're both really good at what we do."

CHAPTER FIFTEEN

Lindsey awoke to her mother's arms around her.

I'm so sorry. It was black ice. I got control, but the car in front of me didn't.

"Are you okay? Are you in pain?" Mom brushed the hair from her forehead, and Lindsey flinched. "Talk to me—what's going on?"

My head hurts. Everything's stiff.

Nothing was coming out of her mouth. Instead it was Jason's voice that answered with uncharacteristic softness. "She's got a concussion. They did a CT scan, but the doctor hasn't read it yet. They're giving her anti-nausea meds, but I don't think she's gotten anything for pain. Nothing's broken, and there don't seem to be are any internals."

This information matched the information in Lindsey's mind. Also in her mind was everything else competing for her awareness: the beep of a monitor in the hallway; the scrape of a chair against the bare floor; the stiff hospital gown against her skin; the pain between her eyes; the smell of antiseptic; the curiosity as to where her clothes had gone.

Again, Mom's fingertips brushed the hair from Lindsey's forehead, and that little movement spiked her pain. "She's getting two black eyes. The airbag went off?"

Jason sounded shaken. "Yeah."

I was being tailgated. He wouldn't back off, and he didn't have space to stop.

Mom breathed, "Thank God in Heaven. We could have lost her too."

Jason spoke really low. "The car's crumpled on both ends. And then they pulled a whole person out of it. It's not something you want to see."

"No." Mom let off a breath. "I don't mean to sound ungrateful to you for staying with her, but you should go home. You look in shock."

"Where's Ashlyn?"

"Parking. She let me off at the door."

Lindsey's thoughts drifted back to her car. She kept picturing the wheel well and how the tire was turned even though she'd been going straight, with the quarter panel embedded in the sidewall. She remembered random things, like the tread on the tire. A blood pressure cuff choking her arm. Swirling lights.

She was cold again, but she didn't move. Her brain was registering things, only disconnected. Sound equipment in a recording studio must be like that. The producer says, "Are we getting a good feed from mic two?" and the equipment knows it has a good feed, but it can't answer. Then someone else gives the answer. It's fine.

Low lights. Low voices. Mom's touch. Light sleep.

When Lindsey heard a new voice, she struggled to focus. "The CT scan showed the concussion, but I'm not seeing any brain bleed or blood clots, so that's really good. When she was awake before, she was dazed but could answer questions. I'm hopeful that while this is serious, she shouldn't have problems recovering."

Mom protested, "You can't just release her."

"Absolutely not. I want her overnight for observation at the very least, but we may not have to admit her."

Lindsey decided to sit up, and suddenly Mom's hands were on her. "Whoa. Stay down."

"I'm okay." Lindsey's throat felt sluggish, but since the doctor was here, she should get information.

Jason's voice broke through. "Should I raise the head of the bed?"

The doctor said, "Do you want to talk for a bit?"

Lindsey leaned on Mom while everyone repositioned things around her. The change in attitude left her unsteady, but Mom felt strong. It was good with Mom. Mom knew everything. "What do I...you know, have to do?"

The question had sounded so clear in her head, so tough to get it out.

The doctor said, "We'll send you home with what we call a brain rest protocol. If you broke your arm, it would be in a cast, but we can't cast your thoughts. You'll need to rest and, in effect, not think about anything for forty-eight hours. After that you'll take it easy until you're feeling better. Limit your screen time. Don't read. Take a week off from work."

"Music?" she said.

The doctor nodded. "Sure, you can listen to music."

Mom snickered. "What she means is, she's a musician. Can she play her instrument? Can she analyze music? Select music?"

The doctor's eyebrows raised. "No, not for at least forty-eight hours."

Lindsey deflated.

The doctor suggested, "Maybe you can play easy pieces?"

Jason said, "If she picks up Suzuki Method Four, within fifteen minutes she'll get bored and start messing around with the Tchaikovsky Violin Concerto."

Ashlyn laughed. Jason added, "Tell me I'm wrong."

Mom said, "You're not wrong."

Lindsey murmured, "Fine."

The doctor said, "As long as you're awake though, I'll repeat the annoying assessment questions."

Lindsey's nose wrinkled. "Annoying?"

"The notes say you told us the questions we asked on intake were 'annoying and stupid.'"

Ashlyn touched her shoulder. "Sounds like you were having a blast when you rolled in."

She'd been right about the questions being annoying. *Do you know where you are?* Lindsey groused, "You want my GPS coordinates? How am I supposed to know what room number I'm in?" to which the doctor murmured, "Yes, this is going to be a long night."

Mom said to Jason, "Speaking of long nights, I told you to go home. You're exhausted."

Lindsey looked over at him, and her heart went out.

Jason didn't look exhausted. What he looked was anguished. She vaguely remembered him upset when they were talking, him telling her something—but the words were misty. Something about her violin and how was going to fix it. Something about hurting her.

Come to think of it, why was he here? He hadn't been driving with her. She hadn't questioned his presence the same way she hadn't questioned where her clothes had gone. When she'd awakened, everything just was. Hospital gown. IV. Jason.

Jason was white-knuckling the bed rail. "I can stay, Mrs. Castleton. You're the one who has to work in the morning."

Mom huffed. "I've texted for coverage, but it's a church. The worst thing that could happen is they have no music for the service and everyone prays for Lindsey. They're not going to fire me for one no-show in twenty years."

Weary and pale, Jason turned to Lindsey. "Well, then, I'm gone. Quit making trouble for everyone."

It was a mismatch. His tone had nothing to do with his words. He didn't want to leave, but he also had no reason to stay. Right before they'd left the venue, they'd been arguing. Arguing was all they did, and now he didn't want to go. Why?

Lindsey said, "As long as I was making trouble for you, pretty boy, it was worthwhile."

Jason smirked at her. "You're fine, shotgun."

And then he was gone. The doctor kept asking questions, but in a weird way, the room felt empty.

At Mom's home on Sunday afternoon, Mom put Lindsey on the couch and drew all the drapes, then dragged over the coffee table and started setting everything on it that Lindsey could ever need. Ashlyn brought pillows and a comforter. Mom turned on the tea kettle.

Lindsey hadn't wanted to eat all day, and even now the thought of tea turned her stomach. Mom would want her to have something, though. Mom-wisdom was generally, "Try a bite and see what your body tells you." In this case, it would be a sip, and Mom would make it sweet and milky.

With the kettle on to boil, Mom returned to the living room. "We need to talk."

Lindsey said, "I know. I need a sub for the quartet, and if I let Jason do first violin—"

"I'll take care of the logistics." Mom settled cross-legged on the floor.

Lindsey sat up. "And I need to contact my students. I can't teach Monday, but we'll see if maybe on Tuesday--"

Ashlyn said, "Look around. Who here is a professional string player who's out of seasonal work right now? I'll ask your students if they'll let me sub until you can get back to them."

Lindsey said, "But we're also supposed to be getting the taxes done, and—"

"Lindsey, let me talk." The stress in Mom's voice drew her up short, and Lindsey stopped cold.

Mom wrapped her hands around each other. "When I went to the impound to retrieve your stuff from your car... You need a new car. It's totaled."

Lindsey tilted her head. "But it was just the front driver's side."

"The car is caved in on both ends. You got hit from the front and the back, and the trunk is in the back seat. Every safety feature engaged, thanks be to God Almighty, and the engine came out of the mounts so it didn't land in your lap. The car is toast."

Lindsey's eyes widened. "Seriously?"

Ashlyn said in a low voice, "That's why you have insurance."

Mom nodded. "Absolutely. That is why you have insurance. Go ahead and be sad about losing your first car, but I'd rather lose the car than lose you."

Lindsey tucked up her legs. "Yeah."

Mom was totally factual. "You should take Dad's car. I would have to sell it anyhow."

Lindsey couldn't remember the moment she hit the car in front of her, but maybe it felt like this, like the impact you knew was coming and could do nothing to avoid.

She needed a car. Dad was never going to drive again, and he had a perfectly good four-wheel drive SUV.

Lindsey sighed. "I don't want to, but it makes sense."

Mom said, "Do it for me. It's a safe car with a lot of years left on it, and I'd feel better if you were in that."

Lindsey ran a finger over the arm of the couch. "You need it sometimes when you bring students to competitions."

Mom shrugged. "Fortunately, I know where you live so I can borrow it twice a year."

Fair enough. "When the insurance check comes in, at least let me buy it from you."

"Done. We'll look up the book value."

Mom drew an unsteady breath, and Lindsey looked away

because this was the distinct sense that after you'd slammed into the car in front of you, there was still a truck barreling down behind.

Mom braced herself, which was never good news, and Lindsey prepared to hear that while they'd been in a hospital forty miles away, Dad had died during the night.

Mom said, "Your violin got destroyed."

Lindsey whipped toward her. "No! That can't be!"

Ashlyn sat on the floor with her arms wrapped around her knees. She must have known, both about the car and about the violin. Lindsey blinked hard. "Which one?"

Mom said, "There was only one. The German."

"But it was in the hard-sided case! It would have gotten thrown forward, sure, but it should have been fine!"

Mom didn't answer, and Lindsey put her face in her hands.

Not her violin. It was hard enough thinking she'd lost her car, but not the violin. She loved her violin. She needed her violin.

Where was the other one? The one Jason defaced? Hadn't that been in the car as well? Had it gotten thrown clear? Was it lying on the roadside?

Ashlyn offered, "Insurance should cover that too."

Insurance would write her a check. Here. Go buy another love. Ashlyn should know better.

"Get it fixed." Lindsey turned back to Mom. "The luthier is really good. He'll take a while, but he'll get it in shape again."

Mom never argued when she could win with facts. "Ashlyn, can you bring it in?"

Ashlyn shut off the kettle, then went out to the driveway.

Lindsey hadn't asked about her violins because of course they were okay. The trunk was a big empty space, and the case was cushioned. She'd strapped down the star violin in the front seat. It should have been fine. Maybe it would be still. Jason had said something about her violin, about fixing it. Maybe Mom wasn't thinking clearly. Maybe

Jason had taken it from the car and Mom found the student violin smashed and assumed the worst.

Except when Ashlyn brought it in, Lindsey didn't even need to open it. It was her real violin, and the case itself had heavy damage.

Ashlyn set to work on the carpet but couldn't get the lid up. Mom told her, "Pry off the hinges. I had to do that before."

Lindsey rasped, "Bring it here."

They put the smashed case on the couch, and Ashlyn wiggled the hinges out of their slots. They came out too easily. Mom must have dug them out with a screwdriver, then pinned everything back together. Ashlyn opened the lid backward, and Lindsey gasped.

Her violin was smashed down the center, right through the waist. The neck was snapped off the body. The belly was caved in. The strings were slack.

Lindsey stroked the wood at the base. "Why?"

Mom didn't answer.

She didn't have to. You could do everything right, and still everything could go wrong.

Lindsey had never deserved any of this to begin with.

She kept her hand on the body, choking back the grief that fought to burst out of her. In the back of her mind was a flat voice saying a violin is just a thing. It's just wood and strings, a solvable problem. Her violin wasn't a piece of history like a Stradivarius. Insurance would cover it.

She was being a brat. Her father was dying, and she was sniveling over an expensive but insured piece of wood. Her father's impending death was the tragedy. Not a totaled car or a destroyed violin.

It never even had a name. Her violin had died without ever revealing it to her.

Ashlyn's eyes glistened. "I'm so sorry, Linz."

Dad had helped pick it out. They'd driven to Boston on a Friday and enjoyed a performance of Hayden at Symphony Hall. Saturday they'd driven to a half-dozen violin shops.

She'd come home with three violins on loan, and at the end of a month she'd sent back two.

Lindsey fought her quivering lip. "Where's the other one? Did you check inside the car? It was on the front seat."

Ashlyn said, "Jason has it."

Mom tucked up her knees. "Your father and I talked about this last February, and he wants you to have his violin."

Lindsey's voice broke. "I can't take Frederika."

"He wants you to have it, and I'm not contradicting him. Of all the kids, you're the best violinist."

Frederika had a glittery gold tone in the light, and it was so responsive, plus it blended amazingly with Ben's cello. But it wasn't hers. It would never sing for her, not the way it sang for Dad.

"I can't. Mom." The headache returned, pounding hard. She wanted to lie down. "I can't be Dad. I can't take his chair as first violin and then drive his car and then play his instrument."

Not without bringing down the wrath of the rest of the muses. Lindsey never deserved what she already had. How could she justify taking even more?

"You can't be him." Mom gathered the disassembled case and splintered violin off the couch. "Lie down. Think about it."

When Mom said, "Think about it," she always meant, "Come to see reason on your own time because I'm not having an argument I can win by giving you space."

Ashlyn stayed at Lindsey's side. In the kitchen, Mom turned the kettle back on.

Lindsey murmured, "If I play Dad's violin, Jason's going to leave."

Ashlyn snorted. "Good riddance."

Mom turned. "Why would Jason leave if you play your father's violin?"

She had no idea why Jason had seemed so attached to Dad's violins, so outraged that someone else might play them. "Remember when he pestered you about not selling his violins? It wasn't the first time. They need to go to someone worthy."

Mom said, "You're worthy."

As if. The retaliatory muses were working overtime to right the injustices. Taking Frederika would trigger Armageddon.

Ashlyn said, "If Jason freaks about this, we'll replace him early."

Jason's face came to mind again. Not just him anxious in the emergency room, but something nebulous that Lindsey couldn't place. Something larger. Him anguished, something about having hurt her. Something about fixing her violin, only he couldn't have known it was broken. It was all nonsense, like the way Lindsey could remember her car at the accident scene even though she'd been unconscious and strapped to a neck board when they carried her out. She couldn't have seen the things she remembered seeing.

Only now she kept remembering the feeling of Jason in a dark room, his fingers woven into hers, him talking in a low voice. His eyes. Most of all, she kept remembering his eyes.

CHAPTER SIXTEEN

The Castleton porch, Monday morning. Jason hadn't felt this awkward in…well, not since California.

It hadn't been awkward over breakfast when he'd texted Mrs. Castleton to ask if Lindsey was okay. It hadn't been awkward when she'd said Lindsey was staying alone. It hadn't been awkward when he'd agreed to sit with Lindsey in case she needed help, nor had it been awkward when he'd texted Lindsey that he was on his way.

It shouldn't require bravery to visit a sick co-worker. No bravery whatsoever. Just walk inside and say, "How are you doing?"

Yeah, right. She'd seen through him in the hospital. She'd been broken and semiconscious, and yet she'd still taken control of the situation.

Feeling decidedly un-brave, Jason opened the door. "Hello? Lindsey?"

There was a text on his phone from Mrs. Castleton: "Just

go inside." That felt so informal, but she didn't want Lindsey to have to get up to let him in. Okay. But here he was, holding an arrangement of orange and white flowers plus a gift bag, and it looked wrong. It looked like he was romancing her instead of doing what you're supposed to do when someone's recovering.

Jason found Lindsey on the couch, under a blanket, lights off. Her phone was balanced on the arm of the couch playing Tchaikovsky's sixth symphony, and she reached up to stop it.

She looked beaten, and Jason's stomach dropped. She had bruising around both eyes, and the care with which she moved bespoke pain all over her body. She could have died.

Looking at her, Jason didn't move. Couldn't. It was worse here than in the hospital. Here he didn't have shock to cushion him. Here was normalcy. You're supposed to be sick in the hospital. He'd supposed he'd find her giving herself a pedicure, annoyed by the restrictions but otherwise fine—not in a loose t-shirt and yoga pants, hair in a messy ponytail, face dark and swollen.

When Lindsey saw what he was carrying, she smiled. "Pretty boy, did you bring me flowers?"

"You're supposed to get well." He carried the flowers into the kitchen, glad for the foresight to have bought the squared-off vase, that way he didn't have to hunt for one now. "One of the first violinists in the Philharmonic insisted you should never bring a plant to someone who's sick because it means you want the sickness to take root in their lives, so that limited my options."

He was babbling. She looked so awful he couldn't think.

"Thank you. But bring them in here so I can see them."

Her voice was raspy, probably because she hadn't spoken since waking up. It was all right. She was going to get better. She had to.

Jason set the flowers on the coffee table so she could admire the palm-sized orange roses, the white baby's breath, the orange Asiatic lilies, the white carnations, and the tiny white rosebuds.

"These don't have roots either." He handed her the gift bag. "I don't know if chocolates heal a concussion, but it's worth trying."

"Thanks." Sleepy, she didn't get all the way up, just propped on her elbow. "You didn't have to do this."

"Your mom thought someone should stay with you." He sat back on the carpet while she removed the chocolate box from the bag. Every time she moved, it was tentative, as though she might lose her grip on space and time. "Are you feeling whiplashy?"

"Not so much. I took an ibuprofen, just in case. Mom made me keep heat on my neck all yesterday, and either it helped or it placebo-ed me into health." Lindsey tried to prop herself a little further, but one of the pillows was trapped behind her shoulder. "They said to lie still doing nothing. I hate it."

"Brain rest for forty-eight hours. You're supposed to be slightly bored." Jason got to his knees and reached around her. "Let me help you with that."

He stood the larger pillow upright. Lindsey shifted backward to half-sitting, and in the midst of getting the second pillow adjusted behind the small of her back, with her face so close he could feel her breathing, Jason kissed her.

He didn't think before doing it. She was right there, smelling of vanilla, battered and exhausted, ephemeral in how close she'd come to simply not existing any longer. He kissed her, and she sank into the pillow. Kneeling alongside the couch, he was half over her chest, one hand in her hair, eyes closed, her arms around his shoulders.

One minute, one bad patch of road—

He paused to breathe. She whispered, "Oh, this is awkward."

"It is." He kissed her once more, long and slow and soft. Then he kissed along the line of her jaw, her neck, the hollow of her throat. There he paused, forehead against her shoulder.

He didn't want to apologize for doing this. She didn't seem to want an apology.

Jason ventured, "Is it... Would it be notably more awkward if we kiss for five minutes versus one?"

Lindsey whispered, "I don't think so."

"Then I'm going for five." He sat up taller and kissed her again, more urgent, more uncompromising. She drew his shoulders up across hers, angling toward him. He had no idea where this was going, why it had started, where it would end. But the feel of her, the warmth, the softness... the neediness to have her close and believe it would be all right.

He reached under the hem of her shirt, but her hand clamped on his wrist. "That's too awkward."

"Sorry." Hands back up around her shoulders. "Upper limit on the awkward."

She nuzzled his neck, and it sent earthquakes through his body. She murmured, "I don't know."

Neither did he. White-hot semi-reclined couch kisses couldn't possibly be post-concussion protocol. He whispered, "We don't have to know."

How much of his five minutes was left? Could he get an extension to ten?

Except then he felt tears on his cheeks, and they weren't his.

Jason jerked back and pressed his forehead against her shoulder. Jaw clenched, he fought fury and a dozen nasty remarks. She could have told him no. She could have said any level of awkward was too awkward. Pulling out the blackmail card was obnoxious.

She might be in pain. He'd run his hand through her hair, and touching her head had been excruciating Saturday night. But she always called him out when he messed up, so if he'd hurt her, wouldn't she have told him to stop? Especially when she'd already stopped him from something else?

He held on, waiting. Figure out her game. Then he could detonate. He'd brought her flowers and chocolate, but if she tried any kind of manipulation, he was out the door.

She shuddered in his arms, and now she was full-on crying. Blast it. She could be so direct about everything, and then—

She gasped, "I'm sorry."

He didn't move. "About what?"

"You'll hate this. You'll hate it so much. I need to tell you first. You'll leave."

Manipulation tactics: in high gear.

She sat up, so he knelt away from her. If she looked bad before, she looked wretched now. He crossed the room to get the tissue box from the far couch. There was one closer, but given how his body felt and how his brain kept kicking like a truck with a bad starter, he needed the space. It would have been even better if he'd walked to the convenience store and bought a box...then kept walking to the post office and mailed it back to her.

He held out the box. "You said you'd never cry over me. I was counting on that."

She took a handful of tissues and buried her face in them. "I'm sorry. I'm all gross. These are last night's pajamas, too."

"I'm offended." Jason forced himself to leer as he got down alongside the couch. "You should take them off."

She half-smiled. "Pig."

She was still fragile. Well, tough. "What am I going to hate enough to leave? You might as well tell me while I still have time to run errands this morning."

Her eyes flooded over again. "In the accident— Mom went to the impound after. The car's totaled."

She didn't need to say another word. Jason's heart went right out of him, and he dropped back on his heels. She wasn't crying over him.

Her violin. Her violin had been in the back.

He'd been her second for long enough that Lindsey knew he'd gotten her cue. She broke down and sobbed.

He slipped onto the couch at her side to hold her. "I'm so sorry. It can't be fixed?"

"The case is smashed. The violin is crushed. It's gone."

As if she'd changed key during an improv session, Jason felt through how they'd play this next verse. He had her student violin on his kitchen table, so at least that was safe. Her German violin was insured, so she could afford a new one. He could drive her to different shops to try them out, sure, but no one wanted a new violin this way. A new violin should come into your life because you'd stupidly fooled around with a century-old Italian and fallen in love, or because you'd tricked everyone into thinking you were competent enough for the Los Angeles Philharmonic.

Lindsey had nearly lost her life. Her violin actually had.

Jason ran his hand through her hair. "In the middle of everything else, that's not fair."

"Mom says—"

Lindsey choked on her words.

She didn't need to finish. There were three professional grade violins upstairs and a violinist dying in a memory care unit across town. *Mom says.* That was what Mom had said.

Jason nuzzled her temple. "You should do it."

This wasn't emotional manipulation. He wasn't even sure why Lindsey would have thought he'd hate it. It wasn't about the kiss. If anything, kissing had made her feel secure enough to cry about her broken heart.

It was... Well, it was strange.

Jason repeated, sterner, "You should do it."

She shuddered. "Can you come with me?"

She couldn't do it on her own. Couldn't tromp into her father's trove and steal the treasure right at the heart of it.

Couldn't do it in front of her mother, even with her mother's encouragement. Lindsey would want to test all three violins, assess them, return to them, examine them, judge them, and then choose one. Or maybe turn down all three—but that was too practical and too cold to do in front of her mother. Bob's heart still beat in each of those violins, and Lindsey couldn't reject her father's heart.

She wobbled to a stand, and Jason helped her zip a

hoodie over her pajama shirt even though that was the last thing he wanted to do with her clothes. She looked too miserable for him to joke about how she kept involving him in her zipper woes. They took a slow trip up the stairs, but even so, she had to lean against him halfway up to get her bearings. Her bedroom was here, but he didn't expect her to go in, and she didn't. Instead they went into the music room. As soon as she could, she sagged against the wall and slid to a seat on the floor.

"Surely you've played all three at some point or another?"

Lindsey tucked up her knees. "A few times. I know how they sound and how they feel."

Jason made his way to the violin pegs, and without hesitation, he took down Frederika. "Did your bow survive?"

"No."

"Nuts. That's a hard thing, losing the whole setup." He couldn't mentally recreate Bob's bow, so he picked the closest. "You might have had to replace it anyhow if it didn't pair well with the violin."

He crouched before her and handed her the violin, but she shook her head. "How can I?"

Jason sat all the way down, and without thinking about it, started tuning. Frederika had a gorgeous sound. "How can you?" First the A string, then the D. Then check the A again. Check both: perfect fifth. "You tuck it under your chin and close your eyes. You draw the bow across." E string: check. A and E together: off. Re-adjust the A. Fix the D. "You listen to the tone. You feel the vibrations right through you."

She didn't even laugh, but at least she uncurled to sit cross-legged. "I'm not him."

"Granted." Adjust the G. Higher, higher, too high. Lower. Perfect. "But if anyone deserves to play his violin, it's you."

G and D together: perfect. D and A: perfect. A and E: off. Adjust the E.

Lindsey whispered, "I was nearly out the door."

"And now you're back in the door. I get it." He put Frederika in her lap, and she cradled it. "Violins remember their songs."

"I'm not good enough. Frederika deserves a special player."

In the middle of tightening the bow, Jason recoiled. "Is that why you thought I'd hate what you were going to tell me?"

She couldn't look at him. He'd broken her. He'd convinced her she wasn't special.

With a hard swallow, she said, "You hated thinking Michael might get one of the violins. You told us to talk to you before selling any of them." She gestured to the wall. "Which one do you want?"

Trying not to let his hands shake, Jason rosined the bow. "I don't want any of them."

He handed it to her, then returned to the wall for the violin in darker wood. "This is the one your parents loaned me. It's got a mellower tone than Frederika, better suited to second violin. It did well by me, and obviously it carried me through the auditions and the first month, but I'm not especially attached to it."

Lindsey's brow furrowed. "Then why were you so insistent?"

"I didn't want Michael to have something he didn't understand." Jason gestured to the strings. "Any of these instruments remembers what was played on them, and as long as we keep playing them, they keep voicing what they remember." Jason turned to her. "Michael would have let them rot or would have sold them to someone who didn't care whose voice he was hearing. You won't let that happen."

"I thought you wanted Frederika."

"I'm fine with my own." He set the dark violin back on the wall. "Have you tried playing her seriously?"

She shook her head.

"Do it now."

She held out the violin to him. "You do it. I want to

185

listen."

It surprised Jason how his hand trembled as he tucked Bob's violin under his chin. Then, eyes closed, he played.

Frederika remembered Bob.

Wood conducts vibrations. Over time, the wood gets more supple in the locations that vibrate the most. The pathways soften. The wood dries out in some areas and picks up skin oils in others. The varnish wears off the shoulder and the neck, a testimony in dullness to the brightness of the sound.

Frederika remembered Bob in the way she responded to the high notes and shifted to the low ones, in the way she trilled and the way she voiced a beautiful vibrato and the way she went dusky at the lowest notes of her range. She replied to just the right pressure with subharmonics that curled through your mind and left your heart longing for a home you'd never seen.

Frederika wanted to play, and Jason played her. Frederika longed for Bob. She was going to get Lindsey.

CHAPTER SEVENTEEN

Lindsey loaded a backpack to spend Tuesday with Dad at the hospital. Tablet, phone, chargers, bottled water. Lunch. A book if she felt up to reading, but there was no way. Focusing was still a problem, and light hurt her eyes. She did have a lap-sized portable keyboard that Corwin had dumped on her last night, saying, "Make yourself useful and play something for him."

Mom dropped her off at the door. Upstairs, a nurse exclaimed, "What happened to you?"

"Car crash." Lindsey offered a smile. "I'm supposed to be taking it easy, so I'll hang out with Dad."

Having finished breakfast, Dad was in the common room with the TV on. Lindsey kissed him. "Hey, Dad, it's Lindsey. What are you watching?"

Dad only shrugged, so Lindsey explained about her black eyes and then joined him to sit with the TV. Then they returned to his room, where he pulled out the keyboard and tried to give her a lesson. They sat together, and Lindsey pretended to learn about chords.

The fluorescent lights buzzed. Lindsey had never noticed them before, but they bothered her.

The PT arrived for Dad's morning exercises. Lindsey waited off to the side with the overhead lights low and the white Christmas lights twinkling. Seven weeks past Christmas and still Sierra refused to take them down: *Dad needs beauty.* Dad did love the lights. There was no harm in letting him think it was always Christmas.

As the PT was about to leave, Lindsey returned to the bedside to continue the keyboard lesson. Dad pointed right at her. "Who did that to you? Who hit you?"

Lindsey raised her hands. "No one, Dad. I was in a car wreck."

Dad struggled up from his chair. "No one hits you! I'll kill them!"

"I'm fine!" Lindsey protested. The PT reached for the nurse pager, but Lindsey pushed past to hold Dad's hand. "Dad, listen, I'm okay. I was in a car crash. No one hurt me."

Dad grabbed her arm so tight that pain shot up to her shoulder. "Tell me! Don't protect him!"

"No one hurt me." Lindsey struggled to wrench free. The PT was calling an emergency into the intercom, and Lindsey twisted until she broke Dad's grip. "Dad, calm down. It's okay. My car got damaged. My airbag went off."

The PT said, "Lindsey, get out of here. Let him get calm."

Two nurses rushed in. "Mr. Castleton," one declared in a no-nonsense tone, "talk to me. What's going on?"

Lindsey fled to the common room. Her breath wouldn't slow, and her head pounded. It dizzied her to reach up to the ceiling-mounted TV, but it was a such a relief when the noise stopped.

Her bag was still in Dad's room. She could ask a nurse to get it, but going back in would just agitate Dad all over again. He didn't understand. He wanted to protect his little girl, and that one sharp emotion was overriding everything else.

She pulled out her phone to call for a ride home, then stopped. Ashlyn and Mom were both teaching classes. Sierra and Corwin would be at their jobs.

She texted the only one she knew didn't have a nine-to-five. "Are you awake?"

Jason replied within a minute. "What's going on?"

Her throat tightened. "I hate to ask, but can you come to Dad's hospital?"

"Is he okay?"

While she was texting "Yes, but," her phone rang in her hand. Jason sounded stressed, but then geared down the more Lindsey explained.

"Okay. Give me half an hour."

"I'm so sorry." Lindsey's voice broke. "But when Mom comes, she should spend it having lunch with Dad, not driving me home. And—"

"It's not a problem. Half an hour."

Lindsey curled on her side on the common room couch, eyes closed, enduring the pounding in her head.

Jason.

He'd been so good to her yesterday, and in repayment she was taking advantage of him. He'd stayed with her until late afternoon. He'd played all three of her father's violins and encouraged her to play them too, but he hadn't scolded her when she'd refused. At lunchtime, he'd made them each an omelet and toast. From the moment he'd shown up with the flowers, he'd been gentle, and that wasn't even to mention the way he'd kissed her.

Jason hadn't kissed her again. Even when he supported her traversing the steps, he hadn't touched her more than necessary. He hadn't drawn her into her childhood bedroom or forced her down onto the couch. Once he'd satisfied himself that she was alive, he didn't need to continue.

It was for the best. Having him in her arms had eased her own desperate fear of dying but ignited a longing for him to get beyond his own selfishness.

He was dangerous. If he could kiss her with feeling, with real feeling, she'd respond.

Even knowing he was leaving in a few weeks, she'd respond anyhow. Dad was leaving her too. Suddenly finding something attractive in Jason would be the stupidest thing her heart could do.

Still, though, he'd smelled so good, felt so good. His arms were strong, his kiss strong, his confidence strong.

Footsteps. Lindsey opened her eyes as Jason hovered at the common room entrance with a pharmacy bag in his hand. He kept his voice low. "Sorry. Were you napping?"

"I wish. My head's pounding."

She started to stand, but he said, "Hang on. Your dad's upset about your eyes, so let's see what we can do." From the bag he pulled out a half dozen bottles and compacts. "Behold! I bought you a whole makeup section."

He spread everything on the couch between them, then put his hand to her chin to angle her in the light. Lindsey crinkled her nose. "Do you know what you're doing?"

"Enough to be dangerous. I watch the makeup artists whenever someone gets done, and there's both science and art to creating a natural look. I know none of it." Jason gave an embarrassed chuckle as he opened a package of makeup sponges. "But let's try. In the worst case, you can wash it off, and then I'll take you home."

This was bonkers, but Lindsey let Jason make the attempt. He started with a concealer that was a little too light for her skin tone. His touch was gentle, his focus tight, his silence beautiful. "Close your eyes," he said, and then it was all about his fingers on her jaw and the sponge slipping along the skin beneath her eyes. She could feel his breath and catch the faint spark of his mouthwash. If he kissed her now, she wouldn't see it coming. Her lips tingled.

He paused, and she opened her eyes to find him staring right at her. He was gorgeous and thoughtful, and she chalked up the effect to her concussion.

"That's a start. Next, foundation." When she closed her

eyes, he applied it all over her face. "We need an even tone or it'll be obvious."

It was a violinist's touch, the slightest bit of pressure able to draw a response. Lindsey shifted, and he pulled back, "Sorry. I didn't mean to hurt you."

"You didn't." It was uncomfortable having him so near and not having him eliminate the rest of the distance. Yesterday morning hadn't been like the elevator. He'd been feeling that kiss all the way through his heart, and she'd felt it too. When she'd realized he'd hate her over the violin, the tears came because he was acting as if he cared, only once again, he'd turn on a dime and spit venom.

The emotional shifts had to be from the concussion. For the past ten months, she hadn't worried that Jason hated her. She'd worn his loathing like a badge of honor.

He paused, then smoothed more foundation over one cheek. "This isn't half bad."

She snickered. "You could moonlight as an esthetician?"

"A few more reviews like I got for Violet Nights, and cosmetology school won't sound so bad." He fumbled with a makeup brush and powder. "Don't be too impressed. I had a wikiHow page open on my phone the whole time I stood there baffled by the makeup."

"I'll feel impressed if I want to, pretty boy."

He dusted the brush in some light powder, and again Lindsey closed her eyes so he could dance the bristles across her skin.

"You want to visit your father." The couch creaked as Jason shifted. "I think it's passable. Here." He turned on the selfie camera and held his phone out to Lindsey. There was some shadowing, but she didn't look beaten. Even in the incandescent lighting, her skin seemed uniform.

She did want to visit her father. She hadn't seen Dad in a week and a half, and every day during camp she'd been jack-in-the-boxed by more reminders of him than she'd ever anticipated. The Castleton kids had all attended that camp. Every other instructor had asked about Dad, and even some of the students had known him. The whole week had ticked down with Lindsey ever more conscious that Dad's days were numbered, and she'd just ripped off a calendar page without seeing him.

Jason had realized it too. And here he was.

She handed back his phone, but then he leaned toward her. Her breath caught. His face tensed, but he didn't pull away.

Their foreheads were close, their eyes down, their lips so near. He was dangerous. He'd kiss her. She would let him because he was being so thoughtful and so careful and so amazing...and then he'd turn on her like a scorpion.

She remembered his eyes in the emergency room. She could almost recreate his words, an unexpected grief, but they were barely out of reach like the zipper on a form-fitting dress. She recalled the sensation of his hands around hers on a stiff cotton sheet, and her wanting him to stay near because for a moment he'd exposed his soul, and it was both wounded and beautiful.

Jason edged back. "Well, showtime."

She couldn't meet his eyes. "The ultimate test of your work. Let's see if Dad notices."

Jason gave her a hand up. With her ill at ease, they went together into Dad's room.

Dad didn't recognize Jason, but he did recognize Lindsey. He didn't remember that only an hour earlier, he'd threatened to kill whoever hurt her. And that hurt too.

Dad faded during the morning. He hadn't had much energy for a while, but the PT exercises combined with his protective rage had sapped it all. They spent long periods in silence, her sometimes messing with his small instruments, sometimes sitting close with her hand in his.

Jason stayed. He stayed with Lindsey until her mother turned up for lunch, and by then Lindsey couldn't focus her eyes. He drove her home.

He didn't try to kiss her again, but he walked her inside. She didn't try to kiss him again, but before he left, she asked him to come back tomorrow.

Chapter Eighteen

On Wednesday, Thursday, and Friday, Jason volunteered his services because a) it meant he was useful, and b) it meant he didn't have to stare at his computer trying to dig out a song that wouldn't come.

Songs weren't parasites, their tendrils shooting out from a hard-shelled spine to coil into your brain and your guts, such that when you yanked them free, they gouged out your insides. Jason kept telling himself that: writing music shouldn't feel like disemboweling yourself. It shouldn't be harder than pushing a boulder uphill. Or pushing a hill uphill.

Instead, Jason drove at dawn to Lindsey's apartment to render her unbruised. He was actually getting good at this, although maybe the bruises were fading. Lindsey still wasn't cleared to drive, so they'd have breakfast together, then head to the hospital in Jason's car.

After that, Jason would stay. "You'll need a ride back,"

he told her the first day. "I'm not family, so I'm the disposable one."

He didn't dare kiss her again. California loomed in his future, and kissing her was an indulgence he couldn't justify, leading to a promise he couldn't keep. Still, though, he held her hand when she was unsteady. When they waited at the elevator and she stood with her head down and her arms wrapped around her stomach, he waited behind with his hands on her shoulders. When he dropped her off at her apartment, he fought the urge to brush his lips over her forehead. She would just raise her face toward his, and he would bend toward her.

He couldn't do anything about the past or the present, but at least he could stop himself from treating her unfairly in the future.

Lindsey couldn't tolerate a whole morning at the hospital on Tuesday. Wednesday, she barely made it through lunchtime with her mother. Thursday, the same. Friday, she and Jason stayed most of the day.

When Bob was asleep and Lindsey was dozing, Jason would sit with the notebook and the gel pen to fool around with song ideas. Whether it was the surroundings or inability, he couldn't come up with anything that stuck. Every time he came close to a breakthrough, he'd look at Lindsey and freeze.

Even without a medical degree, Jason saw Bob was fading. Lindsey must have known it too, but she had only so many usable hours in the day before her eyes couldn't tolerate the light. Bob stayed in bed more as the week went on. He spoke less and recognized less. On Thursday, he spent most of the day asleep. On Friday, he didn't recognize Lindsey at all. He thought Jason was Ben, and Lindsey looked gut-punched. Even then, though, Bob didn't say much, only was so pleased that Ben had come to visit.

When Mrs. Castleton arrived for lunch on Friday, she showed Jason the guest book. "Ben visited last night before flying to Michigan to see his new grandbaby. Bob's still thinking of that."

Jason glanced at Lindsey, sitting alongside the bed with her head on her father's pillow, her hand on his arm, and vertigo swept through him. *How much time do you think he has?* He didn't ask. Couldn't. The man was leaving them. This whole week, his breathing had gotten worse, and his cognitive functions were in freefall. The nurses were doing things to assist his breath, but he was less responsive and didn't want to leave his bed.

Saturday, Jason wouldn't have to take Lindsey to the hospital because everyone else would be around. He could have the entire day to himself to work on that last song and get both Edward and Walt Ingram off his back.

He could string any number of notes together and make a passable melody. This one had to be good, though. It had to revive his career. Whatever he did had to be unassailable, and it had to prove he could play. Prove he could compose. It had to be on a par with Lindsey's song and Bob's song, which he'd finally gotten to a point where they met his approval.

This one had to sound resolute. It had to ring with bravery and hope at a time when Jason felt nothing but cowardice and despair. Maybe it was the hospital surroundings. At home, he could complete it. Start it. Start and complete it. A great musician would sit right down at this table today and get it done.

He reached for his phone and texted Lindsey. "I think I'll camp out with you at the hospital in case you need a ride mid-day."

Lindsey replied, "Ashlyn and Mom will both be there, and Ashlyn's driving me."

He replied, "You don't want to take them from him. Remember? I'm the disposable one."

Jason arrived to find Bob eating breakfast, all smiles. Lindsey was beaming, and Ashlyn looked pleased. "Michael will be here soon," Ashlyn said.

Bob added, "And my mother."

Lindsey looked up. "Your mother?"

Eight years ago, Jason had played at Bob's mother's

funeral.

Bob nodded. "I saw her last night. She was packing for a trip."

Mrs. Castleton looked expended. Even with the relief that Bob was having a good day, she must be exhausted. She stepped into the hallway for five minutes, and when she returned, she said, "Corwin and Sierra are coming. I cancelled my morning classes, so I'll just stay around."

Something tickled at the back of Jason's mind, a detail he remembered from his own grandmother's death, something the hospice nurse had told him. The longer the day went, and the longer Bob was sitting up talking—the more Bob recognized people—the more uncomfortable Jason felt inside his own head.

Sierra arrived with her harp, and Bob exclaimed, "Sierra!" She flung her coat into the corner and pulled over a chair, fingering her lap harp while telling him about her performance at an upscale coffeehouse. Five minutes later, Corwin blew in, and Bob was again delighted. "Corwin! You came too!"

Beneath the windows, Lindsey had two easy chairs facing one another, her legs up on one and her body semi-reclined on the other, her coat and Jason's spread over her to complete the cocoon. She said to Corwin, "Dude, you're awake before noon?"

"As it turns out, waking up is one of my superpowers." Corwin clapped Bob on the shoulder, then leaned against the wall, arms folded. "Or not sleeping at all, like when I got a hundred messages from Mom saying, oh, your sister detonated her car, so I need you to cover all the church services."

Jason pivoted to him. "You?"

Corwin opened his hands. "Me! I rolled in at four a.m., poured a pot of coffee into a thermos, and rolled right back out again."

Jason side-eyed him. "I had no idea you could do that."

"Are you kidding? I'm the son of a church musician. I could do that in my sleep."

Lindsey shot at him, "It sounds like you did!"

Jason glanced at the clock. Bob had been perky for a couple of hours, longer than at any other point in the week.

Michael arrived, making this the busiest room in the hospital. Shoulders squared, Susan Castleton strode right over to him and said, "It's time."

She took a wide-eyed Michael by the hand and walked him up to the bed. "Bob, listen to me. We found Dalton." Her voice cracked. "Dalton's here."

Bob's face changed, and Jason's heart broke.

Lindsey was staring, and Ashlyn had her hands by her mouth. Trembling, Bob reached for Michael's hand, and Michael reached back. Then Bob pulled him, and Michael gave him a huge hug.

"My son." Bob didn't get out more than a whisper. "My son."

Lindsey's lips were quivering. Jason crouched near her chairs, then grabbed her hands.

That detail in Jason's mind had changed from a tickle to a throb: *swansong.* The hospice nurse who cared for Jason's grandmother had told him there were signs right before people died. Some people had a really great day. A lot of people saw their dead mothers.

Clutching Lindsey's hands, Jason watched Bob meeting his son, for the first time aware of who he was—and then Bob was crying. "We've wanted you for so long."

Michael gripped his father's hands hard. "I was looking for you too."

Bob looked him over, astonished and disbelieving. "Do you see him? This isn't another dream?"

"It's not a dream. We've found Dalton." Susan sounded broken, like the last autumn leaf clinging to its branch. "Now we're all together."

They were all together now. But only for now. Jason shifted so he was kneeling behind Lindsey's chairs, arms around her, her hands clasped between his.

Bob said to Michael, "What instrument do you play?"

Michael said, "I'm learning violin," and Bob gasped.

"Tell me. Tell me all about you," and Michael told him while Bob looked delighted. His son. "I knew you were smart," Bob said. "You have a great smile."

Jason's knees ached from the hard floor, but he wouldn't leave. Lindsey leaned back into him so he could hold her tighter, and then she rested her head on his arm.

Bob's energy waned before lunch. Susan ordered pizzas and had Jason pick them up. By the time he returned, Bob was dozing, his breathing shallow. Lindsey remained in the cocoon chairs, also asleep, and Jason laid his jacket back over her.

Susan watched him, eyes watery. "Thank you."

He wasn't sure what she was thanking him for, so he said, "Not a big deal."

Michael and Ashlyn carried their pizza into the common room, and shortly Corwin and Sierra joined them. Susan sat alongside the bed, stroking Bob's hand. She had a pizza slice on the bedside table, but more than a bite, she hadn't eaten.

Swansong. Between the faint breathing and the pallor, Jason was scared for Bob. Scared for Susan.

Jason said softly, "Mrs. Castleton...?"

She looked at him dead-on. "I know."

Jason fell fully silent.

She added, "That's why I called Corwin and Sierra."

Dizzy, Jason sat in one of the metal chairs. It scraped the floor, and Lindsey raised her head. "Oh hey," she whispered. "Pizza."

"Fuel up, shotgun." Jason forced his numb body to plate a slice and deliver it to her. "Feeling better?"

"Not really." Blinking even in the darkened room, she tucked up her knees to brace the plate, and Jason got the water bottle from her backpack.

Mrs. Castleton still wasn't eating, just running her fingertips over Bob's limp hand.

"He's asleep?" Lindsey said. "He was up for a long time."

Jason said, "Yeah. But—"

Susan shot him a look, and Jason fell silent.

Lindsey took another bite, then shook her head. "I can't finish."

Jason took back the pizza. Lindsey swallowed a mouthful of water and then screwed the cap on. She said to Jason, "Would you mind driving me home?"

Jason glanced at Susan. "Shouldn't you stay?"

Susan looked down. "Are you feeling bad, honey?"

Lindsey wrapped her arms around herself. "I'm sorry. Dad's having such a good day, and we're all here, but I'm just taking up space."

Susan looked torn. Jason said, "Wait a little longer. You just woke up, and in a while you might feel better."

Susan said, "You could drive her home and stay with her. If she wants to come back later, could you bring her then?"

Jason gave a hesitant, "Sure," but Lindsey said, "That's a waste of time for him. He's got music to write."

Jason said, "I can write in your kitchen. But are you sure you want to leave?"

Lindsey got up as if she weren't sure which way "up" was, and when she finally had her balance, she tried picking up her backpack. "Quit being a rebel," Jason muttered, positioning her jacket over her shoulders so she could slip in her arms. "I'll carry that."

Lindsey bent to kiss her father, and Jason wasn't sure she wouldn't topple onto the hospital bed. She walked out of the room, tentative, as Sierra was coming in. "I feel lousy," she said in answer to Sierra asking why she was leaving. "I'll see you tomorrow."

Jason carried her backpack so she could take deliberate steps down the hall. He would stick around. If Ashlyn came back to their apartment, no big deal—he'd leave. If he was still there in five hours, he could make dinner or order in.

At the elevator, Lindsey frowned. "Do I look that awful? You're shattered."

Jason shuddered. "You can tell?"

She shifted her weight. "I'm glad Dad was better today. I was worried."

The elevator arrived, and they went to the first floor.

Jason closed his eyes against vertigo. She'd kissed him in an elevator and started all this, and again in an elevator, he was betraying her.

The door opened. He didn't move, and she turned at the door. "You coming, pretty boy?"

He stared at the embossed steel floor. "Your mother will hate me for this, but you'll never forgive me if I don't say it. Your father is dying. This is the end. Your mother knows it, and she doesn't want me to say anything because you're feeling awful."

Lindsey's eyes flared. Her hand shot out to hold back the elevator door. "How can you say that? You saw he was doing better!"

"People rally right before the end. He was seeing his mother. He dreamed about her packing for a trip. It's the swansong, and your mother knows." Jason's fists tightened. "That's why she made Corwin and Sierra come. That's why she cancelled classes today. She's not leaving here until it happens."

Lindsey stepped up close, face livid. "You're lying!"

Jason didn't flinch. "I wish I were lying! I wish he were doing better, but he's not."

Lindsey punched the number three, and the doors closed. "Shut up. Just shut up."

Back upstairs, she paused at the nurses' station as if to ask, then kept going all the way back to her father's room. Throat tight, Jason followed.

When Lindsey walked in the door, Mrs. Castleton looked up at her, and their eyes met. Pain engulfed Susan's face. Lindsey kept staring at her, and then she stalked back to the pair of chairs beneath the window. She dropped her backpack on the floor and climbed in.

Mrs. Castleton focused on Jason. He didn't need to be telepathic to know what she was thinking. *Snake.* As far as she was concerned, he'd harmed her daughter.

Jason sat in the corner and pulled out his music notebook.

Lindsey turned to him. "You can go. I'm not leaving until Mom leaves."

Jason raised his hands. "I'm staying. In case you need someone dispensable."

No one went home. The nurses spoke several times with Susan, and the verdict remained the same: as long as Bob wasn't in pain, she didn't want any interference. A nasal canula helped him breathe, and when he grew agitated around dinner time, they added a morphine drip.

This was a vigil, and no one was talking. Jason and Ashlyn brought back fast food, but nobody other than Corwin wanted to eat. Except then Corwin made everyone eat, especially his mother. "You're not going to be good for this if you're lightheaded and queasy."

At eight o'clock, the pastor arrived to do a final blessing, not only Bob but also Susan. "Don't worry about music tomorrow," he assured before he left. "No one's going to complain about a silent service, and if they do complain, the one they'll complain to is me."

By ten o'clock, Bob's breaths were so light and so infrequent it was hard to tell he was breathing at all. Jason dragged a chair alongside the bed so Lindsey could sleep with her head on Bob's chest and one hand on his arm. Bob rested his other hand on her hair. Sierra was on the opposite side, nestled to her father's shoulder with her head on his pillow.

Corwin finger-picked a tune on the lowest strings of Sierra's harp. Jason wished he'd stop, but at the same time it felt proper for music to usher Bob out of the world. Ashlyn and Michael had cleared the room a while ago, dozing in the common area.

Susan brushed the hair back from his eyes. It nearly wasn't Bob anymore, with his skin loose and his face slack. Sierra got up. "Here," she whispered, and Susan laid down alongside Bob, eyes closed, tears coming in dark silence. Bob shifted, and Susan shuddered. Sierra held her.

At eleven o'clock, Bob stroked Lindsey's hair, and she raised her head. Without opening his eyes, he whispered, "Music. The music plays on."

Susan cuddled him tighter. "It does. I promise."

Lindsey whispered, "I love you, Daddy."

He didn't say anything more. At midnight, with all his children around him, Robert Castleton left the world.

Jason roused from the most uncomfortable sleep he'd ever had, including every airplane ride and every college orchestra trip where he'd shared a hotel bed with two other students. He'd meant to stay awake until Lindsey wanted a ride home. At some point, he'd made the mistake of sitting down, and that was all it took.

It was over. The music was silence.

Blast it, Bob. This wasn't right. This needed to be a prank the universe had played on them all, and now a producer would step into the sound booth and say, "What have you done?" before fixing it all.

Except it wasn't an outtake, and Bob was gone.

Jason shifted, but something pinned him to the corner of the couch. He raised his head, and it was Lindsey.

Now he recalled Lindsey joining him in the deep dark, head on his shoulder. While sleeping, she must have worked her way horizontal, and now she lay across his lap. Jason reached for her hair, then remembered Bob's fingers in her hair, and he drew back. Let her savor that memory.

Instead he rested his hand on her shoulder and tried to buy some more time.

Voices in the hallway. Corwin. "You're not doing this." A softer voice: his mother. Corwin again: "And I don't care. I'm covering for you." Mrs. Castleton must have asked how he expected to play for the church services only hours after his father had died, because Corwin shot back, "And how do you think you're going to play? If they send me home, I'll come back. Otherwise, let them have their freaking pipe organ."

Corwin walked into the common room. "Anyone awake in here?"

Jason forced his throat to work. "Me."

"Awesome. Do not let my mother out of the building or I will murder you."

"I consider myself deputized to keep her here."

"I knew I could count on you." Corwin stormed out.

Lindsey stirred, and Jason rubbed her shoulder. "Stay down. It's just Corwin."

She murmured, "So much havoc starts with, 'It's just Corwin.'"

"Well, he's leaving."

Lindsey pushed up. "Where's Mom?"

"Good question." Jason stretched. "Because I'm supposed to keep her in the building."

Lindsey unfolded herself from alongside Jason, frightening when he remembered the paramedics unfolding her from a crushed driver's seat. She went into the hallway, glancing as she did at Ashlyn and Michael sleeping on the opposite couch. Mrs. Castleton had returned to Bob's room where he was still in the bed. Beneath the dark windows, Sierra was out cold in the seat-cocoon. Susan had unplugged the white twinkle lights.

This was what remained of Lindsey's "we." Bob's death was a blow right at the roots of her community, and it made sense she'd immediately take stock of everyone else. Jason stayed close at her back.

Lindsey hugged her mother. Susan said, "I'm sorry I

woke you up, honey. Go back to sleep."

"As if." Lindsey went to the bedside to stroke her father's hand. "He's cold."

A heaviness sank through Jason.

Susan wrapped her arms around herself. "I keep thinking, if I could just warm him up, things would be okay." She shook her head. "Corwin already said goodbye. After the rest of you get a chance, I'll let them call the funeral home."

Lindsey kissed her father's forehead. "I'm sorry, Mom."

"I'm sorry too."

Sierra sat up, eyes bloodshot as if she hadn't slept at all.

Lindsey swallowed hard. "This isn't fair."

Jason's hair stood on end. The last time she'd said that, she'd offered to trade her life for her father's—and nearly died. "We don't get 'fair' in this lifetime."

Sierra tucked up her knees. "At least he's in a better place."

Lindsey's eyes flashed. "You don't know that. There's no way you can know that."

Sierra didn't respond with anger. "Whatever it is, it's better than this."

Lindsey turned to Jason, wordless, and he held her.

Through the rest of the morning, Jason held her a lot.

CHAPTER NINETEEN

Lindsey went home with Mom. It was Mom's house now. Dad...gone.

You could know the bullet was coming and still feel the pain when it hit. The difference between Dad's death and a total surprise was how the grind of watching him decline had worn them to the bone. Sure, they'd pre-answered all the questions. They'd gotten ahead of the paperwork and the decisions. They'd wrestled with the philosophical issues. Now all that was left was the unremitting agony. Maybe, like that guy with the crushed chest, the train could leave the station and your ribs didn't collapse right away. Maybe you could lie on the platform, pulverized, drawing just enough oxygen that death wouldn't come.

Sierra sat with a mug of tea in her hands. Ashlyn and Michael huddled on a couch, talking in low voices. Lindsey walked to the glass doors and gazed out at the deck. It had snowed last night, barely enough to cover the ground. The sky hung low with a greenish-grey cast that left her wondering about the weather report.

Mom said, "Yeah, it's supposed to snow this afternoon."

Lindsey sighed. "At least no one will look out the window and say today's a lovely day."

Lindsey drifted into the living room, and she lifted her smashed violin case off the piano. Today was already a disaster, but she'd had a thought. A worthless, awful, beautiful, ungrateful thought. On the couch, she worked the case open.

Ashlyn joined her as she uncovered the lid.

"Oh," Michael breathed.

Ashlyn said, "I told you it was destroyed."

"Yeah, but I hadn't... It's a visual of how much force there was in the accident. Sorry. I'm saying it all wrong."

I get it." Lindsey lifted the broken violin onto her lap, her heart cringing as the neck swiveled with a scrape of wood against wood, and it was like handling a corpse with a broken spine. She first unwound the strings, and then with the strings out, she removed the pegs. She disconnected the chin rest, the tailpiece, and the base button. The bridge was already collapsed. "Get me a bag?" she asked, and when Ashlyn returned with it, Lindsey filled it with the broken neck and the splintered body and the collapsed bridge.

While Lindsey was coiling the strings around one another, Mom came into the living room. "I don't know if they'll allow it."

Lindsey hadn't even asked permission. "It's fitting. Besides, the casket is wood."

"True. I'll ask."

Michael looked mystified. "What isn't allowed?"

Lindsey said, "To cremate my violin with Dad."

Michael flinched. Mom took the broken pieces. Without knowing quite what to do with the rest of the parts, Lindsey pulled her cloth bag out of the case and cleared out the compartments. Her rosin. A spare fine tuner. A glittery guitar pick she'd found. A tiny pencil. A bent paper clip for tightening the chin rest. A ticket stub from a concert her parents had played at together. Lindsey tucked the cloth bag into her backpack.

She should have coffee so she didn't pass out. Or...she should not have coffee so she could get a much-needed nap.

Mom said, "I reached Ben on the phone. He's devastated, but I told him to stay with his daughter and the baby. We'll have the funeral Tuesday after next, once he gets back."

Lindsey rubbed her temples. "I'm glad he got to see Dad on Thursday."

Mom said, "He was in an awful position. He knew it was coming, but his granddaughter needs to be celebrated."

The doorbell rang. Momentarily Lindsey's cousin Aileen was hugging her. "I'm so sorry." Then Sierra was there too, arms around them both.

Aunt Jen had brought a crock pot, and Mom helped her get it set up on the counter. Aunt Jen said, "I didn't know what you had for food, but in five hours, that will be a crock pot lasagna."

Mom hugged her. "I'm so sorry. This has been an awful few years. First Kelty, now Bob. How are you even standing?"

Ashlyn and Michael came into the kitchen, and Aileen kept trying to sneak a look at Michael without staring. Catching this, Susan walked over to Michael to take his hand. "Jen, Aileen, this is our other son, Michael. Michael, Jen is Bob's sister—so, your aunt. Aileen is your cousin."

Michael's expression bore the same disorientation Lindsey felt: his thrill to meet more relatives, but also the soul-gutted feeling of having just lost his connection to them. "I'm sorry to meet under the circumstances."

Aunt Jen took his hands, looking him all the way over. "I'm amazed. When they told me last fall—I hadn't even known you existed, but finding you is wonderful. Especially now. Welcome to the family."

No one had warned Lindsey that it would physically hurt to lose her father. Not just the lack of sleep or the headache that would never leave. It was the constant burning of her eyes, the tightness of her throat, the continuous feeling that she couldn't take a breath deep enough. Her arms ached. Her stomach revolted at the slightest scent, but at the same time, she was nauseated because she hadn't eaten. That lasagna was going to start smelling as it cooked, and she'd have to leave.

Except...Jason wasn't here to drive her. Jason had gone home to sleep or work on music (or both, considering how much progress he seemed to have made). He'd stood in the dooryard trying five different ways of saying goodbye, stepping toward the exit and then stepping closer again, almost touching Lindsey and then retreating. "Well, I guess I should go," except he wouldn't quite go. Until after the fifth time, he did go, leaving Lindsey uneasy.

For the last week, Jason had been a fixture. From teaching at the last day of camp to the emergency room to her recovery, he'd been right here. As long as they weren't playing music together, they weren't fighting. He'd actually been thoughtful. He'd enabled her to spend time with Dad. By defying her mother he'd given her, in effect, one last night with her father.

With Jason gone, she ached for him to come back. He couldn't protect her, but he'd made her feel safe.

She got out her phone, only Jason hadn't texted. He was probably asleep, and there was nothing new to report anyway. She shouldn't feel disappointed.

Except her father had just died, and if there was anything she could do to feel better, something that wasn't illegal and wasn't entirely stupid, she was going to do it. Lindsey typed, "Thank you," and then hit send.

A moment later, Jason replied, "You're welcome."

And then, "I'm sorry."

Mom and Aunt Jen drove into the snowfall (along with the dead violin) to talk to the funeral home and the pastor about "the arrangements." Lindsey hated that term. "Arrangements" were sheet music you should perform, not...well, this.

Sierra and Aileen were sitting at the table, Sierra writing a series of thank-you notes to Dad's nurses and doctors while Aileen sat with an herbal tea.

Lindsey said to Aileen, "Are you okay? I mean, you lost your sister two years ago."

Aileen breathed long and deep. "Mom's the one I'm worried about. I feel like I'm the only one she has left."

"And Trey," Sierra said. Aileen had gotten married last summer to a guy she'd met after Kelty's death.

It occurred to Lindsey just then—*How?* With this kind of weight on your soul, how do you even think about starting a relationship? Except had Jason been doing that with her? Slowly getting past Lindsey's defenses because her life was in turmoil, making himself useful, being strong, being quiet when she needed space?

Aileen smiled. "Trey's more about going up on Mom's roof to chip off the ice dams. He loves her, but he's not someone she'll lean on. Not yet." With her elbows on the table, Aileen rested her forehead on her palms. "After someone dies, you learn who cares. I didn't realize. Mom's friends did step up to help her, and I'm sure they will again."

Sierra said, "Yeah, our mom has a whole community here."

Jason had stepped up. Lindsey's breath caught as she thought about him sacrificing his whole week—sacrificing all of last night and most of this morning.

That... Well, it looked a lot like caring.

Aileen traced a circle on the tabletop. "The ones who surprised me most were Kelty's friends. They really came through."

Lindsey said, "Trey was Kelty's friend, right?"

"He knew her, but he knows everyone." Aileen chuckled. "No, it was more that after Kelty died, her friends wanted to arrange a memorial. She had helped start the running club, so the running club decided to hold a 5K race."

Why was that a thing? Lindsey prompted, "Okay...?"

"See, that was exactly my response!" Aileen laughed. "A memorial race? Why kilometers? But she was a runner, so a memorial race made sense, and that's how I met Trey. I know Aunt Susan wants a private funeral, but maybe in six months, you could arrange an Uncle Bob Memorial Concert."

Lindsey picked up her head. "Go on?"

Aileen shrugged. "I don't know anything about concerts. I don't even know what went into planning the Kelty 5K, except every year the club president wants to change her name and move to Providence. But you know how you and Uncle Bob played in those music festivals?" Yes, like their entire career. "You could invite a bunch of musicians, and the ticket price could go to a music scholarship fund."

Lindsey's eyes half-closed. "I wonder how many people we'd get."

She remembered Dad's fingers in her hair, Dad's faint breaths under her cheek. The moment she realized they'd stopped. The heartbeats had ended. The music went on.

Lindsey grabbed a note pad off the counter and started a list. The quartet. Clear Enigma. Sierra's harp. Who else? Enrique would sing if she asked. Declan would play. It took five minutes to fill the page with local bands and chamber groups and soloists who'd had their genesis at the Castleton School of Music.

The lineup would be a mess, but you could staff an entire music festival this way.

Half an hour each? But there were so many. Not

everyone would want to perform. They'd have to donate their time and travel expenses. Maybe fifteen minutes? Fifteen minutes with a few minutes between to set up and tear down. That would still be a hundred hours of music.

Was there any way to gauge interest? Could she start a poll or create a spreadsheet? What was that service people used online, the one where you looked at a calendar and claimed a slot?

Where would they even hold this kind of concert?

Lindsey grabbed her phone and dictated a text. "Mom, where can we get an auditorium?"

Aileen stood from the table, and Lindsey started, having forgotten she was there. "Okay, this is a great idea." She jotted down two more names. "Except we don't wait for summer. We do it now."

Sierra looked up from addressing an envelope. "In the summer, we could do it outdoors."

"In the summer," Lindsey said, "everyone will have performances booked, and no one will want to travel."

Mom replied, "The music school can hold 75."

Would that be enough? "Say we go up in size."

Mom replied, "Town hall. Two-fifty. Saint Mary's High School. 400."

Either would work. Lindsey said, "Thanks."

Aileen was grinning. "You look like a woman with a plan."

"It's a ridiculous plan." Lindsey rolled her eyes at herself. "I like it."

The survey and signup form went live that night. From her kitchen table, Lindsey logged into the school account and sent an email blast with the links. Every current student. Every Castleton Music School alum. Every current and former teacher.

She put it out on her social media and sent it to any musician who had a tangential connection with Dad.

She texted Jason. "We have one more gig before you leave for California."

Jason replied, "I expected that."

She arched her eyebrows as she replied. "Really? Do tell."

Jason replied, "I'm the disposable one. I assume you need someone to play for the funeral."

She blinked at the screen.

Ashlyn wandered into the room at her back. "Hannah's onboard for the concert if we go through with it. She asked for a solo slot too, at least five minutes."

Lindsey said, "Yeah, but make sure she fills out the survey because I'm not going to remember anything."

Ashlyn said, "You okay? You sound stunned."

"I didn't think about music for my father's funeral. I assumed he and Mom had that planned. Jason..." She shook her head. "I'll play if they want, but Jason offered."

Ashlyn sat in the living room, head bowed. "How could any of us do that?"

How had Corwin played the church services this morning? How would Mom climb back into that choir loft and play other couples' weddings? Worse, other young men's funerals? Or would Mom's playing be that much more expressive because she knew the depth and weight of the changes life brought?

"The music goes on." Dad's final words rang through Lindsey's head. When you love someone, you give them the most valuable thing you have. He'd given his life and his music and his career to his wife, and later to his children. Now was his funeral, and Lindsey wouldn't be able to give her music to him.

Jason texted again, "Just let me know what to play and when."

She fumbled with the screen. "Actually, that wasn't it."

This concert was her chance to give Dad back the music

he'd given the world. A chance to gather it all in one place like a bouquet of songs and performances: that could stand as a monument to his legacy. Instead of a eulogy, he could have a festival. Instead of tears, he could have applause.

Jason texted, "Please tell me you haven't accepted a gig now of all times?"

Lindsey replied, "I can't explain. Check your email." Jason was on the alumni list.

Three minutes later, he replied, "Oh my."

Then, "Are you up to this?"

Mom had been more...well, logical about the question. "The reason we pre-planned the funeral arrangements was so we didn't have to make a lot of decisions now."

Contrast to Sierra's response: "All of us can come together in song! It's the perfect tribute to a man who made music his life!" Corwin, when he'd returned from church dressed to the nines, had only looked over the planning with a derisive snort. "I'm in."

Lindsey was still post-concussive, grieving, not thinking very well, and about to lose her second violinist. Organizing a memorial concert was, likely, the dumbest thing she'd ever decided to do.

Lindsey replied, "I guess we'll find out."

CHAPTER TWENTY

Jason logged in to Lindsey's signup sheet and reviewed the chaos.

At every step of the way, Lindsey kept saying, "We only want a fun concert to honor my father," so Jason kept reminding himself not to worry about it. If the goal was getting a bunch of musicians together to take turns jamming, they had a reasonable chance of success. The trouble was keeping the thing from growing too far and too fast.

As of Friday morning, they had an online chat with at least fifty-two thousand comments from nine hundred participants (slight exaggeration) and plans that would have made the organizers of Peace Without Borders grab the nearest chair. Lindsey's general comment to every outlandish suggestion was, "If you can make that happen, go right ahead." When Michael said it really should be livestreamed, that was exactly her response, and an hour later, Michael found a way to broadcast it. Other than securing a hall, monitoring the schedule, and asking a caterer to deliver a steady supply of sandwiches, Lindsey was letting this unfold with a hands-offness that was peculiarly not-Lindsey.

Oh, and Corwin had insisted on a security presence—but he was inexplicably friends with several police officers (that is to say, he refused to explain how he knew them) who were "more than happy" to show up on their day off. "More than happy" probably meant Corwin himself was paying them to attend the Concert of Chaos, but who even knew?

A few people had offered memorial donations that would, Lindsey believed, cover catering and auditorium rental. Although from what Lindsey had said, the Castleton family could open their fridge and cater a concert festival. Everyone in Hartwell had brought a meal or signed up to bring one, and instead of having to feed out-of-town mourners, Mrs. Castleton was actively handing off food to her children and anyone else who showed up.

Jason texted Lindsey. "Sunday afternoon's lineup looks quite amazing."

She replied, "Doesn't it, though?"

Then another notification came in, except it wasn't from Lindsey. It was from Edward. "We need to talk."

Jason set the phone on the table and stared at it. If he didn't touch it, the message would stay "unread" for a few minutes and he could figure out how best to phrase, "No, I haven't come up with an acceptable third song" such that it didn't result in the detonation of his career.

"It's not that I don't have ideas," he could say. "I have an entire notebook full of ideas. It's just that none of them have ignited with that cinematic magic."

That was also a great idea, except his phone rang, and the name on the screen was Walt Ingram. Walt Ingram, calling at six a.m. his time. Dear heaven, this wasn't going to work out well.

Rather than spend the rest of Friday dreading his

upcoming torture, Jason took the call. "Walt!"

"Woodward, we need you out here. Those songs are two weeks overdue. We're about to wrap up filming, and you're one of the cyphers left in the process."

An odd disconnect grew between Jason and his body. His body was on the chair in front of his laptop, his eyes regarding a spreadsheet listing times and musical acts. His ears were hearing Walt Ingram. His heart was pounding, and his limbic system was telling him to flee into the nearest burrow for safety. His brain was...aware but otherwise unconcerned.

Jason's voice said, "What do you want to do?"

Walt said, "I want you out here next Wednesday to film, and I want demo copies of all three songs in my inbox by midnight tonight."

Jason said, "I can get you two by the end of today. The third is proving tricky."

"Not what I wanted to hear."

"Also, I have a funeral to attend on Tuesday. I can't leave before then."

"We'll fly you out Tuesday night. But let me hear those other two because I've got production breathing down my neck, and they really want to get rid of the temp tracks."

It made sense. It made so much sense, and it wasn't as if Jason hadn't gotten this assignment months ago. It was just...months ago. Before December he hadn't been able to think about Ultraviolet Dawn without freezing in the headlights, and until Christmas he hadn't been able to talk about it. He'd agreed to do this in May when the year had spread ahead with the promise that once Jason was out of the crosshairs, the adrenaline would subside and he'd be able to think of the industry without his eyes smarting.

What more could they want? He'd "taken a year off to learn to play." He'd backed out of the limelight and then danced back into it again saying all the right things with the right tones, penitent and humbled by losing his career and his girlfriend.

Jason said, "I understand. I'll get you clean copies of the

love song and the transit song."

"Thanks, man. I'll be waiting."

Five minutes later, Jason managed to text Edward. "I spoke to Walt. I'm getting him what he wants."

Edward replied, "Copy me on whatever you send him."

Yes, of course. Keep tabs on your wayward client as if he's a naughty child. Which was entirely appropriate under the circumstances.

Jason took his violin and the printed copies of Lindsey's song and Bob's song. Lindsey had offered him the music school recording studio, and now it was time.

Lindsey met him with a plate of donated brownies. "Allow me to introduce your sound engineer," and she bowed before unlocking the studio.

No, not Lindsey. Not here. Not now. "You've still got a ton of stuff to organize for Sunday."

"Naturally. I've discovered something, though. If I tell people to organize the thing themselves and then leave them alone, they do what you did with the double-booking and come up with their own solutions." Lindsey winked at him, and Jason wanted to crawl into a hole. "The solution may stink, but I didn't have to do anything about it. That frees me up to offer brownies to visitors at the music school, and afterward, to hit the record button on the other side of the glass. Speaking of which—" She held out the plate, but Jason backed away. He couldn't look at them, wouldn't be able to stand the smell, and couldn't imagine choking one down.

She snickered. "Oh, right, I'm fresh out of plastic gloves. I should have brought you chopsticks."

If only that were it.

Jason took far too long to tune his violin. To set up the mic. To set up the music. He'd played both songs any number of times in his apartment, but here he studied the notes as if he'd never seen them before. Lindsey played on her phone in the sound booth, and every so often she'd turn on the intercom. "You do realize it's going to snow, and we'll be trapped here forever."

"It's going to snow on Saturday," Jason snapped.

"Agreed. At this rate, we'll still be here Saturday night."

He played scales while she sound-checked for him. "Hang on," she said, her voice artificially flat through the intercom. "Okay, try again." Then, "Better. Give me a minute and we'll get you started."

She signaled him to start, and he didn't. He stood there, ready to play, and didn't play.

The recording light went off, and Lindsey disappeared from the window. The door opened, and she was in the room. "What's going on?"

This wasn't a panic attack. After experiencing two of them, Jason was an expert in those. This was more like complete paralysis with none of the doom, none of the crushing chest pain, and none of the panic. He simply couldn't play.

Lindsey walked around to his side of the music stand, and Jason blocked her.

"Ah. It's me. I thought so." She fingered her hair. "I can get someone else to do the recording, but they're going to hear it too."

He closed his eyes. "This isn't what I expected to happen."

Lindsey arched her brows. "Why don't I sight-read it and play through once? Then when I bollocks up the whole thing, you'll feel compelled to rescue your violin from my unworthy hands and play it the right way."

"You're making fun of me." Jason's throat tightened. "It's not that."

Lindsey said, "It's that you don't want to do this at all. It's that those monsters on the left coast traumatized you. It's that every day since you fled to Maine, you've been able to put off for one more day the moment you needed to face down the producers, the critics, the monsters, the fans, and the celebrities who never cared about you in the first place."

Jason's eyes widened.

Lindsey folded her arms. "Whichever jerk said you

needed to take a year off and learn to play—I want him in a ditch on the side of the road. He took something from you that you never even knew you had, and now we're standing in a sound booth with you unable to play your own music in front of your own first violinist, and why? Because someone eviscerated you with words in the pursuit of clicks and views. I hate them, and I wish I could give it back to you."

Jason's mouth was dry. "Give back what?"

"Your bulletproof arrogance. You knew who you were and what you were about. You'd have picked up this violin and played that song like a giant screw-you to anyone who wanted to criticize, and you'd have laughed while you did it." Lindsey's eyes narrowed. "How about this: I'm not recording right now, so there's no pressure. Tuck that thing under your chin and whip through the whole piece at once."

She sat in the corner, knees to her chest, arms around her shins.

Jason met her eyes. "Why are you doing this?"

It came out wispy, uncertain.

Lindsey said, "You've been good to me."

He closed his eyes, unmoored.

She softened her voice. "Or, if that's uncomfortable to hear, you're a massive pain in the behind, and I want to make sure you complete your triumphant return to California with no chance you'll boomerang right back home again."

He'd been good to her?

He'd wiped out her violin's star and hadn't been able to put it back.

He'd dragged her to New York City and kept her there when she wanted to be home supporting her family.

He'd fought her for ten months over who had top chair in her own string quartet.

He'd convinced her she was nobody special when it turned out she was incredibly special—badgered her into thinking she was ordinary when she was extraordinary.

She'd listened to him and somehow concluded she was less fit to live than anyone.

Now here she sat, telling him he'd been good to her, and then giving him an out by being sarcastic.

Jason raised his violin and played through Lindsey's love song. The D minor key, the tension in the transitions, the pauses, the runs that kept getting cut off. What did she hear? She could read his mind. Would she realize?

When he finished, he found her studying him. "Play the second."

He cocked his head. "No wild applause?"

"I believe my opinion is unrequired." She winked at him. "I'm a human microphone, and microphones don't pass judgment."

True, except microphones were the most dangerous instrument in creation. Microphones passed along everything they heard without making excuses.

Jason shifted the papers and played through Bob's song. This was harder, playing the pre-loss song in the week post-loss, two days pre-memorial, four days pre-funeral. He'd written the first draft contemplating the inevitability of suffering, and now he was playing it for someone waist-deep in suffering.

He ended it and gave Lindsey a mock bow. Again, she gave no feedback. "And the third?"

"That's where I'm in trouble. I've got nothing."

She cocked her head. "You were working in that notebook the whole week we spent in the hospital."

Jason's shoulders dropped. "I have fragments. Nothing that wants to be a song."

"Do you want me to tell you why?"

Her gaze was level, but her body language was defensive. Meeting his eyes like a territorial cat, she dominated the room, and Jason wanted to say she might as well, since she knew everything.

The sarcasm wouldn't break the surface of his heart. Jason laid his violin on the chair and sat on the floor of the soundproof room, legs crossed. "Tell me."

"None of that is you. There's a heart to both those pieces, but you've hidden it under ornamentation and virtuosity. Your technique does nothing but muddy up the through-line. The trills, the runs, the double stops, the pizzicato—sure, you can play all that, and you're doing great. You created all that violinistic blitz to bury the heart of the song so deep that no one's going to hear it. Your soul is in both those songs, but you're hiding it. I think you know this, and I think that's why you don't want to finalize them."

Jason glared at her. "Shall I go back to *Suzuki Method Two* and play 'Lightly Row'?"

"No, but can you forget the 'learn how to play' people and start emoting again?" She drilled her gaze through him. "Because you're not emoting at all. You're whipping easily through this technically insane piece that I would have declared unplayable, but it's a chain of stunts. It's plate armor around your heart, and I want to see your heart."

Jason snorted. "My charred, ruined, selfish heart?"

Lindsey shrugged. "If that's all that's in there, then yes, I want to see the charred, selfish ruins. But I think you've got more inside." She sat away from the wall and moved nearer to him. "May I look in your notebook? Do you still have the first draft?"

Jason could only thank his past self for the prescience not to have printed "Lindsey's Song" in the header. He'd been thinking of it that way since the moment he'd written it down.

Lindsey's eyes widened. "Play that."

"I'm not playing that. I've—"

"So help me, pretty boy, play it."

He didn't even stand. From the floor, he played through it, although he couldn't help but add a few ornaments.

Lindsey's eyes were widened. "This is awesome. You should have stopped here."

"And sounded like an idiot?"

"And sounded like a star-crossed lover! Sounded

frustrated and sad!"

Jason said, "It's too simple."

"Simple and emotional. You, my friend, are experiencing a cognitive error. Somewhere along the line, maybe as a defense mechanism, you substituted complexity for emotional engagement."

She reached for his violin, and for the first time, Jason handed it over.

With furrowed brow, Lindsey studied the music, then drew the bow across the strings to play the song he'd written for her. She emoted through the strings and the wood, her touch rapid, her playing clumsy because she was sight-reading—but heartfelt. So much heart. So much joy blended with sorrow.

Jason's breath caught in his throat. She had no idea why he'd written it. She'd never have played it if she had.

She lowered the violin. "Where's the first draft of the second song?" He paged forward to that one, and she played through it too. "Okay, this one needs some help, but not the burial mound you shoveled on top of it." She cradled his violin in her lap, his bow resting on the crook of her arm. "Let's get them cleaned up. When do you need to get these to the movie guy?"

Walt Ingram: movie guy. Jason said, "Midnight, but my computer's at home."

Lindsey handed back his violin. "I'll go with you. I bet we'll also find your third song somewhere in this notebook, and then we'll come back in triumph to get all three recorded and uploaded before deadline."

Jason left his car on the street because his building had exactly four parking spaces: two for the family on the bottom floor, one for the sound-sensitive woman on the second, and the last for him. He waited in his Audi until Lindsey arrived in Bob's SUV, then showed her where to park.

Fear. He was afraid, and at the same time, he felt calm because for a year he'd been afraid alone. Now he had someone to be afraid with, someone shining a lamp to show the way forward.

Lindsey hiked up the steps that bent around themselves with practically no footprint. "Old houses are the best."

"Until the wind hits them and blows out all the candles." He stopped on his landing. "Also, sound travels. If we don't finish before a reasonable hour, my downstairs neighbor will be upset."

Lindsey paused. "How upset?"

Jason unlocked his apartment door. "My violin is audible in her kitchen. She tolerates regular noise, but with both of us playing...?"

Again, trust Lindsey to come up with a plan. Not ninety seconds later, the woman had opened her door to find Lindsey offering her the plate of brownies. "I have the hugest favor to ask." Lindsey pitched her voice slightly higher, and she gave a tremulous smile. "My father's memorial service is in two days, and Jason's been helping me get everything ready. But Jason's on deadline to get a song to his agent, so I was wondering—would it be a problem if we played a lot of music? Maybe even after quiet hours? It would be just this once."

The woman took the brownies. "Oh, you poor dear! Of course! I'm so sorry!"

There were apologies and niceties, and the woman reassured Jason that of course he could play all night if he needed to after being so nice to everyone.

Back in his apartment, Jason murmured, "She doesn't suspect what you really think of me."

Lindsey snickered. "We're all glad for that. But if she can hear you that well, aren't you worried she'll record you playing and post it somewhere, violating your iron-clad nondisclosure agreement? *Listen to what my nice neighbor does with his pretty violin!"* When Jason shuddered at the mention of the NDA, Lindsey added, "Why didn't the director tell you to knock it off with the endless revisions before now?"

"I wouldn't let him hear it before now." In response to her shocked expression, he said, "The last time I did that, I kept waiting for them to call me in to do the real recording, and then it turned out they used my demo."

Lindsey laughed so hard the neighbor woman was going to wonder if they were holding the world's funniest funeral. "Are you kidding me?"

Jason's eyes flared. "That's half of why they think I can't play! I'm out there credited with the theme song for this kid's show, and it's garbage."

"It's not garbage! They saved it before you ruined it!" Lindsey wiped tears from her eyes. "They recognized perfection and ran with it."

Frowning, Jason folded his arms. "I could have done better."

"You could have done worse. That theme song is cute, and it's perfect for the audience." She pointed to the table. "Let's get started."

"Actually, first I need to return this." Jason brought the starless violin from the couch. "I tried to retrieve the star, but the way I got it off—it's gone. I can't even recreate where it was."

Lindsey closed her eyes. "I'm sorry I flipped out on you."

"You said nothing I didn't deserve. I did what I wanted and assumed you'd thank me for it." Jason shook his head. "You were right about a lot of things, and I wasn't listening."

Lindsey unzipped her backpack and pulled out a cloth bag, and from that she withdrew a handful of parts that Jason didn't at first recognize...until the moment he did. "It's not like you did this." Four pegs, four strings coiled around one another, and a tailpiece. "The violin is still playable."

Jason lowered his eyes. "I'm sorry about your real violin

too."

Lindsey shook her head. "It puts things in perspective. We're both alive."

Being alive meant they had work to do. Jason started inputting the basic version of Lindsey's song, but halfway through, she got up and returned with the other case. "I thought you had only the one violin, you filthy liar."

"It's not a real violin." While he kept transcribing, she opened the case to admire his handmade violin. "It was my summer project when I interned with the luthier, but it won't sing."

"Oh, that's a pity." She pivoted it. "Can I tune it?"

"Ten-year-old strings. I wouldn't attempt it without eye protection."

Lindsey had to exert a lot of pressure to loosen the first peg. "If you've got peg dope, I'll play with this for now."

Jason said, "It still won't sing."

"You're not thinking. Your neighbor doesn't want to hear you, and you've made effectively a mute violin." The peg came free, and Lindsey unwound the string. "And look: four orphan strings on the table. There's literally no cost."

The cost was a spare bridge from the student violin case, and by the time Jason was done transcribing, Lindsey had the mute violin re-strung and in tune. Using the bow from her student violin, she played a D scale.

The violin sang out, and Jason's head snapped around.

"Um, dude? That's not a mute violin." Lindsey did a three-octave G scale, and it resonated all the way up to its highest notes. "You made a pretty cool instrument."

It was the same one. It was clearly the same violin he'd made, right down to the mistakes Jason always saw first when he looked at it (and which his parents professed they never saw, no matter how well he pointed them out). He took her bow and played the stripped-down version of the love song, and again the violin resounded.

"It's not a Strad, but it's talking." Lindsey snickered. "It needed some time alone to figure out what it was."

Jason said, "In an attic that was too hot and too cold, where the summers were too humid and the winters were too dry? That should have killed it."

Lindsey rested her chin on her hands. "Adversity gave it a voice."

Jason watched her, throat warm, eyes stinging. "You gave it a voice."

"Not my voice." She met his eyes. "I only helped you unlock what was inside."

CHAPTER TWENTY-ONE

Bob's song was the first they tackled with Lindsey like a drill sergeant. Man, was she merciless. *Does this serve the main line? No? Out it goes. Chuck that. Save this for another song, genius. I'm glad you can play this, but no one will care. That part shines: keep that ornamentation. Enhance this.*

He listened as she kept playing variations, leaning into the emotion every time. Jason burned with embarrassment when he tried it, but she promised it sounded great. She recorded him on her phone and played it back so he could hear himself. (Then she handed over the phone for the video's deletion: she would not be the reason the nondisclosure agreement got violated.)

"My professors at the conservatory would pass out." Jason hit the delete button. "They mocked angsty playing."

Lindsey powered down her phone and left it on the table so he could trust it wasn't recording. Not only was she a drill sergeant, but she'd added a sprinkle of CIA agent for flavor. "It's not angst, and forget the academics. You're reaching for hearts. You can't do that wearing oven mitts." She reached for the notebook and traced a couple of measures with her finger. "Things like this, they're something you can play if you're an unhinged once-in-five-centuries wonder like Paganini. But you're not Paganini, and this movie doesn't require Paganini."

Jason said, "Did you know that was one of the movies we were in negotiations over? Paganini."

Her eyebrows shot up. "Wow."

He said, "Yeah, wow. The internet mob took care of that for me, and I guess the movie got shelved."

"You'd make an awesome deranged virtuoso. But you still need to take stuff like this out of your song."

Once Jason had a handle on her editing technique, they tackled Lindsey's song, running right over the surface of the piece with a carrot peeler and scraping off everything that didn't need to be there.

Jason was in the groove now, so while he worked, Lindsey spent time coordinating concert details. Every so often Lindsey would mutter about fights going on in the group texts, or two bands that wanted to cover the same piece. He opened a bag of cheese puffs, and they ate from bowls using chopsticks. Lindsey thought it was funny, and sometimes she fed him one.

The bowls were empty, and Lindsey's song was pared down to just its beating heart. Now, for song three. "I've got nothing."

In between putting out fires, Lindsey had been flipping through his notebook. "You got good headway on this one before you abandoned it. Play the main line and let me listen."

"It never felt right. The third song has to be triumphant and forward-looking."

"Is it hard writing something you don't feel?" she asked, leaving Jason cringing in his skin because once again, she was seeing right through him. That's what a first violinist does in mid-play, and they were neck-deep in these songs. "Think about when you first left for California, about to take over the world. Can you touch that?"

"Not without feeling like a fraud." Jason played through the notes.

Lindsey dumped more cheese puffs into a bowl. "Part of the problem is it's a complicated feeling, and you're imagining a complicated tune to match. What might serve better is a mismatch. You know how we do difficult music with easy lyrics, or difficult lyrics with easy music? It depends what effect you want, but I think: difficult emotion, easy melody. You've solved the 'entire hive of queen bees' problem, but don't you want people to walk out remembering this song? Then it's got to be streamlined."

"So, this?" and Jason played about half the notes.

She sat up. "Oh, wow. I can hear lyrics in that."

He tried it again. She urged, "Add the D back in," and the third time, she beamed. "There."

Jason adjusted the notation. "You can hear lyrics in that?"

"Can't you? *We're marching ahead.* Put a decent rhythm behind that or syncopate it, and you've got the sensation of ascendancy. It's got momentum." She hesitated. "Change keys. See what happens in A major."

Eventually it was G major that resonated, and Jason dove in. Lindsey, merciless Lindsey, was like Mitzy awarding him exactly twenty-five seconds of solo, except Lindsey was declaring Jason could have three ornaments and fifteen seconds of virtuosity; anything beyond that was grandstanding. "Tone it down, pretty boy," she murmured.

Jason glanced out the window to find snow falling in the full darkness. Maine evenings were glorious, and he had a song in his head and a career in his future. It was dinner time, and cheese puffs weren't going to cut it. He wanted to celebrate. "What do you want for food?"

Lindsey was rubbing her temples. "Oh. I guess we

should eat."

"Aren't you starving?" Jason jotted directions to himself on the score. "This is so close. If I order in, we'll be back at the school by eight o'clock, and I can beat Walt's deadline by three hours. Six hours if he's going by California time." He got out his phone. "What do you want? Say the word and it's yours."

Jason turned to find Lindsey pale, elbows on the table, forehead in her fingertips. "Whatever you want. I'm not hungry."

Blast. She had a headache, didn't she? She'd spent herself all the way, and like the selfish lordling she'd accused him of being so many times, he'd ignored her because he was so involved his own train of thought.

Why did he keep doing this to her? She was thinking of the group, and he was thinking of himself. Then he'd wipe out her stars, trample on her memories, and spend all her strength. At the end, he'd pirouette away to California, and she'd be emptied out.

He wanted better for her. He wanted to do better by her. He wanted... He wanted her.

He wanted to cherish her and focus on her and spend time with her. He wanted to make her happy and give her back some of the good things she'd given him. He wanted to make sacrifices and have her notice them and then have her benefit from them. He wanted her to stay with him and not feel it was a sacrifice of her own.

He shivered, violently shivered, and averted his eyes from her drawn face and her exhausted posture. Wanting all that—that was love.

That was love, and he didn't love her...shouldn't love her...couldn't possibly love a woman he was about to leave. Except all these urges said that he did.

It didn't matter. Stop. Think. First, she didn't love him. He'd hurt her too many times for her ever to fall in love, and he'd already fallen in love with one woman who'd never loved him back. He was done with that kind of thing.

Secondly, romance didn't matter anyhow. In the life he

aimed for, it was about being seen in the right places at the right times with the right people. At no point could love factor into this process. The last time he'd tried to factor it in, he'd gotten his heart broken and the pieces fed to the social media wolves.

Still, as a mere matter of human compassion, he couldn't let Lindsey stay like this. She was beaten, and he'd been the one beating her into the ground.

Jason set down his phone and hugged her. She relaxed against his shoulder, and warmth shot through him. So much for "a mere matter of human compassion."

This was love, and it shouldn't be.

Lindsey sighed. "Don't do that. You're on deadline, pretty boy."

"And you're on my shoulder, shotgun." He tucked her head into his neck, and she slackened into him, her breath light as it if hurt even to do that.

She was in pain, and all last week whenever she'd been in pain, she was also nauseated. No wonder she didn't want to eat. He'd kept her here for more than a full day's work, work that engaged all her brain and her ears and her eyes. In a revenge she didn't know about, she'd just engaged all his heart.

"Come with me." He led her to his bedroom, right alongside his bed. She'd kill him for this, except she was too dazed to protest. "I've figured out what will motivate me to finish the song. I want you to lie down here, in the dark, with your eyes closed."

Her head jerked up, and when their eyes met, her pupils were dilated. She must be in agony. "I'm not doing that!"

His soul blazed with the urge to kiss her. "You need to rest. Your head is pounding, and you're about to puke."

"I'm not going to puke, and you need to finish this up. I'm not getting in bed with you. Plus, I need to talk to the venue—"

"No." Jason couldn't hold out against temptation any longer and wrapped his arms around her. "You're still dealing with a concussion, and you can't push on this or you're going to set back your recovery by weeks, if not months."

Her body was calling to his, and he struggled not to slide his hands down her sides. Even though she stayed tense, she didn't push him away. Jason had as good as won this match. She said, "My mother needs me to get things done."

"Your mother needs you to recover." Jason backed her to the bed and then, when she was at the edge, he tugged down on her shoulders. She ended up sitting on the mattress with him kneeling before her, his hands on her hands. She looked soft, desperate, sad. "Everything will get done for the concert, and everything will get done for my songs. You said it yourself—deputize people to take care of things, and they'll get them done. Your mother's going to rely on you in the coming months. If you wipe yourself out now, you won't be there for her when she really needs you."

Lindsey clutched his hands. "You're on deadline. You have literally hours."

"And I have literally two finished songs. I didn't promise the third one tonight. If you nap for an hour, we can drive back and record."

Lindsey edged forward, but Jason rested his hands on her thighs. "Get in my bed. I have never ordered a woman into my bed, but I'm telling you now: get in bed, shut the lights, shut your eyes, and see what happens. I'll bet you're unconscious in sixty seconds."

Lindsey's defiance melted into defeat. "I just want my headache to go away."

"I'm the biggest headache in your life right now." Wow, that hurt to admit. "Stay here while I go away."

Averting her eyes, she choked out, "I don't want you getting in bed with me."

No, that would make everything hurt even worse. When Jason left Maine, he was going to miss her no matter what, but if he snuggled in and cuddled her to sleep, she'd end up hurting too. "I'm not getting in bed with you. If you prefer, I won't even stay in the apartment. I'll take my violin and leave."

She trembled. "I won't sleep. If you leave, I'll drive home."

"You're in no condition to drive, but how about a compromise? I'll sit in my car for fifteen minutes. If you come downstairs, I'll drive you home. If you don't come downstairs, I'll go to the music school. I'll do the recording, and then I'll come back to you."

There were tears in her eyes. Jason said, "Did you take ibuprofen or acetaminophen?"

She nodded. "Both."

"And it still hurts that much? You're an idiot, and I hate you for not saying anything." Jason sat back on his heels because his self-control was a thread. If he didn't win some distance, he was going to stretch up and kiss her. "I am serious. I have never wanted a woman in my bed as badly as I want you in it right now. Get some sleep."

Marshaling anything that resembled strength of will, Jason walked out of the room. He shut the lights and pulled the door closed behind him.

At ten o'clock, all the lights were out in Jason's apartment, and Lindsey's car remained in its spot.

Jason breathed out long and slow as he gathered his things. Ever since Lindsey's accident, he'd begun buckling his violin through the handle, but his backpack was tucked neatly into the floor space between the front and back seats. If only his heart stayed where he tucked it too.

At the apartment door, he gentled open the lock so it barely clicked. Say what you want about playing the violin, but you learned to apply very small amounts of pressure when necessary. Jason's bedroom door was still shut.

Again, good. He flipped on the kitchen lights and wondered if Lindsey had stirred at all. If she hadn't gotten up, she'd be famished. If she got up now, he could cook for her.

This whole "love" thing was driving him to distraction. While playing Lindsey's song in the recording booth, Jason thought about her the whole time. He'd unleashed all his emotional strain and self-denial until his violin keened with the frustration of finally finding what he wanted and not being able to have it.

Lindsey wouldn't leave Maine. Even if she wanted to give Jason a chance, this was her home—her "we"—and especially now, she'd stay. Their futures lay three thousand miles apart.

Should he try? He wanted to, but every reasonable answer was no. No, she despised him. No, he'd been hateful to her for far too long. No, she wouldn't leave New England. No, he had nothing to offer her. In every version of every scenario, if they got together, the only one who benefitted was Jason.

Torn by loneliness and fascination, Jason had recorded both pieces, touched them up on the computer (but not enough that Walt could dump them into the soundtrack unchanged), and uploaded them to Walt's secure server. Walt had texted back, "Got it. Sit tight while I make sure they open." Jason endured ten nauseating minutes messing up scales before Walt finally replied, "These are awesome! Totally worth the wait! Now get me a third to match."

Jason sat at his laptop. He was about to do something stupid enough that he'd need to write another song by Wednesday.

He pulled up piece number three. The computer played it through his headset, and Jason decided Lindsey was right: he could hear lyrics right there under the surface, and for the first time since last year, Jason knew what the lyrics should be.

Both Lindsey's song and Bob's song were instrumentals.

Now, with his brain alight and his stress relieved, Jason gave this song its words.

It needed only a few adjustments. In just a few hours, Lindsey had trained him well: get the song out and stop upping the degree of difficulty. No SAT words in the lyrics. No nine-part polyphony. He'd recited the words to himself in the car, working on the rhythm and the interlocking rhymes. The snow had swirled over the frigid blacktop on the ride home, and now he watched it out his window as it fell in huge clumps. Close to the house, it slanted left, but further out it slanted right. The world resembled a snow globe, and here was Jason in his bubble, doing something stupid.

He could do this, right? It was stupid in all the best ways. It was ridiculous and extravagant, and he shouldn't. Lindsey had helped him with this song for a reason, and here he was, wrecking everything again.

Well, he was leaving. After Wednesday, he'd never have another a chance to wreck things for her.

An hour later, with the words a perfect fit for the melody, Jason shut down the computer. It was eleven thirty, and Lindsey still hadn't made a sound. When he'd told her to sleep for an hour, he'd figured she'd stay unconscious until dawn, which meant he'd camp in his living room. The loveseat was too small, so he'd grab a spare blanket and pillow and do what she'd done at the hotel.

At his bedroom door, with his hand on the knob, he paused.

His judgment and his self-restraint waved like a tattered flag in the breeze. He was thrilled by unloading those two songs in a form he'd never anticipated, even more relieved that Walt approved, and at the same time he was daunted by the fact that he was going to have to do it all over again with one as-yet unwritten. He loved music again, loved his violin—and loved a woman. Reeling from the brand-new frisson of adoring Lindsey, he'd slip into the room to grab his pajamas and the extra pillow...and he'd never slip out again. He'd slide into the bed with her, which she'd said explicitly she didn't want.

He couldn't give her much in the time remaining, but at least he could give her respect. Jason turned away from the door.

CHAPTER TWENTY-TWO

Lindsey blinked awake. Jason's room.

Completely still, she listened for his breathing. Silence.

Tentative, she raised her head. No sparking bands of light—good. The only thing she could see was the digital clock, and it read 12:15. He'd have recorded and uploaded those songs by now. He'd better have.

Gently, very gently, she extended her leg behind her. No contact with another leg. Slowly, reach for the phone. Find the flashlight. Look.

No Jason.

She dropped back to the pillow, breathing easier. He'd stayed out. She was alone.

Her second thankfulness: that the darkness and sleep had done their job to banish the headache. Third thankfulness: that she felt hungry instead of nauseated. Finally, thankfulness that Jason's bed was comfortable. His blankets were warm, and his pillow smelled faintly of him, which was exactly the right amount of Jason to have found in his bed on awakening. She hadn't even meant to go to sleep, but he'd been right: she needed it.

Lindsey lowered the brightness on her screen and struggled to make out the alert that had popped up. It was a six-hours-old text from Ashlyn. "Planning dinner. Are you eating here tonight?"

Lindsey replied, "Sorry. I crashed at Jason's. I'll come home in a bit."

She'd probably be able to make the drive back. Twenty minutes, though. With snow on the road

A reply popped up. "Yeah, he told Mom when she did the recording for him. Just stay there."

Lindsey replied, "Why are you awake?"

"Probably the same reason as you."

Lindsey smirked. "Oh, you're dealing with a concussion?"

"Well, not exactly the same. I'm thinking about Dad. Dad and everything that has to happen with this concert."

Dad.

All day, whenever there'd been a gap in the work, she'd thought of Dad. Missing him. Wanting to drop by the hospital to hear his voice. Wanting to text a photo to his computer tablet or wanting to get his advice. Thinking of something to tell him the next time they talked, only now they couldn't.

She'd kept hearing her father's songwriting advice coming out of her mouth. She wanted to tell Dad about how quickly Jason's songs had shaped up. All afternoon, she'd remembered sessions with Dad where he'd shown her how to arrange pieces for the quartet, how to make the sound serve the emotions. "He's still a good student," she wanted to tell him. "But maybe that's because you were a great teacher."

Lindsey replied to Ashlyn, "Yeah, I'm a mess."

The transit song haunted her. She'd heard her father in its slow transitions and its impending doom. Working with Jason, she recognized whenever he got it right because of the sob that built in her throat. Even the love song in D-minor didn't bring back her father's death as much as that one, and she had no clue why.

Ashlyn texted, "Jason said you were worked to the bone. Get back to sleep. We'll make everything happen for Sunday, and if it's a disaster, at least it will be fun."

Lindsey texted back, "Hah."

Ashlyn missed Dad just as much as she did. Lindsey was alone in the room, but not alone in the world. She could distract herself with work, but the grief didn't care. The grief would wait.

Lindsey edged open the door and found Jason's entire apartment dark, so she turned her phone back into a flashlight to navigate to the bathroom. When she came out, she swung the light across Jason's living room, and there she found him: conked out on the floor with a throw blanket, and his jacket over the blanket.

Lindsey's heart twinged.

He'd sounded salacious about her presence in his bed, but he'd left her alone. He must be chilly. She'd find an extra blanket and lay it over him.

What was going on? As of Christmas, Jason would have rolled his eyes at Lindsey's headache. He'd have let her drive home. He'd have used the other side of the bed with a pillow between them because she was being ridiculous and nothing would happen. What did she expect him to do, camp on the floor?

Only here he was, doing just that. That wasn't even a pillow, was it? It was a folded-up towel.

She went to get a blanket off the bed, but then stopped. If she tucked him in, he'd wake up. He'd find her kneeling over him, and her guard was lowered. He'd put his arms up to her, and she'd let him draw her down. "Is your head better?" he'd whisper, and then he'd guide her to his side. She'd follow, in no state to hold the line and guard her heart...for all the good that was going to do at this point.

Still, Lindsey had some defenses remaining. She could make sure they didn't kiss again. She could make sure they weren't whispering in the dark, curled around one another. There was one week left. After that, Jason would leave for California to flit around doing Jasonly things, and if Lindsey wasn't careful, she'd be in Maine with a twice-broken heart.

She shut the door again, and this time, she locked it.

It was barely daylight when Lindsey awoke, and again she tested the world for the proximity of Jason. She was still alone. She was famished.

In the living room, he was messing around with his music notebook. She leaned against the wall, finger-combing her hair. "I thought we had you squared away. Yet here you are, creating songs like a musical fiend."

He gave an embarrassed smile. "You're right that there's some good stuff in here. I just need to declutter. We pulled five songs worth of queen bees out of...um, out of the love song yesterday. It'd be a shame not to give each of them their own hive." His eyes were shadowed. "Is your head better?"

"Yeah, thanks." She sat on the floor right where his heart had been six hours ago. "Did you get everything recorded and sent?" When he nodded, she prompted, "And when will you hear back?"

"Ten minutes after I uploaded them. Walt loved them both. Demanded the third. Which I'm not sending."

"Gosh, you're a rebel." Lindsey squinted at Jason. He looked as wrecked as she felt. "Can I ask why?"

Jason shut his notebook. "Of course you can ask why."

A long pause.

Lindsey sighed. "Must you always be irritating?"

"It's easier not having to change strategies." He looked up with a spark in his eyes, and she giggled. "Fine, I won't press the matter, but let the record show that you didn't ask me anything other than whether it would be okay to—"

She stuck out her foot and kicked him lightly in the shins. "I get it, pretty boy. *Why* aren't you sending the inestimable Walt his third song, since it was very nearly done last night?"

"Because I have other plans, plus it's not totally ready, plus two songs were all I promised by midnight. Speaking of which," and Jason flashed her his phone screen as though she could read it from here, "Walt's personal assistant just sent my flight information. They must really want me because I'll have to leave directly from the funeral."

"Crud," Lindsey breathed before she caught herself.

Jason looked up, startled.

She covered. "Long day for you. You're going to travel in funeral clothes?"

"As if that day could get any worse. I'm not looking forward to the jet lag either, but they're giving me one whole entire blessed night to adjust before they expect me to film while the sun rises." Jason slumped back on the couch. "I may use your brother's trick with the pot of coffee in the thermos."

"It's Hollywood. They provide free coffee for their pretty boys."

Jason looked uncomfortable. "I don't suppose you'd ever consider going out to California?"

"For free coffee?" Then Lindsey recoiled. "Oh, does your producer want to create the impression of a love triangle with Mitzy Maxwell? Because no. I'll go to a sound stage in New York to talk about quartets, but enough's enough."

Jason threw up both hands. "No! I didn't mean it that way at all."

Lindsey rolled her eyes. "In the entire year you've been here, you've never said one positive thing about California. If I ever had the slightest desire to go, I don't now."

Urgent, Jason leaned forward. "I'm sorry I gave that impression. California is beautiful. The weather's terrific, and the art and culture scene is so vibrant. There are interesting people and conversations, and there's the Santa Monica mountains. You can put your feet in the Pacific Ocean. I'd like you to see it. You might enjoy it more than you think."

He was selling it hard. Maybe he wanted her to see him in his element, impress her with his connections and his Brentwood zip code. He'd escort her to all the ritzy places so he could feel superior, then pat himself on the back as he kicked her out of his expensive car at Departures, having fulfilled his requirement to introduce culture to the New England violin teacher. Instead of pointing her toward a rickety burger place half a mile off 1A, he'd escort her to a spa in Malibu. Jason claimed his California life was all about buzz instead of feelings, so maybe he'd pretty her up and show her off to the media in order to entice Mitzy Maxwell to reclaim her territory.

Although...that was what Jason would have done in December. Maybe now he really did want to pay off Lindsey with what he considered the trip of her lifetime.

Tentative, Jason said, "Will you think about it?"

"I don't think so." It was too exhausting to do this while she was feeling so warm and he was looking so good. If she went to California, she'd have proof he'd outclassed her right from the start. He was leaving. He'd been clear that he'd never do otherwise.

She got to her feet. "I'm sorry I stole your bed, but you win points for being right."

He smirked at her, and she kicked him again, then went to find her boots.

Now he looked concerned. "What are you doing?"

"Going home. I don't live here."

Jason stood. "No, I'm not letting you do this. Don't walk-of-shame yourself out the front door."

Lindsey paused. "How do you propose I reach my car? Rappel down the back of the building?"

Jason looked pained. "You helped me yesterday. I'd have messed everything up even worse than I already had, and I didn't even give you dinner. At least let me take you out for breakfast."

Lindsey shivered. The two of them out for breakfast was worse than a date—it looked like the follow-up to a date. She forced a smile. "That won't disappoint your thousands of fangirls?"

Jason waved a hand. "I don't have thousands of fangirls. I don't want them. I only want one fangirl."

In the middle of lacing up her boot, Lindsey froze. He sounded imploring.

Jason was looking right at her. She flashed back to his eyes in the emergency room, almost recalled him looking right into her and telling her something...

She broke away. "One very special fangirl, whose wealth can keep you in the life you're accustomed to?"

Jason dropped back against the couch, spent. "Someone loyal and hard-working. Someone who gives her love totally and doesn't hold back afterward. Someone who knows all about music and will write and play it with me long after dark."

It wasn't fair. It wasn't fair that Mitzy had dumped him without ever having loved him. It wasn't fair how he'd gotten so hooked on her that even after all this, he kept clinging to the pipe dream of #Mitson.

Lindsey focused hard on lacing her boots. "She doesn't want you."

Jason stood. "No, I get it. Zero chance is zero chance, and it's my own fault. I'm sorry I made you uncomfortable."

Lindsey snickered. "Shouldn't we both be used to that by now?"

"That's why it's easier just to be irritating all the time." He went into his bedroom to change out of yesterday's clothes.

Lindsey switched to the other boot. She was hungry enough to be dizzy, exhausted enough that she couldn't focus. It scared her how much she'd have let Jason do last night if she hadn't kept her head together. It panicked her when she thought about how undone he'd been when faced with the moment of truth, and how for the first time he'd listened to her criticism—and then accepted it.

With a week left before leaving, why was he vulnerable with her now? Why'd he have to pick his last few days to finally turn into a human being?

He came back out of the bedroom. "There's a diner five miles up the road that does amazing waffles and even better omelets."

Lindsey got her jacket. "Sounds great. You always know all the best things."

As they went to the door, he said, "The problem is, sometimes it takes too long to recognize what they are."

CHAPTER TWENTY-THREE

In the lobby of Saint Mary's High School, it broke Jason's heart to see Lindsey on the brink of tears, and not the kind you expect during a memorial service. Staring at her phone, she said, "No one is going to come."

The weather wasn't playing nice. She'd picked Sunday over Saturday because the forecast had snow on Saturday and sunshine for Sunday. Easy decision. Saturday's snow had held off just enough that it was coming down Sunday morning. The performances started at one, and they'd already gotten five cancellations.

Jason put his arms around Lindsey, and she let him because it had gotten to be a thing since her father's death: he'd hold her, and she'd lean into him. It was something she did, nothing more. Lindsey was huggy with Ashlyn too. She needed comfort.

Jason said, "You kept saying it was about getting a bunch of musicians together to play in your father's memory. It's going to happen. We'll fill in the gaps."

For all that Ashlyn was huggy with Lindsey, Ashlyn always looked perplexed when Jason did it, although not quite as perplexed as Jason felt. Ashlyn said, "Seriously. We have a stage and this many musicians. All I'll have to do is say, 'Does anyone want to perform for fifteen additional minutes?' and they'll be shoving each other out of the way."

Lindsey's phone buzzed in her hand, and Jason let her go so she could get the next cancellation. Across the lobby, Susan was standing in front of a statue of the Virgin Mary. He went to her side.

Susan gave a long sigh. "We don't have statues in the church where I play, but this one—I feel it." She gestured to how Mary had opened her mantle to reveal her heart. It was ringed with a crown of roses and had a sword right through it. "I never noticed her heart before, but that's exactly how it feels."

Jason's shoulders dropped. "I'm sorry."

"It's inescapable. You just close your cloak and walk around, impaled." Her eyes glistened. "Take care of Lindsey. She said she wouldn't stress about the concert, as if that was ever going to happen. She's the definition of stress."

Jason offered, "The weather played us dirty."

Susan shrugged. "Life played us dirty. I expected one more spit in the eye."

At one o'clock, with more than zero people in the seats, Lindsey began the first part of the concert: the student recitals. "Welcome, everyone. Thank you so much braving the snow this afternoon to honor my father."

She looked amazing on stage, again wearing the dress from New York, the waterfall necklace and the champagne-toned heels. Jason kept flashing back to the thrill of unzipping her dress and realizing she was braless. He had to stop himself from figuring out if she was once again in the strapless/backless getup because...well, it would be rude. Rude and frustrating.

The recital audience was mostly parents, siblings, grandparents, and a few friends. The children's chorus performed two songs, and then the students began coming onto the stage. Ashlyn and Lindsey stayed with the littlest ones who were nervous, and one of the six-year-olds ran off the stage because he was scared. Ashlyn sat on the piano bench with one of the eight-year-olds.

Hilariously, Michael Knolwood went on stage with Ashlyn and his violin. "Bob Castleton was my father," he explained, "but because I grew up in a different family, I never learned violin until this year. Technically, that makes me a student of the school. I have never played in public, so please be nice." He and Ashlyn played a duet out of Suzuki Method Three. Michael looked stunned and relieved when he finished, and he said, "Thank you. For the rest of the day, I'll be backstage where I belong."

At two thirty, they announced a thirty-minute break until the professional performances began. It was still snowing, but caterers had set up sandwiches and snacks, and Jason found Lindsey in the production booth at the back with three different computers in front of her. Oh, and also a deer-in-the-headlights look.

Jason said, "How bad is it? Be honest."

"It's not unsolvable. We've lost a few acts that had to drive from northern Maine where they got slammed overnight, and a group from Vermont decided I-89 in the snow was the equivalent of suicide." She looked up. "That's actually what they said, followed by, 'Even long-haul truckers won't do that.' Given what happened to me, I'm not going to criticize." She shuddered. "That leaves five open slots, but all the slots were short to begin with, and the gaps might fill in on their own." She gestured to the auditorium. "The real problem will be having no audience, since every one of those groups would have provided listeners."

Ashlyn said, "A few groups are down a player. I'm going to ask for volunteers to fill in."

From a folding chair on the other side of the room with

the second computer, Michael said, "I've got us set to livestream. Anyone who couldn't make it can still watch."

Corwin had the third computer. "We'll have low attendance, but I've done shows for six people, and four of them only stayed because they were too drunk to drive home. It's part of the mystique."

Crestfallen, Lindsey said, "I wanted better for Dad."

Jason put a hand on her shoulder. "It's fine. We've got people out there already, and you designed it like an open-house so folks could drop in and out."

"Even so." She looked grim. "Dad touched a lot of people. I wanted a lot of people to come."

Jason glanced out at the seats. "Most people don't show up until halfway through the performance anyhow."

Michael snorted. "No, that's what people do in California when they want to say they've been to a thing. Then they leave early."

Jason frowned. "Yeah, I used to find it frustrating when we started to a half-empty house, but it was full at intermission, and at the finale it was half-empty again."

Lindsay kept working at the spreadsheet. "Well, I wanted people to watch and remember my father, and it's not going to happen, and I hate it."

Jason took a slow walk up to the stage, and then backstage to the prep room. Corwin had asked to be the opening group, so his band was getting ready.

Lindsey wanted viewers. Maybe Jason could entice a few. He texted Michael, "Send me the livestream link."

A link appeared. With a sense of futility, Jason put it out on his social media. He figured most of his followers had rage-followed him because they wanted to jeer at anything he did, and the rest of them were #MitsonForever fans who were doomed to disappointment. "I'm performing on and off today at a memorial to the greatest musician I ever knew. Watch me on livestream! {link}" He scheduled that to drop at three p.m., then scheduled other versions to post every fifteen minutes.

Three o'clock arrived. Clear Enigma launched an all-out

assault on the eardrums of the hundred listeners in the audience. Because the different acts had negotiated on the group chat, trading places and coming up with their own lineups, the next act was a punk band called the Tasers.

Michael texted Jason. "Can you add a microphone?"

Jason replied, "Sure, but shouldn't we all have headsets so you can yell orders at me?"

He added, "How many livestream viewers?"

Michael texted, "34. Hardly worth it."

Jason brought the mic to the wing, and between songs he ran it out Corwin and Sean.

In the back, he met Lindsey. "So far, so good."

"I guess." It didn't sound like agreement.

He hugged her. "Hey. You're doing great. Your dad loves you, and you've got this."

She looked beyond defeated, but she didn't argue as she went back to the lobby to intercept an incoming group.

All right, then. As usual, Jason's best wasn't enough, and fate was acting like a jerk. He hadn't wanted to reach for his last resort, but there wasn't a choice if he wanted to help Lindsey.

He walked up a silent hall away from the auditorium. St. Mary's was a typical high school, except for the crucifixes on the classroom walls, with bulletin boards about saving the environment and ending human trafficking. Jason sought out some privacy in which to sell his soul, and he turned up an unlighted corridor, except then the motion-sensitive lights flared on. Sure, let it happen in the light. This wasn't different from every other way he'd messed up his life.

He tried to get a deep breath before he finally went into his contacts, but calm wouldn't come. His hands were shaking, and his voice wasn't going to be steady, but— Yeah.

He pushed the button to make the call. Maybe he'd been blocked. Maybe she wouldn't answer.

She did answer. "Jason, honey! It's been so long! What's going on?"

"Mimi?" His voice was softer than he intended. "I'm sorry to bother you, but I need to ask you a favor."

As the performances continued, the audience grew. People gathered in the atrium, too, talking about Bob and spending time with Susan. Jason hadn't predicted this, that people would treat the concert like an ongoing thing in the background while they spent time talking and remembering Bob—exactly the way dinner guests treated the quartet at a party. In the atrium, parents were spending time with Susan while their children played. Lindsey's Aunt Jen and cousin Aileen were there, along with a number of other relatives. People wandered in and out of the auditorium depending on whether they were interested in the act. The caterers arrived with a second food delivery. Corwin's police friends lingered at the entrance and in the front row.

All at once, strangers began arriving. Some went straight to the auditorium without even saying hello, but others waited in a cluster at the front door. None of them spoke to Susan. Maybe it was good that Corwin had asked for a police presence, although no one seemed menacing. One of the cops joked around with them, looking stern but unworried.

A guy walked into the atrium with an electric guitar and an amp, and the door crowd rushed him. "Back off!" the guy shouted. "Have some respect!" The cops moved to his side while he pushed through, bringing with him a woman with a backpack. "Susan? Susan Castleton? You here?"

Susan rushed to him, and behind her, Lindsey exclaimed, "*Edgar?*"

All at once, everyone was taking video or photos. The guy kept pushing ahead. "Let me through! For goodness sakes, this is a memorial service, not a mosh pit. We'll do autographs later." When he reached Susan, he hugged her.

Jason blinked. Edgar? *Edgar Chantz?* He was a Castleton alum?

Lindsey flung her arms around Edgar. "Seriously? You have a show in Boston at eight!"

In his gravelly voice, Chantz said, "I couldn't live with myself if I didn't come after all. Long as I'm out of here at three-thirty, I'm good."

"Are you kidding me?" she exclaimed. "Where's the rest of your band?" and he just opened his hands and looked around. "Corwin! This man needs a backup band!"

Chaos erupted, and Lindsey went into high gear. Michael and Jason raced down the aisles and shot into the backstage to prep for Edgar's act. Beside himself, Corwin rounded up Clear Enigma, and then Lindsey popped onto the stage. "You guys." Her breath was heaving. "Especially the one *thousand* viewers of our livestream—thank you so much! We've got a special guest right now, someone you know from the top forty and who drove all the way to Maine even though he's live tonight in Boston. May I present—Edgar Chantz!"

The man strode onto the stage to fans shrieking.

Beside Jason, Michael was breathing hard from the scramble. "Turns out about an hour ago, this guy posted the school's address to his fans and said he'd be doing a free fifteen-minute performance. Anyone who could get here was welcome, but he told them to leave a donation to pay for renting the auditorium."

Jason breathed, "Wow."

To have that kind of pull. To do something that awesome with it....

Edgar Chantz calmed the crowd so he could speak. "When I was six, my mother dragged me in front of the principal and said, 'You gotta do something with this boy. He destroys everything he touches, and he's going to spend his life in prison.' The principal wrote a name and a phone number on a sticky note and said, 'Call this guy.' My mom thought it was a therapist, but instead it was a musician. After she finished telling him I was a disaster, the guy said, 'Three lessons, three weeks. Let's see what we can do.' And that was Robert Castleton for you. At the end of three weeks, I had beaten the snot out of my first drum set, and I was a musician for life. I got a guitar for my ninth birthday, and let me tell you, that man bailed me out of more trouble than I ever deserved. All the time it was, think about your music. You want to play in a prison? Good, but do it from the right side of the bars. Bob was wicked smart, and I owe him my life. I miss you, man."

Edgar Chantz launched into a series of three number one hits. Playing bass behind him, Corwin looked to be in heaven.

Mitzy texted Jason. "You never said you knew Edgar! Say hi to him for me."

Jason replied, "Will do. You got us a thousand viewers."

"I'm getting you more, hon, but you owe me big time."

Lindsey came up to Jason, and he slipped his arm around her waist. She said, "A minute after Edgar started playing, the livestream jumped from a thousand to fifteen hundred. We need to follow his act with something amazing."

Jason chuckled. "And here we are, with a ragtime band on the schedule."

"Yeah, they asked for a later slot. I was thinking of leaving Corwin on because Clear Enigma is already up there."

Michael ran up to her. "Linz, do you trust me? If you give me fifteen minutes, I have someone with an online following who wants them."

Jason's eyes widened. *Mitzy?*

Lindsey nodded. "Who do you have in mind?"

Michael said, "A music critic Youtuber named Memento Mortie just saw a mention of us on Twitter. He wants me to put him on a screen at the front."

Jason's eyebrows shot up. "We're going to show a livestream to the audience which you're then going to livestream back to our viewers?"

Michael sighed. "It's bizarre, but you know what? I don't care. We're giving everyone a chance to celebrate Robert Castleton, so let's go for it."

Edgar Chantz left the stage with a police escort, and Lindsey announced that in fifteen minutes, they'd have an amazing Youtuber up for them as a surprise—but while they got that set up, more Clear Enigma.

The auditorium was notably more crowded. This had to be Mitzy's doing. She'd promoted it not as a memorial service but as a free concert. Her fans had responded.

Unfortunately, she'd tagged it #Mitson, and Jason's notifications had blown up.

While Corwin's band likewise blew up the stage, Edgar Chantz asked Susan what the hall rental cost, then signed enough autographs to fund the whole thing with donations. When that was done, he hugged Susan.

She was sobbing. "You didn't have to do this. You drove eight hours just for us."

"I'd have driven eighty hours if I had to. I'm so sorry he's gone." Edgar hugged Lindsey and Sierra. "Cor did great for playing without notice."

Lindsey said, "You made his year."

Jason almost said, "Mitzy Maxwell says hi." Instead he glanced at Lindsey, and his throat seized up.

The cops escorted Edgar and his sole roadie back to his car, while in the auditorium, Clear Enigma finished its second set. Michael took the stage and lowered the screen. "I'd like to welcome our next guest, appearing thanks to the wonders of technology, YouTube star and music critic, Memento Mortie!" Edgar's fans cheered (they shared a demographic?) and then the screen flared to life.

"Hey, Morticians," said a super-skinny guy with spiked hair and an industrial piercing. "Let me tell you all about Bob Castleton, the man who kicked my butt into next Tuesday."

Lindsey came up behind Jason and laid her hands on his hips. "You weren't the only egoist my father tough-loved into submission."

Chills curled up Jason's spine. She sounded so much better now that they had an audience—now that she had proof her father was loved. She squeezed his waist. "This guy's got an amazing screen presence."

Instead of giving in to the urge to turn toward her, Jason navigated to Memento Mortie's YouTube channel. "Whoa. He has half a million subscribers."

Lindsey stiffened. On the screen, Mortie was telling everyone how even when it became obvious that Mortie didn't have a career in performance, he never forgot how Bob could dissect a piece.

Mortie said, "That's how I got into music criticism and started reviewing. So I'm talking directly to my subscribers now. Last week, you awesome Morticians did a fund-raiser for Malaysian earthquake relief, but I'm going to ask you to contribute again. I put up a link in the show description for a fundraiser for the Castleton Music School. Let's get their mortgage paid for the rest of the year so they can do what they do best. Get these folks out in the community putting delinquents like me and Edgar Chantz in front of instruments. Let's get guys like us creating things instead of destroying things."

Susan ran up behind them and gripped Jason's shoulder. "Is he serious?"

Lindsey whispered, "How much do you think a guy like that will raise?"

At the front, Michael was looking like a man about to grab the fundraiser link and stick it on their livestream description as well.

Memento Mortie finished with, "Bob Castleton, a gentleman and a wonder, I salute you. The world is richer for having had you. Specifically, my life is worthwhile because you were in it. Thank you!"

The audience applauded over Mortie's closing spiel about following his channel.

Lindsey grabbed Jason's arm. "Come with me. We need to keep the momentum." She pulled off her heels and sprinted through the atrium to the back corridors. "Ashlyn!" she called. Hannah was already in the back. "Enrique! Someone grab Corwin!"

While Mortie finished up his appeal for everyone to subscribe to his channel, Lindsey gathered her crew backstage. "We've got the highest number of online viewers we're ever going to. If I know him, Michael will get that donation button up on the livestream, so we need to keep those viewers at least a little longer. We'll play 'Love Once More.'"

But Mitzy was watching. His song. Their song.

"Jason, we'll perform it the way we did on the air. Ashlyn, Hannah—support. Corwin—"

Corwin raised his hands. "I know, I know. Let me get Rose because this song practically glows with a keyboard."

Hannah shook her head. "Not me. A cello would snuff that glow right out."

"Understood." Lindsey turned to Enrique. "Can you sing Mitzy Maxwell's line?"

Enrique bowed. "Your wish is my command."

"Good. We're a go."

Jason finally found his breath. "Wait. This isn't a good idea."

Mitzy was watching, and he knew she was watching, and she knew he knew she was watching.

"Don't freeze on me now, pretty boy." Lindsey looked anguished as she took his hands. "It makes sense. Do your solo. Solo for fifteen minutes if you want. You can have a whole hive of queen bees. We're doing this for my father."

Jason's breath shuddered in his throat. He'd stopped doing this for Bob long ago. Now he was doing it for Lindsey.

Well, if Mitzy hated him for it, things couldn't get any worse between them. He already owed Mitzy for all the viewers.

And speaking of owing things, Jason owed Lindsey.

Against his better judgment—against his every instinct, Jason lowered his eyes. "Fine. We're on."

Onstage, Lindsey took the mic. She was holding Frederika, and her dress shimmered in the lights. "I'm beyond thrilled that Mort was able to show up for us this afternoon, and a huge thank you on behalf of the Castleton Music School to all the Morticians who donated. And now— No, I won't bother introducing our next song. I'm sure you know it."

Rosalind Ward burst into the intro of into "Love One More". Corwin joined with his bass, and then Lindsey and Ashlyn slid in as well. Enrique began singing the first stanza, and by reflex, Jason started his violin line.

This was a Castleton arrangement in the way only these people could have done it. The audience began singing along with Enrique, and then Sierra was up on stage beside him to provide harmony. Definitely a Castleton affair: it wouldn't surprise Jason if in the next two minutes they picked up a saxophonist and an acoustic guitar. Lindsey looked and sounded fabulous on Jason's right, and Enrique had the mic on Jason's left. They'd positioned him right in the center, as if he were the headliner.

The players did two verses, and then Enrique sang the bridge which led directly into Jason's solo. Working together, the Castleton-trained performers wrapped around his line and supported it the way Bob had taught them, the same way Jason's line had supported Mitzy's vocals. This wasn't the way Jason and Mitzy had done it, and it wasn't even the way Jason and Lindsey had done it. Every time they played it, with every different combination of players, they transformed the song.

This was how it should be. Music was alive. Music wanted to *be*—wanted to *become.* It didn't want to fall into the past. Instead, the music longed to play on.

Lindsey sidled up next to him, he and she playing back to back, him executing every bit of trickery he'd ever wanted to put into this song and she working hard to hold up her end. The keyboardist had backed off, and so had the viola. Corwin was keeping things real while Enrique was waiting for them to come back around to the chorus.

It was just Jason and Lindsey, first and second violins on a piece that was only ever supposed to have had one violin.

He said, "Take it," and they switched, Lindsey flooding his line with emotion in a way Jason never did. She was joy and bedazzlement and infatuation all at the same time, and Jason went breathless as she voiced the emotions flooding his heart. She only went through it once before signaling everyone else to jump back in. Enrique started the final chorus, and Sierra urged everyone in the audience to keep singing until they ended the last chorus. "Love Once More" was no more.

Their ensemble bowed, but Jason grabbed the mic before Lindsey could. "Thank you! Since you're already on your feet, I let's keep you there. Michael, can you put up those lyrics I gave you?"

As the screen lowered, Jason handed sheet music to Enrique and Rosalind, and then Jason started to play.

He played his third song for Ultraviolet Dawn, the one he and Lindsey had written together. Above his head, the lyrics appeared.

He spoke while playing. "Lindsey, tell everyone your father's last words."

Lindsey's eyes were glistening, so it was Sierra who went to the mic. "'The music goes on.'"

Jason paused playing. "The music goes on, and that's why I want everyone to sing with me." He turned to Rosalind, who nodded. "We've lost a very important musician, but his song plays on. Let me teach you, and then we'll get started."

He and Enrique sang the chorus together. Enrique got it easily. When Jason had turned it into a song, he'd streamlined it even more than Lindsey would have demanded. *Show me your heart,* Lindsey had said, and now, Jason showed it.

> *One last breath, but the light burns strong.*
> *And the music plays on,*
> *And the music plays on.*
> *Now you're gone, and we're scattered like stars.*

But the song goes on,
But the song goes on.

Jason said, "Let's try the chorus again. And for everyone watching on the livestream, I suggest you sing too because it's the only chance I'll ever have to play accompaniment for you."

There was laughter. Enrique was stronger on the vocals the second time, and Rosalind had a better sense of the rhythm as well. Then, behind him, Jason heard a violin, and that would be Lindsey. Lindsey, who'd played this with him over and over on Friday night before Jason had given it words.

The verses were more complicated. Jason had combed Lindsey's interview for exactly how she'd described her father: scattering musicians like stars; doing it for love; re-defining success; creating community. Jason had reached for her admiration and tried to give it a voice.

Sierra stepped to the front for the chorus, raising her arms and encouraging everyone to sing. *Your song goes on.* Jason hadn't written it that way, but Sierra changed it on the fly and now everyone was singing her version. Lindsey played Frederika with tears running down her cheeks.

This was hard. It was wonderful and awful and simultaneously the worst and best thing Jason had ever done.

Michael brought Susan onto the stage during the second verse, and she sang with Sierra. Two hundred voices in unison: it was awesome in a way Jason hadn't anticipated. They cared. They cared about Bob.

In that moment, a gate opened in Jason's brain. He let go of the judgment and the fear. He leaned into his song and emoted like he hadn't for two years. So what if critics said his playing was juvenile and angsty? One of the most important men in his life was gone, and Jason was about to lose one of the most important women, and neither of them knew. Bob never knew how important he was to Jason. Lindsey didn't realize and would never realize that he'd fallen in love with her. If all he could give them was this song, this moment, this *now,* then that's what he would give. "You're burying your heart," Lindsey had said to him, and mid-performance, Jason unburied it.

The moment he finally let go and accepted it all—the pain, the uncertainty, the honor, the loss—it flooded through his fingers and out the hollow instrument between his chin and his heart. For the first time in years, he wasn't just creating sounds. He was giving himself.

They played the chorus three times before ending, and after that final fanfare, everyone was applauding. Susan hugged him, and Hannah took Jason's violin so he could hug Susan back.

Then Lindsey was against him, her face buried in his shoulder. He put his hand in her hair, and everything hurt. Jason hadn't realized until that moment that he was crying too.

Sierra exclaimed to the crowd, "Wasn't that amazing?" and triggered another roar of applause. "Next up, we have vocalist Enrique Almendarez and pianist Declan Hatcher!"

Backstage, a tearful Lindsey rushed away from the others into the prep room. Ashlyn pointed at him, and Jason ran after her.

Lindsey didn't even look at him. Shaking, she lay Frederika back in its case. "You're an idiot!" Her voice broke with tears. "Now you can't use that song. You violated the NDA."

He leaned against the door, and his voice emerged soft. "This is the way the song wanted to be used."

Her throat trembled as she turned to him. "Why? After all the trouble you had—"

Jason neared her and took her hands. "Your father is important to me. You're important to me."

He shouldn't have said that, but they were standing inches apart, gaze to gaze, hands clasped. Lindsey's mouth quivered, and Jason wanted to engulf her heart with his own, bring her with him to California, and shield her from the pain.

He couldn't stay this near and not get nearer. He put his

arms around her shoulders and drew her closer. *You're important to me.*

She looked into his eyes and whispered, "I wish—"

The door opened, and she jolted back. Jason whipped around to look behind him, and it was Michael, wide-eyed. "Guys, you need to see this."

Dazed, Jason found himself holding Michael's phone instead of Lindsey's hand, and looking into a Twitter stream rather than Lindsey's eyes. He had no idea what Lindsey had been about to say, but instead he was seeing what Mitzy Maxwell had to say.

"Oh my goodness, guys—did you see what Jason just did? #SoSweet #LoveOnceMore #MitsonOnceMore? So amazing!!! I just donated $10,000 to the Castleton Fund, and I want you to donate too. {Link}"

What?

Mitzy had done *what*?

Reading over his shoulder, Lindsey drew a sharp breath and backed away. "Oh." Lindsey sounded stunned. "That's...huge."

Michael sounded pleased. "I thought you'd want to see. It looks like she's been driving traffic to us, but I didn't think she had a connection to the school."

Lindsey turned away. "Yeah. It's tangential."

"I need to show Susan. This is incredible."

Michael left, but instead of looking back to Jason, Lindsey finished putting Frederika in the case. It was so mechanical: strapping it down, tucking it in, loosening the bow.

Their moment was shrapnel. Whatever she'd been wishing, she wasn't going to say it now. "I wish you weren't leaving," or "I wish you'd shut up," or "I wish we could be together."

Lindsey was hoarse. "That's why you didn't want to play it? You knew she was watching?"

Jason shivered. "She doesn't sound angry."

"No, she sounds ready to jump you." Lindsey snorted. "Well, you said it's all about how it looks. I'm learning a lot of things look different than they really are." She locked Frederika inside and turned around. "Thank you for the song for my father. He would have appreciated it."

She'd frozen over from the teary-eyed beauty he'd very nearly kissed for the third time. Jason said, "You're mad? Why?"

Tense all over, Lindsey still wouldn't look at him. "Why would I be mad?"

"Because we worked on the song for the movie."

"If you just hamstrung your own career, that's your decision, pretty boy, not mine." Fire and water mixed up in her eyes. "You got everyone to their feet, and you had a strong performance while everyone was still watching the livestream. That's all I asked. Now when we lose viewers because of the jazz and the classical, it won't affect donations. And Mitzy Maxwell donated ten grand because she's a philanthropist."

Jason recoiled. "She does actually donate—"

"I know that!" Lindsey's voice went up in pitch. "I know she spends Tuesdays at children's hospitals and shovels cash at Clean Water Worldwide! She's an awesome person and a terrific musician and a sharp businesswoman! Go back to California and be the other half of Mitson again— it's good for clicks and views, and that's good for your career."

Jason moved toward her. "I don't want to be the other half of Mitson."

She side-stepped him. "Then someone better tell her because she's all set to chew you up like she did last time. I thought you were smarter than that. You certainly told everyone you were smarter than that." Lindsey looked distraught. "I should have known better than to play her song at my father's memorial. It seemed like a good idea at the time, but a lot of things like that blow up in our faces."

"I don't know why she tweeted that. We're through." Jason's voice broke. "Talk to me?"

Lindsey closed her eyes and stood with her fists clenched. Was she hunting for five things she could hear?

Enrique singing a love song. A conversation in the hallway. A cellphone that should have been turned off. A fluorescent light buzzing overhead. Her own exhalation.

When she opened her eyes, she looked sad. "Don't get wrung out by her again. You're worth more than that."

Jason put out a hand, and she took it. "I won't. I know better now."

"Promise me."

He hugged Lindsey, but she was barely enduring his touch. He let her go. "I promise. She tweeted to make her fans excited and get your father's concert more views. She's been pushing our livestream for a while."

Lindsey's shoulders dropped. "Well, I guess after how she treated you, she owed you a favor."

Yeah... About that.

Lindsey stepped back into his arms, and this time she let him hug her for what felt like ages, but it wasn't long enough. He couldn't ask what she wished before, not without sending her away from him. Then Ashlyn and Hannah's voices approached in the hallway, and she backed out. As they entered, she said, "Thank you. For giving my father your song."

"Our song," Jason said before she fully disengaged. "You co-wrote it with me."

Ashlyn called Lindsey over, and Jason took his violin back from Hannah. He ached with Lindsey's absence, so rather than keep feeling uncomfortable and useless, he checked his phone.

He had a text from Mitzy from the same minute she'd tweeted about her donation. "You owe me, sugar, and I know what I want. Come see me when you're in L.A."

With goosebumps all the way up both arms, Jason realized his promise was only two minutes old, and already he wasn't going to be able to keep it.

Chapter Twenty-Four

In the wing offstage, Lindsey was exhausted, but they still had a half-full auditorium, plus people in the atrium. The last of the food had arrived an hour ago, and the sun had set. The treacherous snow had stopped (thank you *so* much). The livestream numbers had dwindled, but as of now donations had covered fees for the catering and all off-duty police officers for a full day's work. Plus, you know, salaries at the school for several months.

Jason.

For crying out loud, Jason.

She'd been one second from opening her heart to him before Michael saved her from embarrassing herself. She'd have regretted it the moment #Mitson reappeared in the world, and being honest with herself, she regretted it anyhow.

Why did Jason have to be so infuriating? Nothing was right. He started his lines at the wrong time, booked clients for the wrong times, and decided to be considerate or even sweet to her all at the wrong time. Like, the time he was leaving. After next week, she was never going to see him again. So why the frontal assault on her heart right now? Why would he take one of the most valuable things he had—his song—and give it over to her father? Why would he pledge that she was important to him when his every action for the past year had screamed the only important thing was himself?

Lindsey needed to shake it off. Sierra was ending her set, and the quartet was on next. Then the finale.

Hannah stood at Lindsey's elbow. "Remember, I get five minutes solo before the rest of us start."

Lindsey gave a wry smile. "If you want our full slot, go right ahead. I'm spent."

"It's actually three minutes and nineteen seconds." Hannah looked sheepish. "I wasn't sure I'd be able to go ahead with it, but it feels right."

From behind Lindsey, Jason gave a concerned, "What are you about to do?"

Lindsey started. "I didn't see you," and she sidled away, battling simultaneous urges to step into his arms and to shove him aside. Mitzy Maxwell had gone radio silent for a year and then chosen the day of Dad's memorial service to grandstand back into Jason's life, a mere three days before he'd fly back to Los Angeles. The worst part was how guilty Jason looked. Even after Mitzy had used him and spit him out again, he was still carrying a torch.

Hannah gave a nervous gulp as Sierra's set ended.

Lindsey put a hand on Hannah's shoulder. "It's going to be perfect."

Michael started lowering the screen, and Lindsey picked up the box of tissues. "We need to go out front."

Jason followed. "Should I be worried?"

He was an idiot. Giving her father that song was an awesome gesture, but he'd wasted it, and now he was being an even bigger idiot about Mitzy Maxwell.

Lindsey dropped into an aisle seat alongside Ashlyn,

pointedly leaving no room for Jason at her side. Instead Jason took the seat behind her and put his hand on her shoulder. Her skin crawled.

No, if Lindsey was tallying up idiots, then the biggest idiot here was Lindsey Castleton, who was letting a guy work his way into her heart because he was treating her nicely as his parting shot before evacuating to California. Doubtless he'd asked if she could visit him just to make sure there was zero danger she would. When and only when he was sure she wouldn't go, then he bragged on how beautiful it was, just to rub it in.

He'd looked so earnest. When she'd refused, he'd seemed sad. None of this made sense. It made even less sense that she was falling for him.

Hannah walked onto the stage. Lindsey pulled three tissues in a row before handing the box to Ashlyn. Across the aisle, Sierra took a seat alongside Mom and flashed Lindsey a thumbs-up.

On the screen, Dad appeared, only it wasn't a photo. It was a paused video.

Hannah said, "Back when I was subbing with the quartet, whenever I needed to get up to speed on a piece, Bob would record a video of himself playing the first violin part and giving me all my cues."

Mom choked on a sob. Lindsey took the box of tissues from Ashlyn and held it across the aisle. Shaking her head, Sierra raised her own box.

Hannah said, "Tonight wouldn't be quite right unless we also had Bob playing one last duet."

She sat facing the screen with her cello. Dad played, and Hannah joined.

In silence, Mom was crying so hard she was shaking. Hannah played with tears of her own, and Ashlyn buried her face in her hands. Lindsey couldn't move her gaze from the screen. Dad, right there. Dad, still healthy, cueing a quartet that wasn't with him, giving Hannah everything she needed to step into her part.

From behind, Jason wrapped his arms around Lindsey to

watch Dad over her shoulder. They'd both played second violin to her father. They'd both gotten these same cues, these same cautions, these same encouragements while he played. It was surreal, and it was wonderful, and it was wrenching.

Last week, Hannah had said, "Do you think I should? Is it too macabre?" and Lindsey had told her to do it, do it, do it, and also to upload every single video so the rest of them could have copies. If she could have, Lindsey would have scheduled Hannah and those videos for the whole afternoon.

At the end of the piece, everyone was applauding. Hannah turned to the screen and bowed to Dad, and as if he could see her, Dad bowed back.

Michael raised the screen so the quartet could take the stage. And this—this, at her father's memorial—this would be the current quartet's final performance together.

Lindsey nodded, and they started, first Lindsey, then Jason.

Jason came in on cue...and at the right volume.

Lindsey was halfway through the first movement before she realized what was happening, that Jason wasn't overpowering her. Like, not even a little. He was actively supporting her line with his own—and then she realized how emotional he sounded. His violin resonated with joy and anticipation in a way he hadn't played since he'd arrived last March.

Lindsey let go then, freer to play her soft parts softer, her expressive parts with more expression. Ashlyn and Hannah were right there, but they'd always been. Every time, it had been Jason fighting the first violin line with his volume and his emotionally flat technique. Now, during their last performance, he'd clicked back into the violinist he'd been for her father. And he was amazing.

They soared through the movement, and it was the same the whole way through: the second violin stayed second. The gentle parts were gentle. Jason never jumped his cue. Everything annoying about him, he'd toned it down. As he played, he smiled.

He hadn't done that either.

They finished, and Lindsey fought tears as they bowed together for the last time.

The other three left the stage, but Lindsey addressed the crowd. "Everyone, thank you so much for coming today, for sharing your music and sharing your memories of Dad. I know he would have been so proud and pleased to see you all here, appreciating his life's work. For the finale, it will be me, my mother, my brother Corwin, and my sister Sierra."

Jason and Michael rolled the piano onto the center stage. Corwin walked to the edge with his acoustic guitar and sat with his left leg crossed under his right, his right foot dangling. He strummed a chord, then started finger-picking through Dan Fogelberg's "Leader of the Band."

Lindsey had been astonished when Corwin suggested this, a song about a musician serenading his own musician father to thank him and say goodbye. Astonished for all of five seconds before she'd exclaimed, "Yes! Of course!" and then formed the rest of the finale around it.

The entire audience responded as she had, going utterly silent while Corwin soloed through the first verse and chorus. In their silence, his notes and his voice reverberated through the auditorium. Then he looked up, smirking. "I bet you didn't know I could do this." Some laughter. He finished the song without stopping again.

Holding her lap harp, Sierra took her place beside Corwin, who changed up his tune into Charlie Puth's "When I See You Again." In her soft, high voice, Sierra performed the lyric version.

While Sierra closed, Susan introduced the piano, transitioning them into James Taylor's "Fire and Rain." Lindsey raised her violin and played in the background.

Still the audience made no sound whatsoever. That was tremendous. That kind of catharsis was an amazing moment. But Lindsey had other plans.

As Mom began the low chords and the keyboard run for

the final song of the night, Lindsey stepped to the mic and sang Abba's "Thank You for the Music."

The lyrics started half-spoken, half-sung. Lindsey wasn't a great singer, but she didn't need to be. It just needed to be heartfelt, and she felt these lyrics all the way through herself. When they reached the chorus, she raised her hands, and her whole family joined with a punctuated, "Thank you for the music." Lindsey urged the audience to join, and above her, Michael showed the lyrics on the screen.

Lindsey sang the second verse, and she got everyone on their feet to sing for the second chorus. Then, with everyone singing, she waved over the musicians in the wings.

Castleton alumni and Castleton-adjacent musicians crowded the stage. Lindsey was singing and smiling and crying all at the same time. Enrique was singing, and Hannah too. Jason joined her on stage, playing at her side. *Thank you for the music.*

Lindsey's father had given everything. Lindsey's parents had given her music, had given her joy, had given her structure and safety and purpose. In return, the only thing Lindsey could do was use their gifts and give them her gratitude.

All these musicians her father had touched—they gathered on the stage and gave all their thanks with their voices and their sounds.

It was the only memorial Lindsey could give her father.

It was the best.

Jason held her while the auditorium exploded in applause. Susan called to everyone, "Thank you so much! Thank you all for sharing your memories of Bob, sharing your love, sharing your support, and sharing your songs. Thank you for sharing our lives."

Jason put his arms around Lindsey, and she pulled him tight.

Jason had given her father one of his most valuable things, a song. He'd given her father a slice of his future.

He'd given everything he had, and then he'd given Lindsey his surrender in the way he played. Jason had given everything, everything—and still she wanted something more from him.

Lindsey's emotions crescendoed until she couldn't resist any longer, and she turned to him. She kissed him. With her heart full and her eyes closed, his kiss crashed all the way through her, rippling through her heart and sparkling through her soul. She'd lost so much, and Jason was giving so much. She would take this moment too.

Thank you for making music, she thought to her father's spirit. *And thank you for making so many other musicians.*

CHAPTER TWENTY-FIVE

No one played for the funeral. Mom didn't want it, not after a lifetime filled with music. They had packed the church, relatives and friends and clients and students and peers. They wore black. They displayed Dad's urn at the front. They had readings and a eulogy and prayers.

Lindsey sat with her family in the front row and more relatives in the row behind. Jason had come, but he wasn't near. Her heart burned. Dad was gone, and Jason was leaving. The world was ending, except it wasn't ending. Only her world. Lindsey would wake up tomorrow and everyone else's world would have rolled ahead. Everyone would drink their coffee and drive to work, pay the electric bill, make dinner, wash clothes, and wait until bedtime when it would be over again for a few hours.

After the funeral came the graveside service. More words, again no music. Jason held Lindsey the whole time, arms wrapped around her, her head on his shoulder.

Everything was over. Everything.

While the guests returned to their cars to attend the post-funeral lunch, Jason stood with Lindsey. In his black suit and black wool coat, he looked amazing. She remained alongside his car with her face in his shoulder, unwilling to let go. As soon as she did, he'd be gone.

He traced the small hairs at the base of her neck. "I'm sorry. I'm sorry for so many things."

She couldn't ask him to stay. He'd put off leaving as long as he could. There had never been a doubt about him going back. He'd park his car at his parents' B&B where he'd left his suitcase and his violin, then take an airport shuttle. After that, who knew? He might do what he'd done when leaving L.A.: hire a service to pack his things and haul his car to the other coast on a tractor-trailer.

Lindsey said, "Will I see you again?" When he didn't answer right away, she looked up. "When are you coming back?"

He looked haunted, and the pain shot through Lindsey like the crunch of a violin getting crushed. "I don't know."

He knew. He was never coming back.

By Tuesday evening, Lindsey had her bearings again. Somewhat. Everything was awful, but they had relatives to distract them and take some of the burden. Her family and friends shared stories about Dad, and it helped a bit to laugh, and it helped a bit to cry, and it helped a bit just to be with other people who remembered.

Jason even texted her. "I figured out how to make the chatty guy in the next seat shut up. He thought it was funny I'm in a suit, so he asked whose funeral it was, har har. I said my mentor and the greatest man I'd ever known. He hasn't spoken since."

A variant of that showed up five minutes later on Jason's Twitter account.

Then he texted Lindsey, "That third piece for the movie? I wrote it on the plane. Only one queen bee."

He sent her the view from his hotel room. He photographed the sunset over the ocean and the artful dinner that room service sent upstairs. He was making a full court press to get her out there, but Lindsey was exhausted. Mom was broken, and nothing would take away the pain. Lindsey wouldn't leave.

Jason texted the next morning, "On set. This is exhausting. Lots of waiting, but I've begun writing again."

The messages slowed on the days they did the filming, and she missed hearing from Jason. Everything got hollow. Lindsey went back to teaching. Jason pushed back his return a few more days because they wanted him in the studio to record the soundtrack. Lindsey had little kids marching to Beethoven while waving colorful silk scarves. She wanted to ask Dad for advice about choosing a new second violinist, and that stung every stinking time. On Monday, Jason's texts stopped.

Indeed. What had she said about the boyfriend who ghosted her last year? "Poof. No more attentive guy." Jason would be apartment hunting right now, or maybe at a spa getting a trendy haircut and a wardrobe update.

Meanwhile she should be violinist-hunting and doing a website update. Should be, but wasn't.

The school had gotten a bunch of enquiries, though. They already had a dozen new students scheduled for trial lessons, and the Brighthead grammar school principal wanted to talk to Mom about how music helped troubled students.

Another Tuesday evening. After thirty-six hours of silence, Lindsey got a text on the drive back to her apartment. "Getting on a plane. Can I talk to you tonight?"

She didn't reply from the car. How long should a flight take from California to Maine, and what time did Jason think she'd stay awake until? He'd texted his flight information. Did he expect her to meet him at the airport?

Ashlyn had already started dinner prep. They'd opted to skip quartet rehearsal tonight on the grounds that they didn't have a performance coming up, and also because they didn't have (sigh) a second violinist. Lindsey really needed to get on that, except it hurt. It hurt having to replace Jason. It felt just like it did last year, knowing she had to login to the quartet's website to update it with all new faces, but unwilling to make the final admission that Dad wasn't coming back. Now Jason wasn't coming back either.

Instead Lindsey set the table. "Two of my students want you to keep teaching them. Are you up for it?"

Ashlyn dumped pasta into the boiling water. "Sure, but how will that work during the summertime when I'm at the ice cream stand?"

"Solvable problem. If we can get them there in the evenings, I'll give you a room to teach in."

Ashlyn sounded worried. "Except then I've stolen two of your students."

Lindsey rested a hand on her heart. "Please note my grievous wounds. If I were bitter and resentful, I'd have told the parents no and not bothered to ask you."

"I'm not much of a teacher, but if they want, I'm game." Ashlyn sighed. "And we need to figure out the second violinist situation. I like both our subs, but I don't think either of them should come onboard full time."

"They've both got drawbacks." Lindsey opened the fridge. "I meant to audition people in February, but between the accident and Dad, it never happened."

"No one blames you." Ashlyn huffed. "Well, except maybe for Jason, but he's out the door now, and he's not wasting time."

Lindsey poked her head up. "How so?"

Ashlyn said, "I follow Mitzy Maxwell's twitter. #Mitson's back."

What?

He *what?* He and Mitzy—?

But he'd just texted her! But he'd promised he wouldn't let Mitzy use him again. But— But he was smarter than that. But he said—

But he'd been leading her on.

She'd been stupid and let him lead her on. Knowing he was leaving, she'd let him hold her and comfort her and kiss her, and her reward was a kick in the face. Jason's attention had felt genuine, but it was never about the feelings. Jason had always been honest about two things: he was leaving, and it didn't matter what he felt.

The pasta timer had five minutes left, so Lindsey opened her laptop. She made enough typos that the address bar couldn't even autocomplete the first two times, but finally she arrived at Mitzy's account. The top tweet was a blurred-out selfie with two faces: "I'm sitting on the announcement you guys have wanted for A WHOLE YEAR! But I'm not allowed to tell yet—and I'm SO STRESSED OUT. :-(#LoveOnceMore"

Four minutes on the pasta timer. As if Lindsey would get even one forkful down her throat.

Further along the timeline were other teases. From yesterday morning, a photo of a violin scroll. "You'll never guess who's here RIGHT NOW!" In the replies, the fans were going crazy, and in her kitchen, Lindsey had nothing left to give.

Jason had texted her every day, every day except yesterday when he'd been with Mitzy, failing to mention that he was sitting atop his throne in triumph as the other half of #Mitson.

It was all about how everything looked, and it wasn't much of a look if you dated a violin teacher.

He'd boomeranged back to being everything he hated.

She re-read Jason's last message: "Getting on a plane. Can I talk to you tonight?"

Tonight. No wonder he wanted to talk to her tonight. Mitzy was dying to announce his return, and he needed to get everything squared away first. Get Lindsey to drive out to meet him at the airport so he could break her heart and then score a free ride home. Or maybe he wanted to have Lindsey at his side so he could soothe her while explaining that everyone in Hollywood led a double life, and she'd still be there for him after Mitzy dumped him again.

I deserve better than that, Lindsey thought, finger hovering over the block option on Jason's conversation. *And so do you.*

CHAPTER TWENTY-SIX

Of course the flight would be late. Jason kept recalculating his arrival time, and it kept getting more unlikely that he'd be able to see Lindsey tonight. She hadn't replied before his flight took off, so he didn't even know if she'd said he could.

She might be holding auditions. She might be spending the night with her mother because the first months of grieving were going to be terrible.

Jason knew better than to stand the moment the plane landed, but he kept fighting the urge. It took too long to taxi to the jetway, too long for them to open the door, too long for the people in the front rows to file out. He took his violin from the overhead compartment and exited, hopeful in case Lindsey had come to the airport.

No one was waiting for him. He checked his phone. Lindsey hadn't replied.

Was she okay? She hadn't mentioned headaches or

nausea, but she hadn't told him she was in pain even when they'd been sitting at the same table. With the stress of the funeral and getting back to work, maybe she was down for the count. Jason hadn't been able to talk to her yesterday. She might be sick. He hadn't asked. It hadn't occurred to him.

Or maybe she was angry. If she was, heaven knew Jason deserved it.

On the other hand, his mother had texted half an hour ago. "Stay here tonight since you're coming in late. Take the blue room."

As if. He'd rather go back to his apartment and sleep in a familiar bed. Mom was thoughtful, but she had no clue about travel.

Also, Mimi had texted. "Well?"

He replied, "Impatient, aren't you? Flight got delayed."

Then he texted Lindsey. "I've landed. Everything okay?"

Midnight. He found his bag, but he didn't find Lindsey. Jason was still on California time, so he was awake enough to get the airport shuttle. During the whole drive, though, he kept worrying he'd missed Lindsey in the airport. Surely if she hadn't found him at the terminal exit, she'd have gone to baggage claim. He could get as anxious as he wanted, but most likely she'd decided to stay home. He hadn't asked her to come to him.

He'd just hoped she wanted to see him too.

Still, why hadn't she replied? He'd expected Lindsey to get angry tomorrow, or tonight if he talked to her tonight. Why would she be cold-shouldering him now?

Mimi's reply arrived. "Of course I'm impatient!"

He texted, "At this point, you're going to have to wait until tomorrow."

She sent him a frowning emoji followed by a tearful one, and he snickered.

Jason longed to get to Lindsey. He needed to talk to her, but what he truly wanted was to see her, hold her, inhale the vanilla scent of her. He didn't even need to kiss her, but he probably would because everything was a mess right now, and she was solid.

Solid and smart, was the problem. In the midst of her grief, Jason was too much work, too damaged, too...well, had done too much damage to *her.* He hadn't told her it was because of her that everything was different for him. His playing was different, his composing, his outlook—his life.

The shuttle crossed the Juniper town line, and Jason wished he could get his feet on solid ground. Travel was annoying. If this worked out, though, he was signing up for a lot of it.

The B&B was dark in every upstairs window as the driver pulled into the lot, but to his dismay, lights shone in the parlor. It was one in the morning, but Mom would want to talk. *How was your flight? Do you want something to eat?* The only one Jason wanted to talk to was Lindsey. It would be rude to just leave if Mom was waiting for him, but still. Jason looked to his Audi.

It wasn't alone. Parked next to it was Lindsey's SUV.

His heart slammed into his ribcage, and he thrust a tip at the driver before grabbing his violin and suitcase. He flew up the front steps and through the unlocked dooryard and into the living room. The parlor's low lights gleamed at either side of the couch, and sleeping on the couch, there she was.

Here. Lindsey was here.

She lay with her head on the armrest, her chin on her hand, her legs tucked up. She must have fallen asleep by accident, spent with the waiting.

Jason went to his knees in front of the couch, dropped his violin on one side and his bag on the other. He reached for Lindsey's hand, then with his other he brushed the hair from her forehead.

She raised her head, and from way down in Jason's core, a smile blossomed out. He couldn't stop it. She was here, right here. He put his arms around her and breathed her into his lungs and absorbed the feel of her against his skin.

"I didn't know you'd be waiting." With his cheek to hers, he ran his hand up her neck into her hair. She was here. Solid. Real.

But she was also tense. He'd melted into her, but she was rigid like a wrought iron fence.

He didn't know what to say. He had a long story and a long explanation and a long apology to make—but couldn't it wait? She'd be furious, and he didn't know how to make it better. After a week away, though, he just wanted to wrap around her and stay that way. Stay. Just stay.

She put her arms around him at last and buried her face in his neck, her breathing jerky.

"I'm sorry. The flight got in late." Jason nuzzled her neck. "I didn't mean to make you wait up for me. I didn't realize you'd be here."

"Your mother told me to stay in the green room, but I asked her not to tell you." Her voice was soft. "In case I left."

"I'm glad you didn't." Burning to kiss her, Jason breathed against her ear. She was here and she did smell like vanilla, and he yearned to get up on the couch beside her and forget everything. "I have so much to tell you."

"Not tonight." Lindsey went tense like a violin string. "No talking. You can break my heart in the morning. I'll hate you then. But I can't right now."

Frozen on his knees before her, Jason couldn't come up with words or a way to move forward. That she'd hate him tomorrow meant to some extent, she hated him now. Except he hadn't told her, and Mimi shouldn't have announced anything.

Jason forced out, "Why?"

Lindsey hugged him tighter. "Please don't."

She ran her lips across his throat, and he arched his neck, thrilling all over. None of this made sense. He kissed her at last, and the touch of her lips exploded through his heart like the world's most urgent yes. He'd wanted this for a week, only now his brain kept misfiring. *You can break my heart in the morning.*

Breathing hard, he pulled back. "Let me explain."

"I asked you not to talk." She met his eyes, and she was devastated. "Once you explain, I'll have no more plausible deniability."

Jason squeezed her hands. "Denying what?"

Her voice cracked. "Mitzy Maxwell."

He recoiled. "Did she announce? She was supposed to wait until I talked to you."

"She's teasing it." Eyes dark, Lindsey looked right at him with a force that sent Jason back on his heels. "She said she's announcing tomorrow. And then everything ends between us."

Jason looked at her knees.

"It doesn't make things better if you tell me yourself." Her voice cracked. "I'm disappointed, but I should have expected you'd betray me for your career. You've been clear all along. This is my fault."

He sat forward. "How are any of my mistakes your fault?"

"I let you get past my defenses. You couldn't have betrayed me if I hadn't trusted you. I fell in love, but I shouldn't have. I had to see you tonight, and tomorrow I'll cut you off." The tears finally came, and Jason's heart broke. "You'll be free to do whatever you want. I can't be your backup plan."

Jason swallowed as she shuddered in his arms. "What if I don't stay in California? What if I go from coast to coast?"

Lindsey pushed him back, offended. "And have a woman on both coasts?"

Jason shook his head. "I don't want a woman on both coasts."

Lindsey's eyes narrowed. "Then there's no job opening for me. Mitson?"

Jason straightened. "What? No!"

She looked livid. "Tomorrow's big announcement? The one she's not allowed to break until you've talked to me first?"

Jason's cheeks flushed. "Did she post that we're back together? Because I'll start a social media firestorm that will make last year look like a cookout."

Lindsey glared. "Do you think I'm stupid?"

"No! What did she say?"

Lindsey fumbled for her phone, but Jason got his first and went straight to Mimi's timeline.

...the announcement you guys have wanted for A WHOLE YEAR!

He breathed, "Holy cow. No, Lindsey, that's not what she's going to announce. Blast it. She's the queen of hype, but no." He clicked off the phone. "Can I explain what's going to happen tomorrow—what's really going to happen? You'll still be angry at me, but at least be angry about the right thing."

Lindsey tucked up her knees, decidedly un-mollified. Jason got on the couch but didn't touch her. He couldn't even look directly at her. "I didn't get back together with Mitzy, and I don't want to. But we recorded a new song."

Unlike Jason, Lindsey had no trouble looking directly at him. "How gullible do you think I am? Fans have wanted that for a whole year?"

Jason huffed. "By the time Mimi's done with the marketing blitz, her fans will think they've wanted nothing else for twelve months."

Lindsey's gaze drilled into him. "And I'm supposed to believe that would make me angry?"

Jason braced himself. "Because I did betray you. When we still had no viewers on the livestream for your father's concert, and you were so sad, I couldn't get more than a couple dozen on my own. That's when I asked Mitzy to promote it. For payback, Mitzy demanded your song. And I gave it to her."

Lindsey pulled back. "What song?"

"The song we wrote together, the tribute to your father, the one that would have been the third song for the movie. *The music goes on.*" Staring sidelong at the carpet, Jason swallowed hard. "That's what she's announcing. It's the first track she's releasing for her new album. We recorded it this morning, and she's going to drop it on Friday. She thinks it'll go number one, and she predicts over the long term, it'll keep getting revived whenever someone wants a go-to tribute song."

Jason closed his eyes. "I'm sorry. I feel terrible about this. I didn't know what to do. I gave you co-writing credit, so you'll make money from it, and any money I make from the song can go toward a scholarship in your father's name. I don't know how else to make it right." He clenched his fists in his lap. "I knew she'd want payback, but I didn't think she'd ask for your song. That song was my gift to you in honor of your father, and I didn't protect it for you."

Hands on his hands. Gentle. Jason opened his eyes to find Lindsey, her expression bewildered. "That's it? That's what you think I'd be angry about? You're not hooking up with her again?"

Jason shook his head. "I'm not. And after a week out there, I don't want to go back. Not permanently. My life is here. You're here."

Lindsey sounded earnest. "Your future is there. Your career is there."

Jason squeezed her hands. "I don't want it. Not if you won't go with me."

She withdrew from him. "Everything—and I mean everything—you've worked for is there."

Jason put his arms around her. "You're my inspiration. You're the reason there's joy in my music again. You're the reason music exists. I love you."

He kissed her until she melted beneath his touch. Intoxicated by the scent and the feel of her, Jason brushed his lips across her temple. "I promise not to break your heart tomorrow."

Lindsey whispered, "We have a tomorrow?"

Jason held her against his heart. "We have as many tomorrows as we want."

Epilogue

Lindsey reached for Jason's hand as Enrique and Hannah arrived beneath the flower arch.

"She's so pretty," Ashlyn breathed as all the wedding guests applauded. "I've never seen her this happy."

Hannah wore an ankle-length white dress and a flower crown with a veil cascading down her back. Stunning in his tuxedo, Enrique paused with her under the arch so the photographer could get a photo of them with the maple trees in full autumn colors.

Jason stood behind Lindsey with his arms around her waist. She relaxed into him, enjoying one of the last warm days before winter would set in.

Enrique and Hannah's wedding had taken place in the church, and because they were keeping things small, Mom had offered the Castleton back yard for the wedding reception. Enrique's brother Daniel had stood as best man, with Parker as a groomsman. Hannah had chosen Lindsey and Ashlyn for her attendants, and then it had been her two little brothers and Enrique's nephew as a trio of ring-bearers. The little ones were racing around the yard now while two of the servers from Enrique's family's restaurant set up catering trays.

Ashlyn said to Lindsey, "You know, it's not too late for you and me to arrange a double wedding...?"

Jason tightened his arms around Lindsey's waist. "Oh, I don't know," she said, flashing a smile at Ashlyn. "You've got your whole perfect scenario set up, with Michael proposing on the one-year anniversary of joining the family and you guys getting married next year on the two-year anniversary. An extra couple would just ruin it."

"Mom would be over the moon." Ashlyn nudged Michael. "Tell her."

Michael said, "Exactly when have I successfully 'told' Lindsey to do anything?"

Jason murmured in Lindsey's ear, "I'm staying out of this."

Lindsey sidled away from Jason. "You'd better. It would be totally rude to get engaged at Hannah's wedding."

Ashlyn said, "I'm already engaged, so I can take notes and make plans."

Mom came over. "I think the bridesmaids are required...?" and Lindsey kissed Jason before joining Hannah.

Hannah looked truly gorgeous as they took more photos. Ashlyn said to her, "Tell Lindsey she needs to get engaged so we can have a double wedding."

With her cheeks pink, Hannah said, "Lindsey, you need to do whatever is best for you and Jason."

Ashlyn huffed. "That's not at all what I told you to tell her. Not even a little."

Lindsey said, "I think I remember saying today isn't about me?"

After the photos, Jason drifted up to Lindsey and ran a finger over the back of her neck. "I don't suppose there's the slightest chance that you're stuck in this dress and require an emergency unzipping?"

Lindsey snickered. "I can get it on and off with no problem. I've done it several times."

Jason traced down her back to the edge of the dress, and she shivered at his touch. "Are you sure? I'd gladly offer my services."

"Ashlyn and my mother are here to help." Lindsey side-eyed him. "I'd never put you in the path of temptation."

Jason gave a disappointed, "Oh. Thanks."

Lindsey laughed.

He put an arm over her shoulder and drew her closer. "Speaking of temptation, remember how you told me not to check my phone today?"

Lindsey wrapped her arms under his suit jacket. He was warm, and she enjoyed it. "I must not have told you, because if I had, you wouldn't be about to tell me whatever you just found on the phone."

Jason said, "Edward says the Paganini movie is a go."

Whoa. Huge opportunity.

Also, unfortunately, lots of time away from Maine.

Jason breathed along her ear, and goosebumps flashed across her skin. "They're talking the whole package. Album. Tour of all the major cities. Carnegie Hall. Lots of time on the East coast." Lindsey turned, and he cupped her cheeks in his hands. "It's worked for six months. We can make it keep working."

He was gorgeous in his suit, his hair teased by the wind, his eyes so earnest. She said, "You keep going out to California."

"And then I keep coming back to Maine." He took both her hands, and she shivered. "I love you, Lindsey. I do want to marry you."

She leaned against him, cheek to his shoulder. "That's going to disappoint your thousands of fangirls."

"I don't want thousands of fangirls." He kissed her forehead. "I want one fangirl."

Lindsey said, "Someone who plays first violin?"

"At least half the time."

She smiled and traced his lapel. "Someone who writes music with you?"

"Someone who writes and plays music long into the night."

Lindsey reached up and put her arms around his shoulders. "That could be arranged."

He pressed his forehead to hers. "I like your arrangements."

Mom was waving them over to the head table. She got a photo of Hannah and Enrique with Ashlyn and Lindsey on either side. Then she pointed to Michael and then to Jason. "Join them."

Jason got next to Lindsey, and in petulant voice he said, "Yes, Mrs. Castleton."

Mom said, "You know, you don't have to do that," and

she gestured at Michael to move closer to Ashlyn.

Jason sounded mystified. "I suspect I'm contractually incapable of calling you anything else."

Lindsey wrapped her arm around his waist. "Someday, maybe you'll call her Mom?"

Jason waited until after the photo to kiss Lindsey. Mom came over to show them the picture on her screen. Enrique and Hannah were at the center, Ashlyn and Michael to the right, Lindsey and Jason to the left.

Hannah sighed. "It's perfect. Thank you!"

Three couples, three families poised to start. On cue, Enrique led Hannah to the tent for their first dance, and the music played on.

THANK YOU!

Thank you so much! I adored writing this series, and I hope you've loved reading it. There's just something about string quartets, plus I just loved the Castleton family so much. I'm already getting requests to give Corwin his own story, so who knows? Maybe we'll be back in Hartwell and visiting the music school.

Would you mind doing me a favor? Please head back to Amazon or Goodreads and leave a review. It really helps authors and other readers when you can do that. It doesn't have to be long. Forget all those book reports you were forced to write in school. Just a star rating and four sentences will do. I would really appreciate it.

Want to hear more? Sign up for my newsletter ("Mondays with Maddie") at http://eepurl.com/dEJjl1 Once a week, I'll send a weird anecdote about my life as well as news about my stories or recommendations of other books you might enjoy. (Plus, if I do write about Corwin? You'll hear about it.)

CAN'T GET ENOUGH OF STRING QUARTETS?

Jane Lebak's **Pickup Notes** was reviewed by BookRiot as one of the best books you're not reading.

PICKUP NOTES BY JANE LEBAK

First and foremost, the main character in this book is a violist. Which is just awesome in and of itself. Why? Because violists are awesome! On a serious note, I really enjoyed this story about a musician whose life wasn't, if you'll pardon the pun, playing out the way she wanted. She was the black sheep in her family because of her love of the viola, even though it gave her a close relationship with her deceased grandfather. Her string quartet finds themselves in the spotlight of the wedding community when the second violinist rips a guitar riff at a ceremony. And it changes them all in various ways. Her family is dysfunctional and seems to have no use for her apart from whatever she can do for them, and her sister is a real piece of work. So if that is a button for you, please be aware of that going in. Her string quartet family is also dysfunctional, but at least they generally care about her. It is a great book that not a lot of people have read, which is a shame, but it is one that truly is amazing and will give you a nice warm feeling, especially if you have a background in music. —PN Hinton

Joey's string quartet has to succeed or she's sunk. Her day job is a grind, and her family is toxic. The student loan payments keep coming. Playing viola is the light in her life.

When her (slightly overbearing) first violinist suggests a new direction for the quartet, they start attracting attention. Some good, some...well, not so good. Worse, the changing musical roles start changing the quartet members' relationships, until Joey stands to lose everything—and everyone—she's ever loved.

Pickup Notes is by turns funny, wrenching, and heart-warming. I hope you'll check it out!

WANT MORE BY MADDIE EVANS?

Twenty miles from Hartwell is Brighthead, a coastal town with a lighthouse, "the statue of lies," and a running club where you just might find your heart's desire while lacing up your sneakers.

In *A 5K and a Kiss*, Aileen is still reeling from her sister's death when the running club invites her to visit. Her sister was one of the founders, and now the club wants to hold a memorial 5K in her honor. Even more, they want Aileen to run it too! She'd like to, but three miles seems a long way.

No problem. They're willing to train her—and by "they" we mean Trey, a bright-eyed guy with a huge sense of fun and a slight problem with being reliable. Can they stay the course and find love at the finish line?

ALSO BY MADDIE EVANS

Peter's about to finish high school in tiny-town Texas and enlist in the army. His family can't afford to send both him and his sister to college, but he's got a plan.

Casey's making her own way across the United States, hitch-hiking or freight-hopping to wherever her next ride takes her. Her life is in her backpack, and her home is 25,000 miles around.

When she and Peter save a litter of puppies together, though, her world starts getting a whole lot smaller...and Peter suspects his plans are going to be wrecked by the most captivating gal he's ever met.